26 Women

a novel

Jeffrey Jordan

www.BoundToBeGood.com

Chapter 1
Stacey Anne Lebeau

My mother, Stacey Anne Lebeau, was born in 1917 and grew up during the depression. After her childhood in the urban midwest, she went to one of the lesser-known midwestern colleges, located in a small rural town. Since Stacey's parents couldn't afford to send her to college, the only way she was going to attend was if she got a scholarship. She got a scholarship because the admissions official saw the applicant was S. A. Lebeau, with a GPA through the roof, from a highly regarded high school in Rivers Edge. He offered Lebeau a full-ride scholarship for four years. The reality was they thought they were getting a male student. When they found out the student was a female, they felt they couldn't back out.

Stacey Anne Lebeau quickly made them feel more comfortable as she steamrolled through her first two years with a 4.0 Grade Point Average. It was more than concerning for the administration when, in her junior year, Stacey opted for a mechanical engineering degree.

Ah, they thought, she had overreached. She'll go down in flames. And it's too bad. She might have turned out to be an acceptable teacher of young children or a nurse.

It was 1940 in America. Stacey graduated with honors, married her boyfriend of two years, James Harrison, and six months later gave birth to me, Richard Harrison.

Mom was frustrated by her life. My Father, Jim Harrison, could try to be anything he wanted, but she would struggle to be a woman who worked outside of her home. The odds were against her. It wasn't enough that she wanted to be a working mom. She wanted employment in a profession thought to be for men only.

With Jim's salary as an accountant and hers, if she could get a job they'd have more than enough to hire a full-time nanny to raise their child. Did I feel abandoned because my mother worked? No. It also wasn't difficult to see that neither of my parents was excited about raising me. Over the years, I heard both of them say numerous times how relieved they were they didn't have any more children.

Stacey Anne passed on to me some desirable characteristics. I like to finish the tasks I take on. I have a natural tendency for organization and planning. I may have learned this from observation, or maybe it was an inherited trait. Still, I assure you I was not taught these things in any deliberate fashion.

Jim passed on what many fathers give their sons, a love for sports teams. In my case, it was our minor league baseball club, the Brighton University football team, and basketball teams. Beyond that, he and I didn't have a lot in common. Where you might think as I got older, we might connect more. It didn't work that way with Jim. I was fourteen when he attempted to have 'the talk' with me. He was more embarrassed than I was and certainly didn't tell me anything I didn't already know.

My parents each moved in their respective professional circles and occasionally shared a few friends. However, no one ever became a close friend of Stacey Anne. Jim told me he limited his close friends to a couple of old Army buddies. Nobody who wasn't 'over there' could understand military experiences.

Two things happened to our family when the Japanese bombed our naval base in Pearl Harbor. Over Stacey's strenuous objections, Jim enlisted in the Navy and left the family before my second birthday.

Stacey got a job as an engineer because the men were sent overseas. When I was older, she was belatedly trying to catch up with our relationship since she pretty much ignored me as I grew up. It was then, during an attempt to treat me like an adult, that she reluctantly admitted she might have never got a job if the War hadn't created the opportunity.

After WWII, it was expected that women would go back to the kitchen and leave their jobs for the returning vets. Stacey had no intention of quitting. Given her value to the company she was working for, no one would force the issue.

* * * * * * * * * *

Dad came home, and it was almost as if he had never left. Betty, my nanny, and my mother's maid fixed a special homecoming dinner for Dad's arrival. I knew what the special occasion was, but it took a cake with the message Welcome Home written in frosting before either Jim or Stacey got it. It surprised him, but he was no more surprised than Stacey since she would have never thought to do something like that for him.

Chapter 2
Jeany and Betty Slotski

Over the years, when I describe my parents to others, some people remark that I was hard on them.

"How could they be so cold and distant? You are a warm and caring person."

I credit the Slotski sisters, Jeany and Betty. They raised me until I finished high school. Betty came to work for us when she graduated from high school. I was almost two years old then. Before Jeany got the position, I don't know how many others tried and failed to meet my mother's standards. Betty was both my nanny and our housekeeper until I was eight.

When Betty quit working for my Mom to marry her boyfriend, who we referred to as my Uncle Dennis, her sister Jeany took over. She remained with us until I went to college. For most of that time, Jeany served as housekeeper and early-evening wine-drinking friend for my mother. Since at this point, Stacey had driven away anyone else who might become a close friend.

The Slotski sisters brought me up to learn how to behave, stay out of trouble, respect my elders, and empathize with others in pain. You name any trait I have, and it came from the patient rearing by these two young ladies.

Jeany is the one that explained the birds and bees to me. She did it matter of factly with no embarrassment or baby words. Vaginas were vaginas, and a penis was a penis. How women and men coupled was demonstrated with books checked out of the library. What happened when they did have sex was explained to me as natural and right. The joy of sex was left out for me to discover by myself. However, I did know how babies were made and a general idea of where the human body's erogenous zones are located.

There you have it: the first three women who made a difference in my life. But there were more. If you want to know about me, you need to know about them.

Chapter 3
Lisa Duffy

Lisa Duffy was one of the few girls I met in 9th grade who was almost as tall as I was. She didn't slouch or try to make herself look shorter. She was tall, lean, athletic, and intelligent. Lisa also was very sure of herself. All of this might be because she had two older brothers. Terry was two years older than Lisa. He was his class' valedictorian and a three-letter sportsman. Her oldest brother, Rudy Duffy, played basketball for Brighton and went on to play in the NBA. Lisa was the first girl I kissed.

* * * * * * * * * *

If you went to a parochial school as I did, you would receive a bus pass each year to use the city bus system. There would be none of those yellow school buses for us. The bus pass worked year-round, and it didn't make any difference where you were going or what time of day it was.

It was good news and bad news for parents. The good news was that since there was no need, they didn't feel the pressure to provide a car for us. We didn't need a car. Not only were cars expensive, but they also weren't convenient in the city. Almost none of the schools had enough parking for the teachers, much less the students. The bad news for parents was that they could never be sure of where we were.

My bus ran downtown directly past St. Richard's High School. After we got off at our school, the bus continued until it dropped off the girls at St Catherine's. In those days, the Catholic schools were not co-ed. The only way the students got together was at highly chaperoned dances, called mixers.

In the mid-fifties, when rock 'n roll' music was just gaining traction, it became a leverage issue between students and school officials, many of the latter being priests, brothers, or nuns. With considerable parental support, the clerics would lobby against rock music. On the other side of this debate were the kids in protest who refused the opportunity to jitterbug or polka. They didn't show up at the mixers they knew wouldn't play their music.

So the battle lines were drawn; no rock music meant no attendance. The peace came after the parents bargained to pick the rock music. Let's just say, for a while, at least, there was no Elvis, Little Richard, or Fats Domino, but lots of Pat Boone and Neal Diamond. There was a competitive element also; once one school played Elvis to draw more kids, the others had to follow. Pretty soon, the censorship more or less faded away.

* * * * * * * * * *

One day I missed my early bus. It meant I would not have time for my morning smoke and a cup of coffee. The coffee was served free by the school.

About six blocks down the route, a girl got on the bus. I was instantly attracted to her. I wanted to get close enough to her to chat, but I was in the back of the bus. She stood near the front of a very crowded vehicle. The next day I took the same bus and stood near the front. It was even more crowded than the day before. When she got on the bus, we were standing face to face, inches from each other. I could smell the toothpaste on her breath.

"Good Morning," I said.

She smiled, "Yes, it is. I love Fall. The crisp mornings. The colorful leaves."

"Yes. How's St. Catherine's?"

"It's fine."

"What are you taking?"

"College Entry."

"So am I...at St. Richard's, of course."

She chuckled kindly at my slight discomfort.

"Funny, I've never seen you on this bus until yesterday, and now here you are again. Did you just move here or something?" she said.

"No. Yesterday I missed the early bus I usually take."

"Oh. So you missed it again today."

"No, today I took it on purpose."

"Really. Why?"

"Because yesterday I saw this nice-looking girl, and I wanted to meet her."

"Oh, How a... How a..." Lisa had this smile like a kid with a secret.

"Romantic?" I said.

"Yeah. I guess that might be a good word."

I looked out the front of the bus.

"Well, it was nice talking to you. This is my stop." I started to move toward the door.

"Nice talking to you." She smiled that smile again, glanced at the floor, looked up, and said, "See you tomorrow?"

"Absolutely. What's your name anyway?"

"Lisa. Lisa Duffy. And yours?"

"Richard, please don't call me Dick, Richard Harrison."

"See you tomorrow, Richard."

* * * * * * * * * *

The day was brighter. I felt like I was more alive than I had ever been in my life. Of course, I had dream girls, but they were TV and movie stars. And yes, I had stared longingly at girls I went to middle school with, and I had imaginary love affairs with a couple of my babysitters, but this was different. At least I thought it was different. I was told my hormones were kicking in, but I couldn't put together the feelings I had that day with body chemistry. Lisa was a girl who told me, albeit subtly, that she had a curiosity, interest, or attraction to me because she saw me once. Maybe she felt like I did. There had to be a reason for that.

Each morning on the bus, Lisa and I had the kind of conversations we all can remember. It's the first date kind of stuff. We talked about the courses we were taking, the teachers we had, the records we liked, and our siblings. The only difference from a first date is you kind of get through those conversations in one evening. In our case, it took several bus rides.

It was a Friday. I remember feeling like I wasn't going to be able to go all weekend without seeing her. It was then I have to admit, the confident and far more mature Lisa Duffy said, "Do you want to get together this weekend?"

I hesitated. Lisa was looking at me with that smug 'got you' look on her face.

"I think that was supposed to be my line," I said.

"Yeah, but I couldn't wait." She laughed. I'm sure the look on my face inspired her. I laughed with her, and I spotted a bit of relief in her expression. It said, 'Thank God, he can take a joke.'

To further confuse things, my stop was coming up, and we hadn't agreed on where or when. Lisa pressed a piece of paper into my hand. It had her phone number on it.

"Call me at seven tonight?"

"Yes."

Two significant steps: she gave me her number, and we're going on our first date.

****

That phone call was shorter than I anticipated. I trailed our family telephone's long cord into the front hall closet to get some privacy. She picked up on the first ring.

"Richard?" She was whispering.

"Yes, how are you?"

"Fine. Do you know where The Diner across the street from the Avalon Theater on Blake Avenue is?" Still, she whispered.

"Yeah. Sure." For no reason at all, I whispered back to her.

"Can you meet me there at one o'clock tomorrow?"

"Yes."

"Good, I'll see you then." She hung up.

****

Okay, I'm a guy. Normally guys don't fuss over clothes, accessories, and makeup. However, I did shower, shave, and apply cologne. I wore my gray dress slacks, a white shirt, and a dark blue v-neck sweater. I used a copper bristle brush on my dusty brown buck shoes.

I got to The Diner on Blake at least twenty minutes early. I couldn't go in since the place was notorious for ejecting students who just hung out while they nursed a ten-cent glass of coke for hours. Lisa showed up five minutes after I did.

"Hungry?" I asked.

"That would be nice."

I was smoking a cigarette.

"Could you put that out for me?"

I was crushing it under my foot before she finished her request.

"Thank you." she leaned over and kissed me on the cheek.

She did it so quickly that if it weren't for the feel of her lips on my cheek, I wouldn't have known she'd done it.

We went into The Diner on Blake and split a chocolate milkshake. The waitress wasn't too busy, so she wasn't glaring at us to move on.

"Have you seen that movie?" Her head gestured toward the Avalon Theater.

I don't remember the movie, but I knew I hadn't seen it. In my family, movies were an unnecessary expense, as long as we had the television set.

"Nope. Have you?"

"No." She stared wistfully out the window.

"We could go if you want to. I have enough money for both of us."

"It would be fun."

Lisa put her hand in mine, and we walked to the theater. I paid the fifty cents we needed to get into the movie.

A Saturday matinee included multiple cartoons and a feature film. The cartoons were still being shown when we got into the dark theater.

She reached over and pulled my head next to her. Then she whispered in my ear.

"There are seats in the back."

I followed her as she walked through the empty back row until we were about halfway in. We sat down. She leaned over again.

"We need to sit in the back because we are both so tall we block the other people's view."

Then she pulled my head toward her and kissed me gently on the lips. Then the following kisses were not so gentle. We kissed and kissed some more. She stopped for a moment, smiled at me, and said, "Make your lips softer, Richard."

Then she demonstrated. I did what she told me. I felt her tongue flicker between my lips. It was unbelievably stimulating for my young inexperienced body.

About twenty minutes later, she said, "I have to go home."

Forget that we never saw the movie; she also didn't explain why she had to go home early.

"What bus do you need?" I said.

She smiled. "The sixty. Same as you."

I told her I would ride to her stop and walk her home. I wasn't chivalrous. I just didn't want to leave her. She insisted I get off at my stop. She pecked at my cheek one more time before I got off, and as the bus pulled away, Lisa looked out through the window and blew me a parting kiss.

****

The relationship between Lisa and me didn't escape the notice of the other kids on the bus. One day, a guy caught up with me as I left the bus and started walking the half block to St. Richards' entrance.

"Hey, Richard." He was a little winded. I stopped walking and waited until he caught up. I had seen this guy around the school. He was a senior, and we didn't have any classes together. I was surprised he even knew my name. We stood outside the entrance of the school, facing each other.

"I just want to give you a heads up."

"Sure, what's happening?"

"Lisa is going steady with Hal Davies."

Davies was the starting guard on St Richard's basketball team.

"It's okay. Lisa and I just talk to each other on the bus. Nothing's going on, you know?"

He smiled. "Good. I just wanted you to know."

I smiled back at him. I was playing it as cool as I could, considering his news destroyed my day.

"Thank you. I'm sure Hal doesn't have anything to worry about."

I laughed. He laughed. We walked through the doors to our school. The guy never talked to me again about anything.

* * * * * * * * * *

Should I bring it up or wait for her to tell me how this would go down? After some thought, I thought I had a solution. Lisa and I continued to meet at The Diner on Blake and then go over to the theater to make out in the back row. We kissed, and I did a little tongue flirting, but she stopped me from going any further. While it was frustrating, it was better than not kissing her. My solution to moving the conversation to an area it appeared she didn't want to go to was pretty simple, but the outcome was potentially frightening.

The next day on the bus, we were in the midst of our twenty-minute conversation when I said, "Hey, there's a mixer at St. Richard's next Friday night. Do you want to go with me?"

She smiled.

"I'd love to, and thank you for asking, but I've already got a date." She kept smiling. I hadn't thought of this kind of response. I took a moment to think.

"Are you upset?" she asked.

"Disappointed would be a better word. I guess I didn't think of you dating other guys. But of course, you do. What the heck was I thinking?" I smiled at her. "Maybe I could cut in and have a dance?"

She frowned.

"I don't think that would be good."

"Really?"

"Yes, if I danced with you, Hal would want to know how I knew you and... Well, I'd prefer he didn't know about us... our relationship. He'd be upset."

I was without words. Well, that's not true either. I had words, but I didn't want to say them.

She went on, "Hal thinks we're going steady. I don't, but he's kind of insistent, and he's my brother's best friend."

"I see." I was still trying to gain my footing. Finally, I asked the most frightening question.

"So if he thinks you're going steady and you don't, what are we doing?"

She reached out and touched my chest.

"We're friends, Richard. Isn't that what we are? Isn't that enough?"

My bus stop saved me.

I smiled at her and said as kindly as I could, "I was hoping for more."

* * * * * * * * * * *

I started taking the earlier bus. I didn't go to St. Richard's or St. Catherine's mixers. People kept asking me what was wrong, so I guess I didn't hide my disappointment very well.

I only saw Lisa once after that when I went to a St. Richard's home basketball game. Lisa had a seat behind our team's bench. I was on the other side of the court. I could look right at her without being obvious.

She didn't look happy, but maybe I wanted her to be crushed by our breakup, so I imagined it. Plus, Hal Davies, her steady, was not playing very well, and we were getting our ass kicked. I wasn't going to get caught in a position where I had to confront her, so I got up to leave with about three minutes left on the clock. Just as I made my way down to the floor, one of the teams called a time-out. It might as well have been a spotlight thrown on me. She looked up, and I know she saw me.

As much as I enjoyed our time together, it all came down to what she thought of me. In my mind, we weren't going to be just friends. I think I was a component in a secret plan of rebellion. For whatever reason, she couldn't tell her boyfriend she didn't want to go steady with him. That had nothing to do with what she felt for me. She didn't think enough of me to give me a choice in the matter. It was all about her, but then we were young teenagers. Everything is dramatic at that age. Isn't it?

Chapter 4
Dedra Cummings

I met Dedra at one of my friend's house parties. Jake's parents were comfortable with the recreation room in the basement of their ranch home full of hot, sweaty teenagers dancing to 'rock n roll' music. They were okay with it as long as they were home. All of the young people at the party knew Jake's Mom or Dad might drop in at any time just to make sure no one was adding anything alcoholic to the soda they provided. And you could count on a parental raid if we played two slow dances in succession. The concern was about us kids having too much close and prolonged body contact.

When I got to the party, most of the usual suspects were already there. I wasn't the only one who met the opposite sex on the bus going to school or who trolled The Diner on Blake for new companions. There was always a friend of a friend or a visiting relative at these house parties. As it turned out, the lonely girl in the corner was Jake's cousin, Dedra Cummings.

I sat down next to her. The dance floor was a mass of my friends doing the "Twist."

"Hi, my name is Richard."

It was as if I woke her from a nap.

"Oh, Hi, I'm Dedra." She almost yawned.

"Dedra, would you like to dance?"

She gave me a sleepy kind of grin.

"Not now. Maybe later."

"Okay, so why don't I know you?"

"I'm Jake's cousin. I'm visiting."

She took the coke I had in my hand and took a healthy slug of it.

"I'm sorry, could I get you something?"

She sighed.

"Yeah, that would be nice."

Again she gave me the grin with a little more energy. I got up.

"What would you like?"

"Coke is fine, thank you."

I came back with a bottle and a plastic cup.

"Thank you. You're a gentleman and a ..."

"I'll take the gentlemen, but I won't risk my reputation as an academic. Okay?"

She laughed.

"I'm sorry, but I can't help but notice you seem drowsy," I said.

"It's the change in time zones. I just flew in from California this afternoon."

"I didn't know you could get tired from flying in from California."

"I don't know about other people, but I can. I lost three hours of time"

"So sorry for you. How long are you going to be here?"

"I fly home a week from today."

We quietly sipped our cokes and watched the crowd switch to another form of dancing. At the same time, Elvis was complaining about the existence of the Heartbreak Hotel.

"Have you visited here before?"

"Once, but I was about five years old. I didn't see much, and I don't remember a lot."

I let that revelation simmer for a moment. Dedra wasn't your brown-skinned blonde California stereotype. Her hair was a burnished brown. It waved but didn't curl. Although she was seated, Dedra appeared to be medium height and build. I noticed her gray to green eyes once she was fully awake. Her oval face was adorned with a slightly turned-up nose. Summing her up? Not spectacular but undoubtedly attractive.

"What do you think about me showing you around?"

She looked at me as if I just crawled out from under a rock.

"Why would you want to do that? You hardly know me."

"Jake is a good friend of mine. I'm sure he and his folks will show you around. But, let's say my tour will be more fun."

She appeared to be thinking.

"Okay, Mister. I'll tell them you offered to show me the city, and I accepted. When are you going to pick me up?"

"Tomorrow at ten o'clock. That will give you time to catch up on your sleep."

"What should I wear?"

"A comfortable pair of walking shoes, dress for the weather, and remember this time of year, our weather can turn cooler quickly. I'll have you home by six to change into something appropriate for doing a little nightclubbing. Does that sound like fun?"

Dedra gave me a shy look that I would see a lot over the next few days.

"Why, Richard! I don't know. Nightclubbing? Jake promised me the Zoo."

"Jake's parents talked him into that choice."

She chuckled.

"You do know them well."

"Yes, they are nice, but a little bit…?"

"Stuffy?"

"That works."

"Is Jake invited to join us?"

"No, and trust me; it won't hurt his feelings. Jake is a great guy socially, but he enjoys his time in the gym. He would gladly swap a day of showing you around for a couple of hours in the gym."

"Seriously?"

"He aspires to be a professional athlete. And he might even do it."

"And you? What do you aspire to?"

"In the near future? I want to be the most stimulating city tour guide you've ever or will ever encounter. Long-term, maybe engineering. We'll see."

* * * * * * * * * *

The following day, I imagined hearing the MaMa's and The Papa's, singing *California Dreaming* in the background as Dedra entered the living room at Jake's house. I had been waiting for just a couple of minutes with Jake's mother, Alice. Alice was trying to get me to tell her about my plans for her niece. She seemed most concerned about my suggestion that later in the evening, we were going nightclubbing.

I made her feel better when I mentioned a new teen bar opening where kids could hang out. To be fair, I never said Dedra and I were going to that teen club. I merely threw the news of its opening into the conversation. I figured that Alice bought the story.

Dedra was dressed and ready to go. Last night's sleepy girl was gone, and in her place was an attractive and pretty sophisticated young lady. Dedra decided that some plaid slacks, a white collared blouse, a powder blue cotton sweater, and white tennis shoes were appropriate for the day's activities and the weather. She hadn't overdone her makeup, but then she didn't need it. With her slightly tanned complexion, her hair pulled back in a ponytail, and her head covered with a baseball cap, Dedra's preparation was perfect.

When Dedra and I walked out of her aunt's home, she looked up and down the street.

"Where is your car?"

"We don't need a car. I have access to a magic carpet."

"Really! I'm going to warn you. I might get airsick."

"Not to worry." As I said this, a bus pulled up to our corner.

"Ah, and so it arrives. ...our magic carpet."

The bus pulled to a stop, and the door flew open. Dedra grinned.

"Indeed. Seriously, how much do I need for the fare."

"No need to worry. I brought you a day pass."

* * * * * * * * * *

First, we went to a baseball game. My hometown has a triple-A minor league Chicago Cubs team. They were playing a doubleheader that afternoon.

Not only did Dedra enjoy the game, but it turned out she was pretty knowledgeable.

"You know your baseball," I said.

"I play softball for my high school team."

"Ah, a jock no less."

"Sorry, I'm a scholar-athlete. Women don't need a..."

"My mistake, of course." She enjoyed my discomfort.

Sitting in the stands watching the game with her was a different experience for me. I reasoned that Dedra had a lot of experience with young men. She wasn't shy and undecided. Having a conversation with her was smooth and pleasant even when serious discussion sprang up.

"So why are you visiting your Aunt and Uncle?" I said.

She paused only a second, then pulled her gaze off the field and looked at me.

"My parents are finalizing a divorce this week. The judge ruled that I'm old enough to choose which parent I want to live with. I thought that I might make a better decision if I wasn't in Los Angeles. You know, kind of getting away from the battle."

I waited so I could absorb what she shared with me. I didn't know anyone who was in a family that had gone through a divorce. It was one of those moments that told me I wasn't at the kid's table anymore. This situation in her life was adult stuff. Dedra was the one who opened up the door to that room for me.

"Christ, I'm sorry. I mean...I can't even imagine what you're going through."

"I will tell you, and I didn't ask for it."

"What happened? Why do your folks feel they have to split up?"

"Hmm. How do I answer that?" Tears began forming at the corners of her eyes. She wiped at her eyes with her sweater's cuff.

"Sorry," I said.

"You don't have to apologize." She pulled herself together.

"Look, you're a nice guy. I liked you from the moment I met you, but in a week I'll be gone. You will forget my name and what I look like. Or, maybe my story is one you remember because you will tell the story so many times you can't forget it. Either way, we have no future."

I scrambled for positivity and said, "Wait, you don't know that. What if I get accepted at UCLA or Southern California? What if…?"

"Pigs fly. You're what... a sophomore.?"

"Freshman."

"Hah. I should have read that childish romanticism in those dreamy eyes." She laughed, reached out for my hand, and held the back of my hand to her breast. She leaned in close to me and whispered. "Are you a virgin, Richard?"

I looked back at her. We were so close I could only see her eyes. I nodded, yes.

"Maybe we should do something about that." Then she put my hand back on my lap and turned to watch the game.

We had hot dogs, peanuts, and I took her to The Diner on Blake for a milkshake after the game. At this point, I could go toThe Diner on Blake and the theater across the street without getting upset thinking of Lisa Duffy. But on this occasion, I wouldn't have minded if Lisa showed up and would see me with this California dream.

* * * * * * * * * *

I had taken a job busing tables at The Manitou Supper Club. After the dinner crowd thinned out and the kitchen closed, the owner, Sammy D'Amato, brought in musicians to entertain. It transformed the place into looking like the jazz joints you see in the movies. I talked to Sammy about bringing Dedra to the club for the music.

"This girl. Is she someone you want to impress?"

"Yeah, I guess."

"Come in at about eight o'clock. You can have dinner on me and then hang around to hear the music."

I couldn't believe my luck.

"Thank you, sir."

"One thing."

"Yes, sir."

"Don't order any booze." He laughed and patted me on the shoulder.

* * * * * * * * * *

That evening, I picked up Dedra at seven-thirty. She was in a dark blue dress and high heels. She had her hair wrapped in what she called a French Twist. She had applied a little more makeup and put on diamond earrings and a string of pearls around her neck.

With her heels on, she came up to my height. We walked down to the bus stop, and her heels clicked off our steps in time. When we got on the bus, she noticed that we weren't the only ones dressed for the evening.

When we got to the club, I could tell the crew was alerted to what was going on.

"Mr. Harrison, right this way, sir."

We were seated at a ringside table. The menus were both guest versions, meaning they didn't show the prices. The service was as always excellent. They didn't hold back because their busboy brought his date, and no one let on that they knew me.

"Wow, I'm impressed. Does your Dad own this place?" she asked.

"I wish. They are doing me a favor." She looked at me for more information. "On any other night, I'd be busing dishes here. The boss is taking care of this."

As it turned out, the band that night played dance music. My mother's maid and my former nanny, Jeany, was patient with me when she taught me how to dance. It paid off that evening. Dedra and I didn't dance every number. However, we didn't pass up any slow dance songs and enjoyed constant close body contact. During one of those numbers, she laid her head on my shoulder.

"Friday night, I'm going to be home alone. My aunt and uncle are going out, and Jake has a date. They said it was okay if you came over to keep me company."

"Sounds nice. I'll be there."

* * * * * * * * * *

That Friday night, I showed up at 7:00. Dedra was in the kitchen, preparing a green salad. I sat at the breakfast bar and watched her work.

"I've made a decision," she said.

"Decision?"

"Yes, I'm going to live with my father."

She turned halfway from the counter and looked at me for my reaction. I wasn't sure what to say.

"it's none of my business, but I'm curious. Why?"

"Because I blame my mother for breaking the family up. Right now, I can't help but be angry when I'm with her. I don't want to wake up and go to sleep angry. So I should create some distance until I don't feel that way."

She cooked a simple meal. We had the green salad with oil and vinegar dressing, pasta marinara with garlic bread, and Italian sausage. After dinner, I helped clear the table and grabbed the dish towel. She told me I didn't have to do any of it. I reminded her I was a professional.

I was standing next to her when she took the towel from my hands to dry her hands. She backed up to me, took my arms, and wrapped them around her. She laid her head back on my chest. I leaned down and kissed her neck. She took my right hand and placed it over her breast. I closed my fingers gently. I realized she wasn't wearing a bra. I could feel her shiver. After unbuttoning her blouse, she put my hand on her bare breast. After a few moments, she turned and embraced me. I put my fingers under her chin and tipped her head up for a kiss.

"God, for a virgin, you are a great kisser," she said. I thought, 'Thank you, Lisa Duffy.'

She tipped her head back, and we kissed some more. She unbuttoned her blouse completely and helped me understand where to put my hands and what they should do to bring her pleasure. I am lost and unsure of what I should do in this world she has me in. And yet, I had no desire to leave it. Even with my eyes closed, I sensed a flash of light and automatically opened them.

"Dedra, someone just pulled into the driveway."

Walking toward the front windows, Dedra gathered her open blouse and began re-buttoning it.

"It's my aunt and uncle."

I turned on the television set and flopped on the couch. Dedra quickly joined me. We sat a discrete distance from each other, and we tried to seem genuinely surprised when they came through the front door.

After their dinner at a restaurant, the movie they went to see had sold out. They joined us in the living room. We watched a black and white film starring people who were by that time twenty years older.

Dedra and I had another half hour alone when Alice and Jim went to bed, and Jake hadn't come home from his date. Still, without saying anything, it was apparent we couldn't go back and resume what we had started.

As she ushered me to the front door, she tried to say goodbye, but it was hard for both of us. We had crossed a line. There should have been a path we could use to take the next logical steps. And yet, tomorrow, she would get on a plane and put thousands of miles between us.

I begged her to let me go to the airport with her in the morning. She was adamant that it wasn't going to happen.

"Why? It's not going to make either of us feel any better. It's not going to change anything. Kiss me and say goodbye."

I kissed her for what seemed like minutes. No matter how long it was, it wasn't long enough. I went through the door.

"Richard," she said.

"Yes." I turned back to see her backlit form in the doorway. It was the last image I would have of her.

"You didn't say goodbye."

I hung my head.

"I'm sorry. I can't."

She stood without saying anything for a moment.

"Well, at least that romanticism in your dreamy eyes isn't childish anymore."

* * * * * * * * * * *

I was a wreck for weeks. Short-tempered and moody, I wasn't fooling anyone. Jake leveled with me after a period of my moping. He told me that Dedra had been quiet and un-conversational on the way to the airport.

"She thanked everyone in the family for their hospitality, but she didn't sound like she meant it. On the way home from the airport, we all commented on Dedra's mood. My mother told us about Dedra's parents getting a divorce and that Dedra had decided to live with her Dad. My Mom was unhappy with both the divorce and Dedra's decision, but she tried not to express that to Dedra. Mom meant it as an explanation of Dedra's unhappiness, but I knew better. When Dedra and I were out of my parents' earshot, she told me how surprised and confused her feelings were for you. You know she's a senior in high school, don't you?"

I shook my head, no.

"She told me that her confusion was based on why she fell for you so quickly. She couldn't tell if she saw you like the solid ground in her life that was uncertain, or was it love at first sight? She sent me a letter. There's a note in it she asked me to give you."

He pulled it out of his pocket and gave it to me. It was in a small envelope like an RSVP reply to a wedding invitation. I put it in my back pocket and didn't read it until I got home from work. In the feeble glow of the single bedside lamp, I opened the note.

Richard.

"When you left that evening we spent together; I was at a loss to explain what meeting you had done to me. So much was happening, my parent's divorce and starting college this fall. And then there's this surprise: this guy, Richard. We are so young. Who knows what would have happened if we could have continued to be together.

"But I want you to know these things. You were my quiet in the storm. You were a friend when I needed one. You are more of a man than you think. I tell you all of this so you will know that even if I weren't carrying all the baggage I have, I would have fallen for you anyway."

Chapter 5
Rebecca Marley

I took my regular bus home on a Sunday night from my extra-busy job at The Manitou supper club. I was tired. The weather was turning from cold winter to wet, fresh early spring. I couldn't help but notice a young lady struggling to get on the bus with too many grocery bags. I got up and moved to the front to help her.

While she paid her fare, I moved some of the bags to an empty seat across the aisle. When she sat next to me, she said, "Thank you. I don't know what I was thinking about by buying all of this stuff in one trip."

"Your welcome."

She extended her hand. "I'm Rebecca, and you are..."

"Richard, don't call me Dick."

She chuckled.

"I don't suppose Rick is good either?"

"I prefer not."

"Listen, I don't know where you're getting off, but I'm leaving the bus on 18th street. Would you consider helping me carry this stuff home?"

"Sure. I could do that."

Rebecca settled in her seat. The 18th Street bus stop was still a long way to go. Rebecca could have been Hispanic, Native American, South Sea Islander, or Inuit. What she was, was exotic and sensual to a white kid like me. Since she is bundled in a long winter coat, I couldn't see her figure. Her angular face held big brown eyes, full lips, a narrow petite nose, with cheeks flared just a bit. Her smile was luminous.

When we got near her stop, I began gathering as many bags as I could. She nodded and picked up the two bags that remained. We didn't have far to go. Rebecca lived in a four flat in a primarily residential district about a half block from the bus stop. She set down the bags and began going through her backpack for her key.

"You don't have to haul this stuff up to my apartment, you know."

"It's okay. I've got it this far. I might as well take the stuff upstairs unless you don't want me to."

"No, I appreciate your help. I've got to get one of those carts. You know. The baskets with wheels like a roller bag you travel with only they have room for groceries."

At this point, she found her keys. We made our way up a relatively narrow stairwell to her apartment door. She stopped and stared at me.

"Oh, I guess you'd rather I just put everything down and leave. I get it, Security. Don't blame you," I said.

I started to put the bags on the floor.

"No, no, no. I trust you. `How old are you?"

"Fifteen."

"Oh, my God! You're jailbait."

I laughed.

"Yes, ma'am, I am. If you want to look at it that way."

She laughed with me as she opened the door.

"Come on inside. I just wasn't sure if I should offer you a drink or soda."

"Wait a second. How old are you?" I said.

I was standing on the edge outside of her galley kitchen because it was too small for the two of us. She started putting some things in the refrigerator and freezer.

"Old enough to be your older sister, smart-ass."

She pulled a can of coke out of the refrigerator and held it out for me.

"If you drink more than two, I'll have to ask for your keys."

"That would make sense If I had a car?"

Gesturing me toward a couch in the living room, Rebecca sat in a chair arranged in a conversation setting across from the sofa.

We began with small talk. When I asked what she did for a living, the conversation became more interesting than a stream of small talk.

"I teach Art at The Community College."

"How cool. I love looking at art, but I'm never sure what I'm looking at."

"What do you mean by that?"

"For instance, I'm looking at a painting that other people tell me is so great, and I think I don't see what is so fantastic about it."

She got up and walked to a large bookshelf arrangement she had on one wall. She was taking some time to find and select a couple of books. She handed the books to me and then sat down next to me on the couch.

"Page through these and show me what you like."

It took a few minutes, but finally, I showed her a page.

"I like this one by Degas. I have seen some of his pictures in other books. I kind of like most of his stuff."

"Okay. First, this painter's name is French. It's pronounced 'day gah,' not 'De gas.' He's one of an influential group of late 18th century painters that we refer to as The Impressionists."

She turned the pages and offered me the book again.

"What about this one?"

"Yes, I like that one too."

"Why?"

"It's a picture of people having a party. I can imagine myself in this situation."

"Okay, how about this one?"

"It looks like a house painter's drop cloth. It doesn't mean anything to me. It's just spilled paint."

"It's a painting by an American painter, Jackson Pollock. We classify his work as abstract art. Generally, if the work doesn't move you and you don't understand it, it's not your fault. Maybe if you were to take a course in art appreciation, you might understand his work better, but you may continue not to like it."

"Okay."

"Do you have any talent for the arts?"

"Hell, no. I can't draw a straight line."

She smiled at me. I liked it when she smiled, particularly when I made her do it.

"When I mean the arts, I'm talking about performance, music, sculpture, not just painting. Do you take photographs?"

"Not really. I've always wished I could draw, but I'm no good at it."

"Would you like to learn?"

"Yeah, sure."

"Okay, tell you what we could do. I owe you for being such a gentleman. What evening next week would you be available for dinner? After dinner, I will get you started on learning to sketch."

I thought to myself. What is my work schedule?

"I could do it on Tuesday."

"Tuesday, it is."

We chatted a little more. I think we both realized that it was already late. Rebecca saw me to the door. As I started to leave, she put a light hand on my shoulder and kissed me on the cheek.

"My knight in shining armor."

Then with her hand firmly on my shoulder, she guided me out the door.

I went home and went to bed. I suppose drinking the cola with all of its caffeine may have made it difficult for me to fall asleep. However, I believe it was the feeling I got from being with an attractive, intelligent woman and liking how she treated me as an adult. Besides, as we Catholics are prone to say, "I was having bad thoughts."

* * * * * * * * * *

When Tuesday came, I made some lame excuse to my mother about an after-school activity. She had her bridge club that evening. My Dad wouldn't worry if I didn't stay out too late. I killed time at the library between the end of classes and my dinner date with Rebecca by doing the homework I needed to do for my classes the next day. I was at the door of her apartment building promptly at six o'clock. When she opened the door, she was smiling.

"There you are. I'll have dinner ready in a few minutes."

As I entered, the smell of food cooking prevailed over my first scent of her perfume. She was wearing some red pants that looked like they were from a two-piece suit. The blouse was ivory-colored and billowed. I looked down at her bare feet.

"Do you want me to take off my shoes?"I said.

"If it makes you feel more comfortable."

I took them off.

"Do you need any help?" I said.

"No, thank you. Do you cook?"

"I picked up some stuff working at the restaurant. I've helped with food prep from time to time."

"I'll bet your mother appreciates that."

"My Mom, no. Nobody gets in her kitchen but her. Dad and I can warm up leftovers if she's not home. But other than that, I wouldn't dare touch anything in there."

There was a small drop-leaf table that she pulled away from the wall. She set the table with a complete service setting, including a wine glass. I sat down at the dining table because I could watch and converse with her as she finished cooking and plated our dinner.

She put the plate in front of me, sat down at her place, and casually poured us both a glass of red wine. The dish had a portion of chicken and pasta with a marinara sauce. On the side, she had fixed a mixed green salad with a creamy dressing.

"This looks delicious. Thank you."

"My pleasure. I'm so glad you got home okay the other night. It was so late. I'm sure you were tired." I smiled.

"What's so funny?" she said.

"It's just that I was tired the other night. We had quite a crowd at the restaurant that evening. But I did have trouble sleeping right away."

"Really? Why is that do you think that?"

"I don't have to guess. Let's just say you made quite an impression on me."

She laughed so hard she had to put her fork full of food down on the plate.

"Oh my, am I going to be safe from your amorous feelings?"

"Yes, ma'am. My inexperience in love matters provides me with enough fear that it appears I'm paralyzed into a state of permanent gallantry. You are safe with me and from me, my lady."

If this sounds ridiculous coming from the mouth of a fifteen-year-old, you're right. I anticipated this conversation and concocted that response. Rebecca gave me the opening, so I let her have it.

She just stared at me for a second. Then her expression brightened.

"That was brilliant. I'm impressed and flattered."

We turned to our food, which was fabulous.

* * * * * * * * * *

Fortunately, she never refilled my wine glass, and I did not drink all of the wine she'd poured for me. Still, I was a bit fuzzy-headed when I sat down on the couch after finishing the dishes. Rebecca went down the hall. When she returned, she had a paper bag. She pulled out a sketchbook, a box set of pencils, an eraser, and a pen-like object called a smudging tool.

"Let's start with a few practice and hand training exercises."

She instructed me on how to hold the pencil, depending on the line I was trying to draw. I practiced drawing shapes, circles, and lines of different thicknesses, both light and dark, depending on the pressure I put on the point. I learned when to sharpen the pencil and how to do it.

"You're doing pretty well."

"I'm doing better than I thought I would."

Okay, let's have you do something simple. Try sketching the magazine lying on the table."

Once I got the perspective lines drawn, she pointed out the direction of the light. I began moving from the rough sketch to a more representative image by filling in the details and tried to shade in the subtle gradations of light.

"My goodness, it's ten o'clock," she said.

I looked at my work in the sketchbook.

"Yeah, I should be going."

I put the tools and the sketchbook in the bag.

"I should buy a sketchbook and stuff so that I can work at home."

"No need. That is my gift to you. Carry it with you at all times. First, I suggest that if you see something serious you want to sketch, take some photos of your subject from different angles. Then pick out the one you like and sketch from that. It freezes the light's direction and eliminates the subject's chance to move and change the angle."

"Thank you for getting me started. I enjoyed this. I hope I can bring you what I do, so you can help me get better."

"No need to worry, my knight in shining armor. Do you want to come next Tuesday and we can work some more?"

I could have only dreamed that last part, but she was serious. When I got home, my mother wasn't back from her card game yet, and Dad had fallen asleep in his chair watching television.

* * * * * * * * * *

The following day my mother was scurrying about the kitchen fixing breakfast for my Dad and me.

"So, how did it go with your school club last night?" she said.

"It was great. I'm learning how to sketch."

I pulled the sketchbook from my book bag and showed her my sketch of the magazine lying on the table. She glanced at it as she continued to work on breakfast.

"Why does it smell like perfume?" she said.

"Okay, ah, I guess the girl sitting next to me might have been wearing too much."

So there we have it. I belong to this fictitious Art Club at the school. I have an excuse to visit Rebecca as much as she'll tolerate me. I'm feeling good.

* * * * * * * * * *

For the next few weeks, I have dinner with Rebecca every Tuesday night. After dinner and an enjoyable conversation, she continues to teach me to draw. She looks at whatever I've done during the week, and then I work on something while I'm there. Rather than be constantly looking over my shoulder at the same time I draw, she often grades assignments or does other work for her teaching position.

"How about I cook for you next week?" I said. Her smile beamed.

"How nice. Do you want me to shop for the food, and you fix it?"

"No, I'll pick it up before I come over. Is there any way I can get in here earlier so I can have dinner ready when you come home?"

She left the room and came back with a small ring with two keys on it.

"Don't lose em."

I smiled as I took them.

"By the way, what do your parents think of your work?"

"My Dad doesn't say much, but my Mom thinks it's cute that I'm learning something artsy."

"I'm sure your parents will be proud of your talent. You do have a talent, you know. I'd like to meet them someday."

I paused and looked at the floor.

I looked up, and she had a funny look on her face.

"Richard, your parents, know where you are spending your time on Tuesday evenings, don't they?"

"If this is the location for the High School Art Club, yes."

Her face caved in with worry and fear.

"Oh shit!"

"Look, I'm sorry…"

"Richard. I don't think you realize how bad this could look."

"Yeah, I guess."

"Whoa. Okay, can you tell them…"

"No, that's not going to work. How about if I tell them that you volunteered to help me because you saw my work and it showed promise. Otherwise, I have to admit I deceived them. It's going to look worse than it is."

"Alright. Okay, but they have to know that you're coming here. Enough with the High School Art Club. Does your high school even have an after-school art club?"

"Yeah, but I'll be damned if I know when or where they meet."

* * * * * * * * * *

I went home with the story that a teacher who thinks I have promise is tutoring me. I told my folks this while they were trying to watch their favorite television program. They both appeared to listen, but I know they weren't. They both nodded when I asked if it was okay with them. I didn't feel it necessary to tell them I was doing this with a single woman in her apartment.

* * * * * * * * * *

The following week I got to Rebecca's apartment a little after 4:30. I knew where everything was because I had helped with the dishes. I had a piece of salmon. I applied a rub of salt, pepper, and dry mustard. Then I put the fish in a bowl with honey turning it every 15 minutes. I went to work on getting the asparagus ready for roasting in the oven. I painted the spears with olive oil and lightly sprinkled garlic salt on them. The rice I made with vegetable stock.

I will admit to her that I bought the cherry tarts with buttercream frosting glaze on them. The head bartender helped me select the wine. He was kind enough, no make that brave enough, to give me a bottle.

"Is this that beautiful girl you brought to the club that night?"

"No. No, she went back to California."

"Too bad. That girl was a stunner."

"Yes, she was."

I was setting the table when Rebecca got home. She marveled at what was going on.

"Tell me your folks know where you are?"

"Yes, they do, and they are fine with it."

I might have overdone the enthusiasm, but she bought it.

I'm not sure if Rebecca was trying to establish borders. Still, I suddenly started hearing references to a guy named Rod during dinner. She wished Rod could cook and how lucky my girlfriend is because I do. I wasn't going to lie to her. So I told her my girlfriend loves my cooking. Since I considered Rebecca, my girlfriend, and she had just told me how good the dinner was, I wasn't lying.

* * * * * * * * * *

That evening, I asked her if I could sketch her. She had consumed two glasses of wine. Perhaps that, and the relief that we weren't hiding what we were doing from my folks, made her more inclined to submit.

"How do you want me to pose?"

I wasn't stupid enough to tell her the truth that my preference was for her to pose naked reclining on the couch.

"Why don't you sit on the chair and give me a three-quarter look to work with."

While I worked to get the perspective sketched in, we talked. I wanted to know more about my competition.

"Tell me what Rod does?" I saw her eyes squint.

"He's a drama teacher at the college."

"Wow, he must be interesting."

"He is a nice guy," That was faint praise from my standpoint.

"Are you thinking about marriage?"

"God, I hope so. We've been dating for over a year. He's very protective of me."

"I'm going to ask this, but it's none of my business. Are you open to living with Rod before you get married?" I thinking that if Rod wouldn't, I would.

"It's funny you'd ask that. Rod and I talked about it last weekend. He stayed overnight on Saturday."

She was looking at something in the kitchen, so she didn't see me flinch.

"He brought it up. I wasn't surprised. He had been staying over more and more. We go to the same place to work every day. And then, there would be someone to help carry groceries, so I wouldn't have to depend on the kindness of strangers."

She glanced at me.

"While I believe you can not replace me. I understand the convenience it would afford," I said.

"I told him I would think it over."

"So, where are you right now?"

I could tell she was mulling it over.

"What do you think?"

"I think my girl and I are too young to make that decision."

"Richard!"

"Okay, I don't know the guy, but this much I do know. It's great if it makes the relationship better, but if it makes it worse, it makes it harder to separate. You'll still be working at the same place. I know I'm young, but I have been in love. Believe it or not. I've been hurt. So I know the risk."

She didn't look at me.

"Tell me about you...the girl who hurt you."

I told her the story about Dedra. Before I could stop it from happening, I was tearing up. She got up from the chair, came to me, wrapped her arms around me, and hugged me to her breasts.

"Quit. I can tell it's too painful."

I was embarrassed, but I couldn't stop the sadness pouring out of me. It felt strange. I didn't realize how much Dedra had meant to me and that I was still carrying it around

"No, I've never told anyone how I feel about that situation. It will do me good."

When I got more control, I finished the story.

"God, that is so sad. Does your present girlfriend know about this girl?"

Well, if it was true twenty minutes ago, It's still true. If only in my mind.

"She thinks it's sad."

****

It was three weeks later. It was Rebecca's turn to cook. When I let myself into the apartment, I noticed that several boxes are being packed. There was no smell of cooking, and it was clear to me that Rebecca had been drinking.

In the last couple of weeks, we had been on good terms. She didn't talk about Rod, nor did she ask me about my girlfriend. My sketching was improving, and she was encouraging me. Rebecca surprised me and framed the sketch I did of her. Then she surprised me again with a framed drawing she did of me.

"Fair is fair, my knight in shining armor."

But that night, there was a palatable pall in the room. She mumbled an unintelligible greeting through her wine-soaked consciousness. As I stood outside the galley kitchen, she uncorked another bottle. I saw an empty bottle in the recycle barrel.

"Good evening, teacher."

"I didn't cook. I ordered a Pizza from Lockland's." She was noticeably slurring her words.

"Shit, I didn't know that was fair. I would have done that weeks ago."

"God damn, if you don't want it..." She was yelling at me

"Hey, you're upset. What's going on?"

"It's none of your business."

"Okay, would you prefer I leave?"

She looked at me for a long time.

"No, don't leave. I need to be with someone. I guess I'm lucky you're here. I'm sorry I snapped at you."

She looked at me. Her body was weaving back and forth as if she was having trouble keeping her balance.

"I'm moving," she said.

"I guessed." I turned to the open boxes and opened my arms.

"Yeah, I'm moving." The buzzer for the entrance door persisted in the background.

"I'll get it."

"Wait," she waved a ten-dollar bill at me.

"Nine-fifty," The delivery guy said.

I got three bucks out of my wallet and gave it to him with her ten.

When I got back upstairs, I found her slumped in the chair. The glass of wine was dangling in her hand at a dangerous angle.

"Honey," I said.

She looked so sad and vulnerable.

"Yes, Honey." She silly-drunk grinned.

"It looks like you might spill that wine."

"Oh." She looked like she just woke up.

She put the glass on the table and gave me her drunken grin again.

"Okay?" She sought my approval. "Are you going to take care of me now?"

"What do you say we eat while the pizza is hot."

"Great idea."

She was hungry because she ate over half of the pizza and some apple pie I found in the kitchen.

"We broke up," she said. "It was Rod's idea to move in together, and when I told him I decided it wouldn't be a good idea, he got upset. We started to argue. All of this crap came out about what he resented in our relationship and how I didn't appreciate him. And then I cut the cord. I told him I enjoyed the company of one of my students a hell of a lot more than him."

She sighed. "It was the last thing I said to him."

I hesitated, " So who is..."

"You, my knight in shining armor. You are the student I enjoy being with more than him. And you know what's fucking sad? The separation over these last few days has convinced me that he wasn't a boyfriend as much as a bad habit. And that is my fault, not his."

She pointed at me with her arm extended. Then she crooked her finger, summoning me to her side on the couch. I went to her. She put her arm around me and pulled me close. Her face was inches from mine.

"You know something. I am so close to just tearing off your clothes and fucking you. And I know you want that too. I can see the lust in your eyes sometimes when we're together. But I can't do it. It's just so wrong for so many reasons."

Besides the embarrassment of having an erection, I was shaking uncontrollably. The thought that this beautiful woman would take my virginity was undeniably exciting. I could feel the warmth of her body. Her right breast was crushed against my chest. Her leg pressed next to mine.

"Besides, I can't let you have me because it's my time of the month. You know, I'm a mess down there. But there is something I can do for you."

She pulled me down on the couch, opened her blouse to expose her breasts, and offered them to my lips. While I eagerly enjoyed my access to her, she zipped open my trousers and took my genitals into her hand."

When the desired result of all of this concluded, she got up, buttoned her blouse, took my hand, and led me to the bedroom. Lying down in bed, she pulled me in next to her, spooned me, and either fell asleep or passed out. I couldn't tell the difference. After a half-hour or so, I couldn't rouse her from her sleep. I couldn't stay with her, so I slipped out of bed, made myself presentable, and went home.

* * * * * * * * * *

It was two days before I got the nerve to call her. She sounded cheerful enough, and she invited me over. When I got to Rebecca's place, I found that she was definitely in the final stages of leaving. Initially, I thought she was just moving to another apartment in Rivers Edge. Actually, she was going to move out of state. I would later harbor the belief that women didn't break up with me; they just left town to get away from me.

She had fresh coffee in the pot and served me a cup. We sat on the dining chairs and rested our cups on the floor because the table was being used as a packing station.

She told me about her new position at some school in the midwest I had never heard of, but it was more than one days travel to get to it. Then she got uncomfortable.

"Listen, the other evening? I apologize for my condition. It isn't how I want you to remember me."

I thought to myself that apology or not, it would be hard for me to forget.

"To be honest, I don't remember much about it, but I was a lush. I might have said some things that were hurtful or embarrassing?"

That surprised me. The possibility of her blacking out never occurred to me.

"What's the last thing you remember?" I said.

She sighed. "Oh, I don't know."

"After you ate most of the pizza and some apple pie I found in the refrigerator, I helped you to your bed and...well, it appears you passed out. You didn't say anything to hurt my feelings or insult me. Mostly you just went on and on about you and Rod."

"Hmm, I'm sorry."

"Look, you were hurt and angry. I get it. You don't have to be sorry for me."

We talked some more. Rebecca didn't promise to stay in touch. I wouldn't find out her phone number or address unless she gave it to me, and she didn't offer it. It was good-bye forever. It wasn't as bad as Dedra, maybe because I never saw any future that I shared with Rebecca. Or possibly, I was getting used to the pain of breaking up with someone who I liked. One unanswered question? Was she that drunk? Or did she know what she was doing all along?

As time went on, I realized that I thought about Rebecca a lot. I got past almost having sex with a woman, and my thoughts became more about the time we spent together. I valued what she taught me. It wasn't just that she opened my mind to talent I didn't know I had and the possibilities presented. It wasn't just that she treated me like the adult I wanted to be. We had good times together. I missed that.

Chapter 6
Audrey Becker

Summer romance: numerous movies and TV programs portray this as a common experience that viewers always embrace. In the summer between my freshman and sophomore year of high school, I took a day job lifeguarding at the municipal pool beside my work at the restaurant. I usually worked the 9:00 am until 2:00 pm shift five days a week. My co-worker who took over the chair at 2:00 was a girl named Audrey Becker.

Audrey was a small girl. I figured about 90 pounds. She was about five feet tall with a head of brown hair that faded in the sun to a reddish shade. Her face was long with a mass of freckles that splashed down over her turned down nose and cheeks as if a can of spray paint exploded in her face. She had gray eyes and a small, puckered mouth.

My job duty was more for keeping order more than saving lives. For the most part, the mothers kept a close watch on their little kids. I didn't get too many teenagers. The young hormonally-charged middle and high schoolers generally didn't come to the pool until later in the afternoon. The few of them that I got on my shift were the biggest problem. They ran after each other, snapped towels, and splashed water all over everybody. All of these things were against the rules, and they knew it.

After a couple of days of changing the guard, I recognized that my dialogue with Audrey was pretty cryptic. I'd say something like, "Hi. I've been watching the little kid in the red trunks. If he falls in the pool, his mom won't notice. She's too busy talking with the other moms. See you tomorrow. Have a good day."

To this, Audrey would nod to acknowledge she heard me, put on her sunglasses, tip her visor lower on her forehead, and climb up into the chair without so much as a word passing her pouting little thin lips. I didn't bother to take it personally because I knew it was pretty much how she acted with everyone.

But I remember Rebecca telling me what a nice guy I am. Audrey didn't notice or didn't share that opinion. The unfriendly daily rite became more irritating every day that passed.

One day I climbed down but kept myself between her and the ladder.

"What did I do that pisses you off so much?" I said.

She was surprised, and it took her a moment to gather herself.

"You didn't do anything to piss me off."

She must have thought that was going to be it. She started toward the ladder. I blocked her way.

"Do you realize you haven't said a word to me all summer until just now?"

She got this smart-ass smile at the corners of her mouth.

"I haven't got anything to say to you."

"Okay, just thought I'd ask."

I let her pass me on her way to the ladder.

* * * * * * * * * *

The next day I didn't greet her. I didn't pass on any cautions. I brushed up against her shoulder as we passed each other.

"Hey, you bumped me," she yelled.

I kept walking.

* * * * * * * * * *

That evening, I got a call from Ernie, the person who scheduled the lifeguards. He asked me to fill-in on Saturday for a lifeguard taking a week off to go on vacation with his family. I agreed to do it.

"Listen, Richard, what's going on with you and Audrey? She said you ran into her on purpose this morning. You know, like you were trying to knock her down."

"Hmm. I don't even remember touching her. Should I apologize?"

"Well, that might settle it. You don't remember touching her, huh?"

"Nope."

"Is she ticked off at you for something?"

"Look, I thought the same thing. I can't get a hello out of her all summer. So the other day, I asked her about it. She told me she didn't have anything to say to me."

* * * * * * * * * *

I'd have to wait to apologize because Audrey asked for a day off. A guy named Andrew subbed for her. I hung around for a little while.

"Andrew, see the big guy over by the lounge chairs?"

"Yeah, I know him. What's up?"

"He's been bothering those girls, and they aren't enjoying it."

"I'll talk to him if he keeps it up. He's a little socially retarded, if you know what I mean?"

I left Andy to handle his friend.

* * * * * * * * * *

The next day, I showed up at 2:00 for my fill-in shift. When I came out of the changing room, I noticed that no one was in the chair. I saw a crowd down by the lounge chairs. I walked down and saw Audrey was nose to nose with my problem guest from the previous day. He was in her face and yelling.

"You. You ain't kickin' me out of the pool, bitch. You ain't nothin' here. What right you got to order me around?"

I walked up behind Audrey. The kid looked at me, and I could tell he knew he was in trouble.

"Problem, Audrey?" I was standing just behind her. She looked back at me.

"This guy is bothering those girls." She gestured with her head. "I told him to stop or leave the pool. He didn't stop."

"I guess that does it then. Please leave, sir."

"Hey, I'm not leavin'. I didn't do nothin', and they ain't gonna say I did."

I could tell the girls were concerned about getting involved with this dispute.

"Okay, I'll tell you what we're going to do. I'm going to get a police officer over here. Then we can all go to the park office and look at the surveillance films, and we will determine whose right and wrong, okay?"

Audrey got a smile on her face. He looked like a guy that got punched in the nuts. He grabbed his towel, kicked his feet into some sandals, and left. The crowd drifted apart and went back to enjoying the pool. Audrey walked beside me back to the chair. When we got there, I faced her.

"I understand I bumped you pretty hard yesterday. I want to apologize. I didn't intend to bump you. But if I hurt you in any way, I'm sorry."

She was looking at the ground underneath the ladder.

"Look, I'm kind of a bitch these days. There's a lot of shit going on in my life. I seem to take out all my anger on other people that don't have anything to do with it." Her honesty surprised me.

"Okay. We're good then?"

"Yes, we're good. And ah...thanks for stepping in over there. I'm impressed. You were smooth. I didn't know we had film surveillance."

"We don't, but I knew those girls were intimidated. They weren't going to turn him in." I softened my voice so as not to be overheard.

"Look, if you need to talk to someone about what's going on, you should know I'm a pretty good listener."

She snickered. Then she looked serious.

"You know you might be the right guy to talk to. Let me think about it."

* * * * * * * * * *

For about a week after that, our conversation wasn't necessarily long or personal, but it was friendly. Then Audrey mentally T-boned me at our Friday shift change.

"Do you have Sunday off?" Audrey said.

"Yes."

"I live at 450 Cromwell. Do you know where that is?"

I wasn't familiar with the address, but I knew the neighborhood. This young lady was from a wealthy family.

"I can find it. Why?"

"I'm inviting you to brunch at my house. I'd like it if you could help me with a decision I have to make. You said you'd listen to me."

"Sure. I will try to help if I can. What time?"

"Ten o'clock. Bring a bathing suit."

"Sounds good. I'll see you then."

* * * * * * * * * *

On Sunday morning, I walked my bicycle up the curved entrance driveway to the Spanish-style home. I kicked the stand down on the bike and walked to the front door. Audrey answered it. She smiled at me, and then the smile faded when she spotted my bike behind me.

"You didn't drive?"

"I don't even have my license yet." I smiled. "Why do we need a car? I mean, I assumed we were having..."

"No, it's fine. Why don't you walk your bike around the side of the house to the back."

When I got to the end of the walkway to the backyard, I was in this magical world I only saw in movies. The pool was big enough to swim laps. The furniture around the pool was probably more expensive than what my parents had in our living room. Audrey was standing by the bathhouse.

"You can change in here. Do you drink coffee?"

"I do, thank you."

I put on my bathing suit, and when I came out of the changing room, she was sitting at a patio table. On the table was a tray with a coffee carafe, some mugs, milk, and sugar.

"Help yourself."

I poured the coffee. I knew it was different from what we drank at my home just by the smell. I didn't bother with my usual milk and sugar.

"What did you want to talk about?"

"Let's enjoy the morning."

We discussed our schools. Audrey attended a non-religious college prep school that was expensive and exclusive. She was the only person I knew that went to that school. She got a grin on her face and asked, "What do the kids at your school think of my classmates and me?"

"What you probably can guess. You're snobby, rich, and pampered."

"What do you think?"

"That you're snobby rich and pampered."

She squealed with laughter.

"You don't pull your punches."

"I am kidding, of course. I don't know you, any of your friends or classmates, so I have little to judge you. As far as my classmates go, I'm sure they think pretty much the same. Frankly, I can never remember anyone having any conversation about your school."

"Wow. That's disappointing. We spend all of this money trying to incur your envy, and no one notices?"

"Hey, we're too busy with our noses to the grindstone trying to impress our parents and teachers. We don't have time to think of you guys."

"Well, you're not missing much, in case you ever do think about it."

"Like what?" She got up.

"Let's eat. I've been preparing all morning long. I have to make sure you eat before we talk."

"Really! Why?"

"You might end up running from here screaming. I don't want to get stuck with the food."

She was smiling, but I noticed some slight discomfort, so I passed on making the remark that came into my head.

Audrey had been at work in the kitchen. There was a stack of fried bacon strips in the warming oven. Alongside the bacon was a bowl of hash-brown potatoes. She pulled a pitcher of grapefruit juice and a bowl of whipped eggs out of the refrigerator. Audrey seemed to be a little confused about what to do with the eggs.

"Do you want me to fix the eggs? I work at a restaurant."

"No, kidding. Where do you work?"

I stepped in and took control of the frying pan just before it would blacken the butter she had put in it.

"The Manitou."

"Oh, my parents go there all of the time."

"I've never seen you there."

"No, I don't go there. My parents do."

There was more than a hint of anger in that remark.

"So, you cook there?"

"I help in the kitchen on occasion, but mostly I bus dishes. I can't wait tables until I'm older."

"This is what you aspire to, being a waiter?"

"As long as it helps me get through college."

I was slowly stirring the eggs to finish them but not dry them out.

"Why do you work at the pool? You can't need the money," I said.

"Like my mother, I work to get out of the house. You wouldn't believe how this kind of money will bore you if you let it."

"I see now that we're talking about your reason for inviting me."

"Down, boy. We'll get there. Enjoy your breakfast."

* * * * * * * * * *

We talked about where we wanted to go to college and what we wanted to study. Audrey wanted to study law. I said engineering. I will be applying to Brighton State. She was hoping for one of the Ivy League schools.

I helped her clear the table and load the dishwasher. Apparently, there was no such thing as leftovers in their house; uneaten food went into the garbage can. After we finished cleaning the kitchen, we went outside to the patio.

Audrey took off her robe. She had on a two-piece bathing suit. Models and Hollywood stars wore these suits called bikinis. No one I knew wore them. Yet, there she was. She was, as my grandpa would say, "skin and bones." She hardly had enough curve in her hips to hold up the bottom. Her body showed just a hint of breasts. It was only the determination in her eyes that betrayed her age to be over ten years.

We swam. I swam laps. Audrey dove underwater and swam as far as she could before surfacing for air. After a time, she got out of the pool, patted herself dry, and laid down on a lounge chair. After a few more minutes, I joined her. Lying down on the chair next to her, I could see she had her eyes closed beneath her sunglasses. I said nothing. I don't know how much time passed before she spoke, but her voice was quivering.

"So, you've seen my problem."

I waited, but she said nothing.

Finally, I said, "I'm not sure what you mean?"

"Don't go brain-dead on me. I'm a young woman, seventeen years old, almost eighteen in the body of a child. I'm smart. My test scores are at the top of every measure. My friends tell me I'm old beyond my years."

Again I waited. She said nothing.

"I don't know what to say, Audrey. I know we didn't get off to a great start, but I like you. I think your friends are right. You're smart and mature. And let me say, you can't help the way you look, which in my mind isn't bad, by the way."

She sat up and moved her legs to sit sideways on the lounge chair facing me.

"Really! My body isn't bad. Okay, explain to me why I haven't ever been asked out for a date. Tell me why I have never been kissed. Nobody has grabbed my ass in the hallway. I've never heard a boy make a crude remark about how it would be to have sex with me. You see, most of the girls I know would hate it if they hadn't gone out on a date, been kissed, or even groped by a guy. With me, my friends pretend they can't understand why I miss it. Or that's what they tell me. They know, but they don't know how to tell me without hurting my feelings."

She was choking back tears and trying to control the rage. I sat up, reached over, picked up one of her hands, and put it between mine on her lap.

"People can be jerks. Often we're faced with situations where we don't know how to react. I can't explain why your body isn't more... more womanly. I do know that guys are attracted to women who are more...more seductive in their appearance. Maybe we aren't mature enough to see you for the person you are rather than a sex object we might want."

She was tearing. She mumbled something.

"What?" I said.

"Would you kiss me?"

I reached for her. She pushed me back.

"Do it as if you mean it," Audrey said.

I took her hand away and gathered her into my arms.

"Tell me when to quit when you've had enough."

Given that I had little experience and she had none, it probably was pretty comical to watch. However, as we said in those days, we went all the way. As we made our way from the pool to the bedroom, we got completely naked and ended up in her bed. We laid next to each other after our sexual activity came to some conclusion, thinking the same question most lovers have the first time.

"Are you okay?" I asked.

"Yes. It was a little painful, to begin with, but I liked it."

"Aren'' you supposed to be bleeding or something?"

"Horseback riding took care of that." she smiled.

"How do you feel?"

"Honestly?"

"Yeah."

"Like, I want to do it more."

I put my mouth next to her ear and mumbled something to the effect that she was a wanton trollop and an unforgivable slut, who captured my soul. Her laughter echoed through the empty house. She wiggled out from underneath me.

"I get to be on top this time," she declared.

****

Audrey and I got together a few more times after that. I learned that she was so upset with the world and everyone in it, because Audrey felt she disappointed her parents. Complicating that relationship was the fact that she was adopted.

We both had aspirations that left no room for each other in our lives. We made out a lot for a month. I can tell you I was paralyzed with fear the first time I bought condoms.

When we went back to school, that was pretty much it for our sex life together. Although, I did take her to one dance at her school. It was a riot. Her friends didn't know what to say to me. They looked at me like I was something they were looking at through a microscope.

I warned Audrey that our date wouldn't help her reputation. Her schoolmates would think that she picked me up on the wrong side of Rivers Edge because no one would date her. She explained to me that one of her friends talked her brother into asking her to the dance. Audrey knew he didn't want to do it. She turned him down, explaining she already had a date. She thanked me for covering for her.

I think we both knew there would be a time when our friendship wasn't going to work. Remember, she was two years ahead of me in school. I know that when she went East to school, she was dating another guy. I was dating someone else, so everything worked out.

But there is one thing I learned. Never judge a woman by her looks. Audrey might not have been centerfold material, but she was an exciting lover. Once I got to know her, I still wasn't sure of my feelings for her. It was a feeling of friendship but not love. It was something in-between that I never felt before.

Chapter 7
I Never Got Her Name

It was the fall of my sophomore year in high school. I was trying to adjust to my life without Audrey. I learned there weren't too many women, like Audrey, that we're satisfied with having sex with no commitment or at least the chance of being 'The One. '

Another shock to my sheltered life in middle-class America was what was going on at home. My Dad started a new job. He wasn't making as much money as he had with his former employer. They didn't explain the reason for this change. Later, I learned that my parents almost divorced over it, but I'll get to that part of the story later.

The impact on me was they couldn't afford to send me to a private Catholic school. There I was one warm early fall day walking into the Public School building where Catholic's relationship with God wasn't in the curriculum. Of course, I no longer believe any of that crap they fed us when I was in Catholic grade school.

I went to my classes and met some of my schoolmates. It was understandable that they held me at a distance for some time. They didn't know me. Many of them had been going to school together since kindergarten. There were a fair amount of boys and girls going steady or exclusively not dating others, as we said in those days. Meeting girls was like going through a minefield. You never knew who was going with who or what kind of reaction you'd get from your mild flirtations. I didn't have a wingman to steer me away from the girls who were spoken for.

Besides these problems, I worked more at the supper club, so I didn't participate in normal after-school activities. I didn't go to football and basketball games. Nor was I invited to the "Sadie Hawkins Dance: which was a girl-ask-boy tradition. As far as Prom was concerned, I didn't go. I was clearing the tables where some of my classmates had entertained their dates with a pre-prom dinner. To be fair, while my day-to-day life wasn't typical of most teenagers, it wasn't terrible.

I'm a pretty outgoing guy at this point in my life. I think my experience working with adults in a place where adults go to relax made me behave older than my years. I saw people at their best and their worst: adults who drank too much, men on the prowl, women looking for the comfort of a man's embrace. I observed greedy people, nasty people, and outstanding people. However, to the regular customers and to the men and women I worked with, I was still just a kid until late one Wednesday evening.

* * * * * * * * * *

A regular customer requested that his group be allowed to stay late to celebrate whatever they were celebrating. This meant I was working past the standard kitchen closing time. Most of the waiters had left for the evening. The kitchen help was down to the dishwasher, and the guy that took out the garbage and mopped the floors. After an hour, the party began to break up, and I had to clean the area.

One of my jobs was to separate the bar glassware from the dish ware. I would collect the bar glasses on a designated tray and take them to the bar to be washed and shelved by the bartender.

On my trip to the bar that evening, I saw a woman sitting at the bar alone. She wore a stunning dress, deep blue in color. The dress was attractive because it defined a gorgeous figure. Her shoes were high heeled silver to match her bag. Her hair, a deep black, cascaded about her shoulders like a hood from a coat. The sparkle in her eyes might have been put there from the alcohol she consumed, but I doubt it. She wore simple jewelry, Including a bracelet-watch, a strand of silver necklace with a small bauble hanging from it, and what looked like a birthstone ring on her right hand.

The bartender asked me if I would watch the bar while he used the bathroom. I agreed and began washing the glassware. The scrubber and rinse tank happened to be across from where the woman was sitting. When I started cleaning the glassware, we were eye to eye.

"Good evening," I said.

She looked up from her drink and smiled. Her subtle red lipstick enhanced her lips without being loud and obnoxious. I was in lust big time.

"Indeed, it is. How are you this evening?" she said.

"Excellent. Thank you for asking. And you?"

"Okay. Long day, but a good one."

She gestured with her head toward the dining room, "Noisy crowd out there earlier this evening...and unusual for a Wednesday evening in particular."

"Yes, they were celebrating some kind of sales goal they met."

"I see."

"May I ask what you do that made your day seem so long?"

"I travel. I represent various shoe companies. Sales."

She nodded her head as if she had to let me know that she was finished.

"Sounds interesting."

"It is. I like it. But the drawback is not feeling at home anywhere. Even when I'm home, it feels just like another stop on the circuit."

"Hmm, I can relate a little bit to that. I just started at a new school. I have trouble fitting in, partially because I work, so I'm not a typical student. Maybe it's not the same as your situation, but I do feel somewhat adrift."

"No, I think it is similar. My advice is to make the best of it. Keep yourself aware of what's going on. You never know what might happen."

At that point, the bartender came back from his bathroom break.

"You have a good evening," I said to the woman.

"What's your name?"

"Richard."

"It was nice talking to you, Richard."

* * * * * * * * * * *

I didn't want to leave, but there was no reason for me to stay. I had to get going. It took me another half hour to finish my chores. I got my jacket, cap, and gloves from the locker room and went out the back door into a frigid night. At the end of the alley, I took a right-hand turn to go to the bus stop.

The woman from the bar was standing in the street next to a car. She had her hands on both hips in frustration and looking about.

"Hi. Are you in trouble?" I said.

"Yes, I had the car washed today. The locks are frozen. I can't get the key turning to open the door."

"Hold on a moment. I can help you."

I went back into The Manitou and picked up a box of matches off of the bar. When I got back to her, she was stomping her feet, with her arms wrapped around her body, fighting the bitter cold.

"Can I use your key?"

She handed the set of keys to me with the door lock key between her fingers. I put the key in the lock. She was right. It wouldn't budge. I struck two of the matches and put their flame below the extended part of the key. I did that twice, holding the matches until they started to be uncomfortably hot on my fingers. I tried the key again, and the lock clicked. The heat from the key melted the ice. I stepped back and opened her door for her.

"There you go."

"Thank you." She extended her hand. In her hand was some money.

"You don't have to…"

"I insist," she said. "I have another favor to ask."

She said this as I pocketed what turned out to be a ten-dollar bill.

"I think I've had too much to drink. If you drive me to the hotel, I'll get a cab to take you home. Deal?"

"Sure."

I wasn't about to tell her I only had a temporary license, and according to the law, I shouldn't be driving at that hour of the night. She was quiet on the way to the hotel. The only thing she said on the trip was that she was embarrassed. When we got to the hotel, she said, "I've got to eat something. Do you want to join me?"

* * * * * * * * * * *

Thinking back at this point in our meeting, I wasn't sure if she intended to seduce me. If she was, it was subtle. There was no physical contact and no flirtatious behavior. We went to the hotel's cafe, where she ordered a sandwich, chips, and a coke, and I asked for eggs, bacon, toast, and milk.

"Do you travel at all?" she said.

“No, I’ve never stayed in a hotel.”

We had both finished our meal and gathered our coats to leave.

“Come on upstairs. I’ll show you what one looks like.”

I didn’t say anything, and she didn’t wait for my reply. She put her arm in mine and walked me to the elevator.

When we got to her room, she opened the door and motioned me in. When the door closed, she locked it and put the chain in place. Dropping her coat in a chair, she walked up to me and looked me in the eye.

“Do you know what could happen next?”

"Yes.” I probably sounded like I was panting.

“Are you okay with this?”

"Yes."

She put her arms around me and laid her head on my chest.

“I have needs. Don’t worry. I’ll help you. We’ll both have fun.”

And so it began.

She wanted our experience to be slow and, as she put it, sensual. I guess my experience with her framed my definition of what sensual means for me. It seemed like it took hours. She whispered her "needs" in my ear and showed me how to satisfy them.

I realized right away her being drunk was an act. She was sober and alert. When I thought we were through, she rolled off of me, laid her head on my chest, and looped her leg over mine.

“So, what are you studying?” She breathed into my chest. Her fingers were slowly running up and down from my chest to my groin and back.

“College entry curriculum.”

Her head snapped up.

"Don't you take those in high school?"

"Yes. I'm a Junior," I lied.

She peeled back off of me and laid flat on her back next to me.

"Jesus H. Christ! You're in high school? I could be in huge trouble if this got out, you know?"

"I guess you could, but I'm not going to tell if you don't."

"Yeah. What do you want for that?"

I don't know why that made me so angry, but it did. I rolled toward her and propped my head on my left arm.

"What the hell do you think I am? When you invited me to your room, I knew what would happen. You're a beautiful woman. I was thinking about how fortunate I was that you might want to have sex with me. I don't expect or want anything else."

She had pulled away from me. I think she thought I might do something violent.

"Okay, I'm sorry," she said

It was quiet for a time.

"How are you?" she said.

"Fine, I'm sorry if I snapped, but…"

"I get it. I challenged you. It's just that I thought you were older."

"I guess I should be flattered."

"What you should be proud of is what a considerate lover you are."

"You liked that, huh?" I said.

"I liked it a lot."

" Do you want more?"

"I thought you'd never ask."

* * * * * * * * * * *

I never thought about getting in trouble. She was the one who would be in trouble. In this state, she could be charged with rape even if I said I wanted to have sex with her. It was only the next day that I realized I didn't know her name.

Did I see her again? No. I never did. I suspect that she might be concerned that I might tell someone, and the situation might blow up in both of our faces.

Looking back, I'd say I was conflicted. I know I'd daydream about living with her and thinking how wonderful that might be, but it was mostly about sex. Since our entire time together was mainly about sex, what else could I think? Realistically, how could a guy my age and a woman like her have anything like a normal relationship? I got over most of what I felt about her, but honest to God, I can't forget her.

Chapter 8
Dina Marshall

My high school ran on a four-quarter system. Fall, Winter, and Spring were mandatory. Summer was for aggressive students who wanted to finish high school faster or students who failed a class during the regular year and needed to make up the credits.

During the junior year, the Winter segment, I went to my English class and sat next to Dina Marshall. When I said I was sitting next to her, I must tell you that I thought she would probably prefer sitting next to some of her friends in the class, given her initial choice. But Dina was late for class. When she came into the classroom, the only seat open was next to me. To further frustrate Dina, Miss Demond made a seating chart to learn her students' names more easily.

We couldn't change seats. Miss Demod told us, "And no, you can't ask me to make an exception to allow me to move you because if I do it for one, I will be spending the rest of the day moving all of you."

From the moment I saw her, Dina intrigued me. Dina was a classic beauty. She was tall and willowy with an oval face, brilliant blue eyes, and natural blonde hair. She sat straight at her desk, paid attention to what was going on, and took notes. Her note-taking, from my viewpoint, looked impossibly neat and complete.

****

On the second day of class, I was already in my seat when Dina came in. Before she sat down and as she put her books on the desk, she said, "Hello, I'm sorry I don't recognize you. My name is Dina Marshall."

"Dina, it's nice to meet you. My name is Richard Harrison. I just transferred to this school in the fall."

This probably sounds as if I was calm, relaxed, and collected. Realistically, I think I stuttered a bit and was looking down at the floor. Generally, I probably looked like a hick.

"I hope everyone welcomed you properly," she said

"Dina, I think I detect something of a British accent."

"It's a curse, I'm afraid. No matter where I go, I unconsciously pick up the local accent. My father taught in Britain for the last couple of years. We just returned to the States this last summer."

"What a great experience that must have been."

"It was, but I'm glad we're back in the States. I need to concentrate on my studies. I want to go to Stanford. I need to work on keeping my grades up. Britain was kind of a distraction. We were spending weekends visiting historical places, going to the theater in London, and popping over to France on holiday."

"Hmm, I guess if you were going to be distracted, that would qualify as worthwhile distractions."

"Oh, yes, I don't mean to sound like I'm not grateful for the chance. My goodness, who knows if I'll ever get the chance to go back?"

* * * * * * * * * *

About a third of the way through the semester, we were required to team up on a research assignment. Rather than seeking someone out, I just waited. I was counting on the fact that there were a couple of other strangers in class. After all of the cliques were paired off, I was sure that I would be matched with another of the undefined and not significant. Then I got a tap on the shoulder. It was Dina.

"Richard, do you have a partner?"

"No, I don't. Do you?"

"I do if you're keen for it." She smiled

Dina was more familiar with research methods than I was. She patiently taught me how to perform the tasks with skill and in an orderly fashion. I was a quick learner and soon able to carry my share of the load. We had several sources for our assignment. We used the school library and the local main public library. Also, her father got us into the University Library. Dina was our leader. I have to say I would have been lost in this process without her.

"Listen, we've got all of this information from the research and our reading notes. Why don't we use my house as our main base, so we can get it all sorted?" she said.

"Fine with me, if it's okay with your folks."

"I asked them already, and it's fine with them. They are keen to meet you."

I still couldn't ignore the British usage, but I had to quit calling her on it.

* * * * * * * * * *

The first meeting we had at their house was right after school. While we set up shop in her father's home office, her mother was busy putting together an evening meal. I found out they expected me to be their guest.

The evening meal was served promptly at six-thirty. The conversation was nothing like the dinner chat at my house. Truth be known, we hardly had family meals at my home anymore. It seems each of my parents had something going on that didn't permit scheduling a family dinner. While I knew there was tension between my parents, I had no idea how acrimonious their relationship had become.

Dina and I worked off of a portable blackboard that her father used to prepare his lectures. We roughed out an outline on notebook paper and then began transferring it to the blackboard. We took each section and began filling in the text and foot notations. This process would end up taking about five different evenings of about four hours each. During this time, we were never interrupted. Her parents neither checked on us nor bothered us.

"I have to tell you your parents are trusting. If I were at anybody else's house, their parents would need to check every once in a while."

"They trust me. I assume you're going to behave yourself?" She was teasing me.

"Yes. Yes, of course. I mean…"

She got phony serious, "What do you mean, young man?"

"Okay, I get it."

We laughed together.

"You are a nice young guy, Richard. I hope our friendship isn't preventing you from having a...girlfriend or something."

"No. I don't have a girlfriend. I consider you a friend. I mean, you would be a fantastic girlfriend, but you don't seem to need me for that...ah, that kind of relationship."

She put down her pen, set her elbows on the table, and put her hands together in front of her.

"Maybe in light of all of the time we've spent together lately, I've sort of taken you for granted. I value our friendship, Richard. You're a mature, intelligent person, and you've treated me with so much respect. You have no idea how much that means to me. I know that I look like the stereotypical dumb blonde. Since the third grade, I have lived with that. It's bad enough kids pick that up, but teachers and… well, it's been a problem. It's needless to beat that drum more than it already has been."

"I'm sorry you've had to experience that."

"The bright side is you, and I don't have that problem. I know that, and I've told my parents that I trust you. And they trust my judgment. So, let's get back to work and kick this paper out of the ballpark, shall we?"

I frowned at her.

"I said something wrong?"

"It's hit it out of the ballpark, not kick it out."

****

Our relationship was like nothing I had experienced until that time. For a time, we were almost inseparable. Everyone thought we were a couple. More than one guy let it slip how lucky I was and how he would love to change places with me. I never implied that Dina's and my relationship included sex. I don't kiss and tell. I had the feeling no one would believe me if I told them we weren't having sex or that I had never even kissed her.

My parents loved her. I swear my Mom started planning the wedding. If I had told my mother that Dina and I hadn't even held hands or kissed each other, she would have brushed it off and felt nothing but joy. Good Catholics didn't have sex until they were married.

We did date. I took Dina to the movies and out for dinner on a couple of occasions. I was still putting in a lot of hours at my job. I suggested that maybe I should let my buddies know that they wouldn't be making me mad if they wanted to ask her out, but she said no. Everything was just fine.

"If they were anything like you, but they aren't, are they? Not that they aren't nice guys, but unlike you, they don't understand me, and I doubt if they would learn."

"Dina, You say I understand you. I like you. You're a great friend, and I value that, but I do not understand why you don't want to meet other guys. They would take you to dances and the school games. You could have even more friends than you have. I don't understand that." She just smiled and stared back at me.

"Not that what you and I have isn't enough for me, I..." I was stammering again.

"And there it is."

"What."

"I can count on you, Richard. We're friends, and I don't have to have sex with you to earn or keep that friendship. That's what makes us special. That may not make sense to you, but it's essential to me."

* * * * * * * * * * *

Once again, a woman I cared for didn't break it off as much as she left town. Her father took a position with UCLA that spring. It seemed to me that they left Rivers Edge almost overnight. Before they left, Dina and I got together for lunch at The Diner on Blake.

"I'm so sorry to see you go, Dina."

"I have to say, Richard, I've gotten used to this constant moving, but I must say our friendship is making this tougher."

"I'd like to keep it going. Will you write if I do? Maybe a phone call now and then?"

"Yes. Yes, let us do that."

Did she keep her word? Yes, she did.

* * * * * * * * * * *

Soon after Dina got to Los Angeles and started her classes at Stanford, she wrote that she had found a new friend. She hoped it would be as good a relationship as we had. The friends name is Sam, and Sam is studying to get into law school. She told him about me.

It was strange. I didn't move on from Dina and my relationship. I realized that she had, but I didn't feel compelled to look for someone for me as long as I was getting her letters. Eventually, I did, but it took a long time.

Then Dina called me on after about six months had passed. She made a phone date by leaving me a voicemail. Could I be available for a private phone call with her? She mentioned the date and time. When I called the number back, It went to voicemail. I told her I'd be available. I was apprehensive. Why did she ask for a 'private' phone call? Did she think I was letting people listen on the line? I imagined all kinds of things.

I worried that she had contracted some kind of fatal disease. Maybe she talked about me too much, and her boyfriend told her she had to cut me loose. On the brighter side, perhaps she and Sam were getting married. Of course, that brought up the why. Was she pregnant?"

I had to wait for about a week. We agreed that I would call her since it was a workday for me. I was working a split 10:00 am until 2:00 pm and then 5:00 - 9:00 pm. I called her at 2:30. She answered on the first ring.

"Richard?"

"Yes, It's me."

I listened as she breathed into the phone for a moment.

"So, what's the big news?"

"I didn't want to write this to you, but I feel it's important that you know that Sam and I are lovers."

The relief poured off my shoulders like over wet cement. Oh yes, there was a little bit of why not me, but it wasn't all of the negative crap I had been imagining. And then, it was as if Dina read my mind.

"So if I know my Richard, he's thinking, why him and not me? Right?" She sounded like she was trying to hold her breath and talk at the same time.

"Guilty, your honor."

"Okay, I'm trusting you with huge news. I'm feeling guilty because I've known something about myself for a long time, even before you and I became friends. My lover, Sam, is a woman. Her name is Samantha."

She waited for what seemed like a long time. I was stunned and didn't know what to say.

"Okay, that's a big surprise to me, but...it does explain a lot."

"Richard, you have to know that I was using you as a shield from revealing my sexuality when we were friends. I feel terrible about it, and I..."

It was easy to hear how difficult this was for her to share this with me. I guess I surprised myself how quickly I went from "why not me" to how can I comfort her?

"Dina, I'm not sure what would have happened if you had told me, but I don't feel used. The mere fact that you feel you have to tell me now tells me a lot. No, Dina, I'm happy you've found someone, and for the record, Sam is a lucky lady to have you."

She was sobbing on the other end of the phone.

"Richard, I was so afraid you were going to hang up and never speak to me again."

"What.. and kick in the teeth of the only woman that helped me get the first and only A grade I've ever earned. What kind of a jerk do you think I am?"

She was laughing-sobbing now.

"You are special."

The voice wasn't Dina.

"Richard, I'm Samantha. I'm here to support Dina in case this didn't go well. She's pretty broken up over your understanding. She was so sure you wouldn't understand or be able to forgive her for keeping you in the dark."

"I'm here for her. She can count on it."

Sam and I talked for about fifteen minutes. By then, Dina had regained control. We talked some more. After that, I got short notes, pictures, and longer letters from both of them. It's not as often now, but at least once a month."

* * * * * * * * * *

The funniest part of all this was my mother. Occasionally, she'd ask, "Richard, whatever happened to Dina?" She'll say this as if I'm going to remember Dina, call her up, and start going together again. I won't tell Mom the truth.

Did Dina use me? I did revisit that question for a while after I first found out about her being a lesbian. I finally concluded that nobody could use you if you don't let them. Besides, if I'm honest, I loved her. I didn't know what love meant then, but now I know what it's like, and I know that I did love her.

It was a critical moment for me. I recognized that there was value in having a relationship with a woman even though you couldn't or wouldn't have sex with them. I was slowly beginning to recognize that women always had a different responsibility in their relationships with men than men had in theirs with women.

Women had to be careful and critical. Anything they might do that would signal they were open to a relationship or even casual sex, if they intended it or not, could be misunderstood. Further along, this will be important for me because of a woman I would meet who would significantly change my life.

Chapter 9
Arliss White

The Manitou had a new boss. As the owner's son, Tim D'Amato had worked every job in the place and knew how hard the jobs could become. To learn even more about the business, Tim left Rivers Edge to work in other restaurants in New York, Los Angeles, and Las Vegas. Tim knew he would come back and take over eventually. It was a matter of when his Dad, Sammy D'Amato, needed him. Sammy's cardiologist settled whatever doubt there was regarding when Tim's homecoming would take place. The call went out when Sammy found out about his heart condition. After a few weeks on the job, Tim called a team meeting.

"I'm looking at growing this business. It will take some investment and cause some short-term disruption, maybe even a short-term closing.

"Here's the plan. The storefront next door is available. I want to rent it and turn it into a banquet facility. I'm not sure all of you know how many parties and wedding receptions. We have to turn them down every year because we can't physically handle them.

"So first, we secure a lease on the next-door property. Next, we design the decor of the party room. In addition to redesigning the dining space, we have to expand the kitchen. We can't have our table dinners waiting for a party of two hundred to be served. I'm not sure that the kitchen work might require us to close the restaurant for a while.

"Here are some options for that time. Salaried help can take a vacation with pay. Wait staff and hourly staff can work on the redecorating and equipping the new facilities. For this transition period, the wait staff will work for hourly wages comparable to hourly workers. Then there is the clean-up after construction. We'll need painters and people to stock cabinets with new and freshly washed dishes, silverware, and linens.

"I wanted to let you know what's going on, and I'll keep you in the loop as things proceed. Any questions?"

* * * * * * * * * *

I took some of the hours doing all kinds of work on the expansion, but mostly I did my regular job until we did close the business for five days.

What changed is that after a three-week period where we hired and trained our banquet staff, we started the new banquet part of our business. That is when I ran into Arliss White.

Arliss was a round-shaped person. It wasn't that she was fat. She might have been about twenty pounds overweight, but it was spread out over her body pretty evenly. Her facial features were round. She had a broad smile, large brown eyes, and full lips under an upturned nose. Arliss had short legs and a quick stride, and that is how we met.

I was bussing a tray of dirty dishes from the main dining room to the expanded dishwashing area when Arliss came around the corner on her way to the kitchen. The collision wasn't that hard, but it did cause me to tip my tray and the sound of breaking dishes, as always, stopped work in the kitchen for a moment.

Arliss was confused and frightened. I began cleaning up the shattered dish and glassware at once. It wasn't my first experience with this kind of event.

"Can I help you?" she said.

"No, I've got it."

"I'm so sorry." I smiled at her.

"Don't worry, it happens."

"Not to me, it doesn't. I feel like such a dope."

"We're cool. I got this, and you can do what you were going to do."

"My name is Arliss."

I put the broom I was using in one hand and extended my other hand to her.

"Richard."

"Nice to meet you, Richard. Again, I'm sorry."

She continued into the kitchen.

* * * * * * * * * *

After work a couple of weeks later, I came upon her in our new break room. It had been a while since I had seen her. It surprised me that those working in the traditional dining room often didn't interact with the Banquet staff.

"Hey, Richard." She had a loud, penetrating voice. That kind of voice was excellent for entering an order in the noisy kitchen, but it could be a lot to take in the break room's quiet.

"Hi, Arliss. How's it going?"

"Good. I owe you for my fuck-up, man. Can I buy you a drink?"

"No, Arliss, I appreciate the offer, but I'm not old enough to drink. I wouldn't want to get you in trouble."

"No, shit. You're Jailbait?"

"You're not even the first person to notice that, Arliss."

"My God. Okay. Okay, I'll buy you a milkshake."

Her face beamed with excitement.

"Sure, why not."

"I promise you're safe with me, Ricky. Normally I'm a real slut, but I don't want to go to jail over it. The question is, am I safe with you?" I laughed.

"We're good, Arliss. I wouldn't offend a lady of your class with any kind of crass behavior."

She laughed. One of the waiters stopped by Arliss and leaned down to whisper in her ear. I knew he was telling her that I was Richard, not Ricky.

* * * * * * * * * * *

I met her at The Diner on Blake. Arliss strode in on her short legs, pulling her body through the door and into the booth where I was sitting. She used her inside voice.

"I haven't been in here since I started having my period. How's it going, Richard?"

She pronounced my name slowly with a wicked smile on her face.

"I guess someone told you I don't like my name shortened."

"Indeed, is there anything I can do to you that isn't offensive?"

"I keep telling you. We're good. I am not offended."

"Good."

I caught the waitress's eye. I ordered a chocolate milkshake.

"I'm driving, so I'll have a diet coke."

Even the waitress smiled.

Arliss and I swapped work stories. She seemed to like the job. She was surprised that I had been working there as long as I had been.

"So, you're a senior in high school?"

"Yes. I'll be eighteen in February. I'm going to start waiting tables then."

"Oh God, Richard, I don't know if I can wait that long to get my hooks into you."

"Down girl. How do you know that I'm not going with someone?"

"Ah, that won't last long. I grow on people."

I laughed and added, "I have the feeling you persist ."

If we had any other substantive conversation, I don't remember it.

* * * * * * * * * *

When I had my eighteenth birthday, Tim pulled off a surprise party. Tim had started a European tradition in our kitchen. The staff assembled for The Chef's Dinner. The Chef would introduce new dishes that were either being offered on the menu or were being considered. The point of this dinner was to inform the waitstaff of the ingredients of the meal and why it might differ from what customers might have experienced in other restaurants.

We were free to criticize the dish. If we didn't like something about it, including how it was plated, we were encouraged to speak up. Observing some of these dinners, I noted that the respondent had to have good reason to criticize. Just not liking something didn't get you very far.

That evening, Because I had arranged to have my birthday off, the crew assembled to celebrate it. Still, I was unaware of this ruse actually two days before my birthday. Because we were periphery players, the guys from dishwashing, two kitchen staff, and I would traditionally serve the meal. With a big grin on his face, Tim stood up to explain the dish.

“Tonight, I’m offering you something truly unusual. Tonight, we are celebrating Richard’s eighteenth birthday with his favorite meal, according to his mother.”

Everyone began clapping. I’m sure my face was red with embarrassment.

They served Pizza from Melloni’s, the pizzeria down the street. The biggest surprise that was one of the servers was my Mom. Another was Tim’s Dad, Sammy, who addressed the group.

“Richard started working for me when he was fourteen. He told me he was fifteen. He made me promise he could become a waiter when he became old enough. Richard, I want you to meet Charles. Don’t call him Chuck. Your job is to train him on how to bus dishes between now and next week so that you can start your new position as a waiter.”

Everybody went nuts. I found out from a couple of them later that most everyone knew in advance. If I had been paying attention, I would notice that a couple of people who had the night off were there. When everybody had eaten and finished telling Richard ’when he was younger stories,’ we went to work. Charles was a young black kid who was eager to do a good job. He was happy with the pay even before telling him that he would get some waiters’ tips.

Charles and I were finishing up the closing chores when I turned to find Arliss standing behind me, her hands resting on her hips.

“I understand you’re not jailbait anymore.”

“Legally, not for two more days.”

“I’ve waited months; a couple more days will be easy. Well, not easy but tolerable.” We both laughed.

“Seriously, I’ve got to get you drunk and unable to resist my advances. When are we going to do this?”

"What are you doing next Monday?"

"Changing your worldview on romance, handsome. Let's meet at Romero's."

* * * * * * * * * *

I'll spoil the story here, but you have to know what I know. Arliss is all talk and no action. We aren't ever going to have sex, but that is not what is vital about Arliss in my life.

Most guys think they can't have a woman friend because there is always sex in the air. I must not be an average guy because I love Dina even though she's gay, and I'm friends with Arliss.

I have to say Arliss is the older sister I never had. My mother loves her and knows Arliss and I aren't going to be anything other than friends because Arliss and Mom had a long conversation about it. As it turns out, Arliss needs a family, and without making it formal, she became part of mine.

Chapter 10
Jennelle Hartland

At this point, my life becomes more complicated. I'm waiting on tables at The Manitou. There are my classes at the local Junior College. After I graduated High School, I don't think the ink was dry on my diploma when my parents told me they were getting a divorce. They told me that I could choose to live with either one of them.

I thought it over. I discussed it with Arliss, Tim, and Sammy D'Amato. I even called Dina and Samatha. With almost unanimous agreement among my consultants, I decided that I could rent a place of my own as long as I was doing well at the restaurant. My parents were upset with my decision and tried to talk me out of it, but I stuck to it.

I have a room at a rooming house. Lee Ann Sedgewick, the owner, is very nice as long as you pay your rent. My place is large, well-lit, and airy. It has a sink, a small refrigerator, and a toaster oven. I share a bathroom with three other men. We aren't allowed to entertain guests anywhere but in the living room on the first floor. I never see anyone entertain down there except Lee Ann.

My day consists of getting up to attend classes at the local branch campus of Brighton University. I can complete my undergraduate work there and transfer my credits to one of the other four-year schools. Which University I choose to complete my degree might depend on my major. Since I've given up on going into engineering, I haven't made up my mind. I've taken the required courses needed to work toward a liberal arts degree.

Tim D'Amato wants me to think about the Hospitality Industry. He's told me he's thinking of expanding his father's business to more than one location. He told me that he could use a guy like me in his organization. Tim is flattering, to say the least, but do I want to work in the restaurant business my whole life? I'm undecided. Some days it seems like a great idea; other days, not so much.

* * * * * * * * * *

Depending on the time of my classes, I study before I attend class. Most of the time, I study at the library at school. I don't like to study in my room because it starts to feel claustrophobic.

The one thing I do in my room, besides sleep, is to continue work on my skills at sketching, drawing, and painting. Not only does it keep some balance in my life, but I'm beginning to get better at it. As for the need to balance my day-to-day life, I just couldn't settle for a menu of only work and school. Art was my dessert. I looked forward to it every day.

As for social life, I have time on Friday and Saturday evenings after work. I can walk down to Romano's, the bar for the locals, and hang out with the other people from The Manitou and the neighborhood. It could get late before I got home, but I didn't have classes the next day.

The crowd at Romano's included Arliss. When I decided not to live with either of my folks, Arliss had invited me to share an apartment with her, but we couldn't work out the money. Half of her place was twice the cost of my room and didn't even consider the utilities. Arliss and I were still at the best pal's stage in our relationship. She kept in touch with my Mom, and to some extent, with my Dad. I hate to admit it, but Arliss was better at keeping up with my parents than I was. I was still pouting over their divorce.

Mom and Dad were both consistent about why they divorced. Remember that my Dad changed jobs. He took a position with another company that paid him less money. I never got the whole story. Finally, he admitted to me that he had an affair with a woman he worked with. When he broke it off, the woman retaliated by exposing him to his boss and my mother. My mother explained that she admired my father because he tried to rectify the situation by leaving the woman. Still, he'd broken a bond of trust that couldn't be repaired.

I felt sorry for him. As he put it, he paid a high price in his attempt to right a wrong by doing the right thing. That made sense to me, but not to my mother or his former boss. By the way, the woman with whom Dad was involved was the boss' sister.

Arliss tried not to talk about my folks too much, but she kept harping about my duty to keep up a relationship with both of them. She was assuming the big sister role that we all would recognize as time passed.

* * * * * * * * * *

I was paddling my life canoe upstream on a slow-moving current on a branch of a river in the journey that was my life. Suddenly my life changed. I was sitting in my usual spot at the library. My study session began at 8:00 am. I had three classes in a row, starting at 10:00 am and finishing at 1:00 pm. I was getting ready to go to my first class when Jennelle came to my table.

"Excuse me. Could I ask you something?" she said.

I looked up. Jennelle was medium in height. Her curly brown hair was sneaking out around the perimeter of a knit cap. She had eyes that matched her hair, a bit of a turned-up nose, and a generous mouth. Her pink jacket was waist-length. She had on blue jeans and fashionable pink boots. I didn't recognize the voice she used with me, but I later realized it as that mommy's voice women often use when talking to their children.

"Sure, what can I do for you?" As someone trained in a restaurant, the answer to a request for help is an automatic yes.

"I notice by the books you have that you are taking an art appreciation course."

I nodded. I didn't say anything because she didn't quit talking long enough for me to answer.

"I'm thinking of taking the course next semester. Two professors teach it. Which one do you have, and what do you think of him?"

I waited a bit, thinking that she might not be through talking despite the question she posed.

"I have Tomlinson. The students I've talked with thought Gray had an attitude about being too good to teach entry-level students who were not majoring in art. I'm doing well in my class, and I think Professor Tomlinson is a good teacher. He lets you know what he expects, and he has a good syllabus."

"Thank you," she said.

"I'm sorry, but I have to get going to my next class," I said.

"Me too. May I walk with you?"

"Certainly. Miss...?"

"Jennelle Hartland." She smiled. "Richard Harrison. Nice to meet you."

So we walked and talked. I can't remember how it happened, but we ended up meeting for lunch after our last class.

Jennelle learned a lot about me because she asked the right questions and listened to my answers. I'll admit that being with an attractive young woman was a nice change of pace. I don't think it was a tough interview. I was babbling like a brook.

"Are you free on Sundays?" she said.

For me, Sundays meant sleeping in late, brunch at a restaurant near my rooming house, relaxing with my drawings, and maybe watching a game on the TV downstairs with my fellow rooming-house residents.

"I often have free time on Sunday afternoons and evenings," I said.

"Would you like to attend a film with me at the theater on Sunday? I think the film begins at 3:00 pm." Her eyebrows raised as if to emphasize she was asking a question.

"I'm free at that time. Sure. Should I meet you there?"

"You can pick me up at about 2:30. That should give us plenty of time to get to the theater."

She handed me a piece of paper with an address on it. I looked at it and calculated the bus trip.

"So that you know, I don't drive. We'll have to take the bus."

She looked away from me and mumbled a slight "Hmm." Then she turned back and looked directly at me with a small smile.

"That should be fine. I'll see you then."

She left me sitting with the check.

* * * * * * * * * *

When I picked her up, it was apparent by looking at her apartment, she was living with other women, but none of them were home. She told me that they all went skiing up north for the weekend.

The film was a documentary on the demise of certain species of animals in Africa. Not to diminish the seriousness of the problem, I thought it was a bit boring. Still, I wasn't going to challenge her taste in a film on our first date.

I took her out for dinner, and we chatted like magpies about our lives and dreams. She continued to be very good at finding out a lot of information about me. After I had time to review the day, I realized I'd learned nothing about her.

Jennelle and I fell into the ritual of having a coffee or lunch during the week and then date on Sunday afternoon. We went to museums, theater performances, and movies. One time, we just walked for about two hours before we had dinner.

After our first date, she encouraged me to give her a hug and a kiss on the cheek when I got her home. Then she would always stand in the doorway until I was out of sight.

I assumed she would go inside. On one occasion, I realized I had offered to carry her wallet, and I had not returned it to her. I quickly went back to her apartment. I saw her walking down the street. I hailed her, and she turned around to walk toward me. When she realized why I was coming back, she made an excuse that she had to get something at the grocery store and how embarrassing it would have been not to have money. I let her go on her way, and I resumed my trip home. I thought nothing of this incident until much later.

The following week she asked me if she could cook for me instead of going out. I agreed and showed up at 2:00 pm. She had snacks out on the coffee table and the game on the TV. The 'girls' were gone for the weekend, and they wouldn't be back until Monday morning.

"I know how much you enjoy your football." She ushered me to the couch. "I'll be in and out preparing dinner."

Even though Jennelle spent most of the day in the kitchen, Jennelle seemed to have an uncanny perception about when my beer was empty or the potato chips were gone because I don't remember wanting for either of them.

When the game was over, the hot meal was on the table. We had a cordial conversation during dinner. I was helping her clear the table and washing the dishes when she dropped a bomb.

"Richard, while I admire your respect for me, I think we have to face it. We are either going to the next stage of this relationship or thinking about breaking this off and looking for other people. If you want to, we can go upstairs and have sex?"

At the time, I'm sure my face just telegraphed shock and disbelief. Sure, I'd thought about having sex with her, but given that she was living with other girls and I couldn't entertain her in my room, I was loath to bring it up. I'm sure I stuttered an answer.

Jennelle was generous in seeing to it that I enjoyed our lovemaking. Still, even with the joy and unexpected opportunity to have sex with this attractive young woman, it seemed just a little strange. Yes, there was that feeling of seeing a woman baring her body and emotions to me that excited me. But there were moments that it felt like she was going through the motions, and she was not sharing in the feelings I was having.

* * * * * * * * * *

After that Sunday afternoon delight, as Jennelle was to put it, we were going together. In other words, we were exclusive. I was okay with it, but more and more, I felt the imaginary hand on my chest that kept a certain distance between us. We didn't talk about our families, friends, the past, or even the future. It was like we were living in a romantic comedy of some kind. We were just before the script gets to the 'guy loses the girl part,' which occurs only before 'the guy wins the girl' and fades to a happily-ever-after ending.

She made an excuse that she was going out of town with the girls for a weekend. It meant I wouldn't see her for about ten days. I was sitting in the library researching a paper and appreciating Dina's teaching me good technique when a guy walked up to the table.

"Have you got a minute? I'd like to talk to you." I didn't recognize him.

“Sure, sit down. What can I do for you?”

“Actually, it’s more about what I might be able to do for you.”

He reached out from his seat across from me, put a bookmark on the page I was reading and closed the book. I was surprised at his behavior, but he gave me a friendly smile.

“You’re dating Jenelle Hartland, right?”

“Yes.”

“How much do you know about her? I know you’re probably sleeping with her, but what do you know about her?”

I looked at him for a long time then I answered his unusual approach and question.

“Why do I get the impression that you are her former boyfriend, and you might be a little pissed off for some reason. Maybe it’s because she’s moved on, and you weren’t ready. Right?”

“Let me cut to the chase,” he said. “She is my daughter’s mother.”

He didn’t smile smugly in the ’got yah’ way you might expect. He looked sad if anything. I tried to recover from my disbelief without becoming combative.

“I didn’t realize she had been married.”

He gave off the humph of disbelief.

“If only that were true. No, my friend. Here’s the way this goes with Jennelle. She scopes you out for a few weeks. If she decides your good breeding stock, she takes you to bed. When she’s pregnant, she weeps crocodile tears, so you feel duty-bound to do the right thing. She will expect you to pay for the expenses, comfort her as she goes through the pregnancy, and assist her in the delivery. Any talk on your part about getting married will be met with the excuse that things are too stressful for her to decide.

"Then after the baby comes. She will put you on the birth certificate as the father. That is key to the next step. She will drop you like a barrel of toxic waste and sue you for child support. Any attempt on your part to get joint-custody will result in her asking for a court order to leave her and the child alone because you're violent and unstable."

I laughed.

"Great movie pitch, man. I know Jennelle lives with a couple of girls. She doesn't have a child."

"She doesn't live with those girls. If you check it out, you'll find that she housesits for them and takes care of their dog. You are right about one thing: she doesn't have a child."

"I thought so."

He smiled, but his smile had sadness around the edges.

"She has three children. All of them have a different father."

He pushed a piece of paper across the table.

"My name is on the top; the other two are her other... let's call them donors. We've tried to get some access to our kids, but it's been difficult and expensive. Good luck. If she isn't pregnant yet. I would drop her immediately if I were you."

I looked down at the list. He had address and telephone information for all of them. When I looked up, he was already walking out of the library.

* * * * * * * * * *

I considered calling these guys. Still, common sense told me if this were some kind of plot to discredit Jennelle, they would be ready to back Gerald, the guy I met in the library. No, I was going to ask her myself.

The next time I saw her was in the library. I was sitting at the same table where Gerald and I met the weekend before. She came up with a smile on her face.

"Miss me?"

I smiled back.

"Bunches."

"What did you do while I was gone?"

"Nothing much. Oh, I met a friend of yours. As a matter of fact, it was right here." I gestured to the table in front of me.

"The guy was telling me some tall tale about you being the mother of his daughter. He got more than a little angry when I told him I didn't believe him. What the hell did you do to him anyway?"

She started shaking and sank into the chair across from me. Her arms were wrapped about her body like she was warding off the cold.

"He's a terrible person. I found out that not only was he violent, but he was engaged. He was stringing me along just for the sex." She started to tear up.

"The bastard. Listen, why don't we skip class today and go to your place. You can tell me the whole story. Or if it bothers you too much, we can talk about our future. Either way, you might feel better." Her eyes began to dart around.

"Normally, I would take you up on it, but I have an exam. Can we put it off until the weekend? Honestly, I'm okay. It was just a surprise to learn of Gerald showing up in my life again. That upsets me."

"Sure. Whatever you say. Just...You are okay, right?"

I hoped my disbelief didn't show through.

* * * * * * * * * * *

I waited. She never called and never showed up for our date that weekend. I decided to check in with her. I went to the house where she claimed to be living. After I rang the doorbell, a woman I'd guess who was in her late fifties answered the door. I asked for Jennelle. The woman told me Jennelle wasn't there. I wondered when she might be home. The woman said Jennelle didn't live there. Her explanation supported Gerald's. Jennelle occasionally house sat and took care of their dog. Jennelle recently told her she wouldn't be available to house sit anymore as she moved out of Rivers Edge.

I wondered if I would get a phone call or a court order regarding my child's birth for a while. After a couple of months, when nothing happened, I thought I had escaped the problem. After a year, I was sure I had.

But I didn't escape the situation without some soul searching. Why am I so gullible? How easy it had been for her to trap me. Arliss had been merciless to me, using her observation about how I always used my dick instead of my brain.

* * * * * * * * * * *

Part of what troubled me was a sense of sameness in my life. The routine I got into was so repetitive. The evenings I spent at Romano's were predictable and not very memorable. Some might think this seems to be a selfish and minor complaint, but I was young, and I wanted some adventure. Later, when I moved further away from home to attend a state college in Brighton, I would long for those uneventful nights with my friends in a bar.

My experience with Jennelle was frightening. I was no longer shy about purchasing condoms or using them. The year after Jennelle left, which I assume she did to find fresh grounds for operation, I allowed myself to think about being a father. What if I and the other suckers ganged up on Jennelle and got custody of our children? It was daydreaming at its highest level. I never did a thing about reconnecting with her other victims. The exciting thing is that in my daydreams, my child was a girl.

Chapter 11
Regina Marsh
Coleen Bero

While I lived the days waiting for some indication one way or the other that I was the father of Jennelle's baby, I was cautious about my social life. But I was still young, dumb, and horny.

Coleen Bero burst onto the scene at Romano's about two months after Jennelle exited my life. Coleen was the kind of woman who preferred playing basketball with the boys. She was a tall girl with a more substantial body. Coleen made it clear that she could out bullshit, drink, and battle with you. Coleen didn't wear any makeup, and her hair was cut short. Her uniform was an untucked loose men's shirt, blue jeans, boots, and a smile. She knew how to tell a good joke. After we got used to her, she was generally liked. We had to get used to the fact that Coleen didn't tolerate fools. She'd call you down if she disagreed with you.

Romano's wasn't known as a pick-up bar. However, the fact was not lost on anyone that Coleen always left the bar with her gal pal Regina Marsh, never with a man.

Regina Marsh, Coleen's constant companion, was a complete opposite and a more traditional young lady. She dressed in skirts, blouses, high heels, and nylons. Regina was also tall but willowy and fragile compared to Coleen. She was quiet, but most of us thought that was because Coleen sucked all of the conversational oxygen out of the room and left nothing for Regina. Most of the regulars at Romano's, including me, thought that they were a lesbian couple. Often when Coleen was holding court, I would end up chatting with Regina. Coleen noticed but didn't seem to care.

I found that Regina was a bright girl who was also a student at my college. Unlike me, Regina knew what she wanted to do with her life. Regina was aiming for law school. She had an internship working with lawyers at a prestigious law firm. Her job was to help them with research for their pro bono cases. She loved it because she got to go to court with the attorneys. Regina was an overflowing cup of kindness. She admitted to caring too much for some of their clients who probably didn't deserve it.

Regina never flirted with me, but she always sought me out if they got to the bar after I did. She often commented that she missed seeing me if I didn't show up. One evening, Coleen, Regina, and I were standing together around a high-boy table, sipping our beverages and bullshitting about the Brighton University men's basketball team's chances. Regina typically said little about that kind of subject. That conversation was mainly a verbal ping pong match between Coleen and me.

For quite a while, I thought I might ask Regina for a coffee on campus. I enjoyed her company and conversation. While my thoughts might not have been entirely free of lust, I knew even then that a lesbian is a lesbian, and no man will change that. During a brief and infrequent lull in the conversation, I made an awkward request.

"Coleen, do you mind if I invite Regina for a coffee at school?"

Coleen's head snapped to attention. Her face graduated from the half sneer and animated thinker to amazement. Behind Coleen, I saw Regina's face light up with a smile.

"Why the hell ask me, Richard? She's standing right behind me. Ask her yourself." Coleen was almost laughing when she said this.

I turned to Regina, and before I could rephrase my request for a date, she said, "I'd love to. When do you want to meet?"

“See, that wasn’t hard, was it?” Coleen roared and slapped me on the back.

* * * * * * * * * *

When we met the following week, Regina set me straight.

“Coleen and I are used to people thinking we are a lesbian couple. Christ, if I didn’t know better, I’d believe it myself. Just the way we look and act is pretty typical of what people think about lesbian couples. But I assure you neither of us is gay.”

After that, Regina and I often had coffee on campus and continued our conversations at Romanos.

Again, the three of us were standing around one of the high-boy tables. Regina left us to visit the lady’s room. Coleen motioned me closer and spoke in a quiet voice that demonstrated no emotion and carried no further than my ears.

“You know it’s a damn shame, don’t you?” Coleen said.

“I’m sorry. What’s a damn shame?”

“Someone as beautiful and as passionate about life as Regina, and she’s still a virgin.”

I had been leaning in close to her to hear her over the karaoke performance. I pulled back to look Coleen in the eye. I was immediately on guard. Was this a joke? Her expression was serious.

“Well...yes, I guess I agree. You’re not pulling my leg, are you?”

“I’m serious as a proverbial heart attack, man.”

“Wow. I’ve got to believe she’s had her chances.”

“Oh yes, many of them. She’s been waiting for the right guy.”

“Laudable. She has her standards.”

"Regina thinks she's found him."

"Lucky guy."

"Yes, you are. Come over for dinner tomorrow night. Be at our place at 5:00 for cocktails."

As smooth as a pickpocket, Coleen turned and walked toward the stage to take the microphone for her turn. As Coleen left, Regina reappeared.

"Oh my God," Regina said. "What's she going to sing?"

I'm sure my mouth was still hanging open. Unable to say anything, my lack of response was covered by Coleen beginning her version of 'Baby, It's Cold Outside.'

****

I was unsure of what might go on during our evening for cocktails and dinner. Was there going to be more? If Regina decided I was the "one', what did that mean exactly?

I was at their door at 4:58. I wasn't inclined to consider what, out of my limited wardrobe, I would think appropriate for what this dinner invitation hinted at. When I caught myself agonizing over which underwear I should wear, I stopped. I decided to let things go where Regina wanted them to go. I still couldn't get my mind around the idea that she picked me. If this was going to be an elaborate joke, I had to be prepared to be the butt of it.

Coleen opened the door and made a theatrical arm gesture welcoming me. I walked through the narrow entry hall into the living room on my right and with the dining room on my left.

Their house was a neat bungalow-style home with gray siding, dark red shutters, and a walkout basement. It was surrounded by well-thought-out landscaping.

The dining room table was set for three. There was the recognizable smell of beef roasting in the oven and the sound of the Brubeck Trio playing on the record player. I sat on a small couch that could hold two. Coleen worked at a dry bar, scooping some ice in a highball glass, splashing scotch whiskey over the top, and cutting it with seltzer water.

"Regina will be down in a moment."

Coleen was dressed in dark green loose-fitting slacks, a white blouse, some discrete jewelry, and beaded slippers. It was evident that she could present herself in a strikingly desirable way if she cared too. I noticed that some of their artwork bore Coleen's signature.

"I like your work." I head-gestured toward the wall across from me.

"Thanks. It's a hobby."

"I don't know. If I had enough money, I'd buy it."

Regina came in from the kitchen. She brought with her the slight scent of her perfume and the vague smell of roast beef. She also had on the loose-fitting slacks pants. Hers were a deep caramel brown; the blouse was beige. Regina's jewelry was a bit more elaborate than Coleen's. On her feet were dark brown flats.

"Hi, Richard." She smiled. "Thanks for coming."

I got a hug.

"My pleasure. I like your house. Who designed your landscaping?"

"He's sucking up, Regina. He's offered to buy one of my paintings," Coleen said.

"Most of the landscaping was in place when we bought the house last year. We are working on a vegetable garden in the backyard and replacing some of the perennials. Do you like gardening?" Regina said.

“That was my Dad’s domain. The only thing I learned about yard work was how to start the lawnmower and properly mow the lawn. Properly was defined by my father.”

“Fathers!” scoffed Coleen.

“Am I getting the hint that you didn’t get along with yours?” I said.

“True, True. Don’t get me wrong. My father didn’t abuse me, nor was he particularly mean. No, he wasn’t...he wasn’t there for me. He couldn’t forgive me for not being a boy. That’s the best way to say it.”

Okay, things about Coleen were becoming more apparent.

“Richard, I uncorked the wine so it could breathe. Do you want to pour? I’ll get the roast.”

Coleen said, “I’ll get the potatoes and vegetables.”

At dinner, Regina sliced and served the beef. The rest of the meal was passed among us.

“This is an outstanding meal,” I said.

“Says the waiter from the fancy restaurant,” Regina said.

“I experimented with the roast beef last time we entertained,” Coleen said. "This one is the cook tonight." She gestured toward Regina.

“I’d have to say, you’ve learned well,” I said.

I was glad that the conversation steered clear of gossip about people we knew at Romanos residents. I questioned Coleen about how she came to become an artist.

“I’ve always sketched and scribbled drawings. When I got to high school, our small town didn’t have any art courses, but my mother found me a teacher. She taught me how to use oils and acrylics.”

I told Coleen, “I know what I like, and I like your work.”

Regina said, "I do too. I keep telling her she should try to sell some of it."

I responded, "Regina and I have shared something about what we want to do in the future. I don't even know what you do, Coleen."

She was midway through chewing a piece of roast beef. I waited.

"I'm working with *Later Years*. It's a non-profit. We work with Seniors getting the care and services they need."

"Good for you. It sounds like a necessary and good organization. I have to say I never heard of it before."

"We're new. Individual donors fund us. It limits our growth. One of our goals is to secure government funding."

Coleen excused herself and went into the house's back portion. As soon as she left, Regina put her hand on my arm.

"She's a tough lady. She didn't tell you that she started the service when an uncle of hers died trying to take care of himself on the streets. They knew he was homeless, but nobody in the family could find him. Coleen's family is wealthy. She talked them into giving her money to start this non-profit. She's upset with them. They let her know last week they were through financing her. Coleen is lost. She doesn't know what to do. She can be combative when things are not working out."

"I'm sorry to hear about this. Is there anything any of us can do to help?"

"Have you got ten thousand dollars you don't need?" We both smiled.

"She won't be back," Regina said. She resumed eating the little that remained on her plate.

"Is it because I got her talking about what she does?" I said.

"No, my goodness, No. She just left the house. I heard the backdoor close. "

"Yes, but she'll be home a little later."

"Yeah. She might be needing a little lovin' if you understand me."

"I see." I poured us more wine.

"You know, she'd do whatever she needs to be your lover, don't you?" Regina said.

I stopped with the glass of wine halfway on its way to my mouth. I put it back on the table. I brought my hands together and propped my elbows on the table.

"What's going on here?"

Regina laughed. It sounded a little forced and nervous to me.

"What do you think is going on?"

"I know this sounds crude, rude, and damn right embarrassing, but tell me, are you a virgin?"

She first looked down at the table. Then she mirrored my posture by bringing her hands together, tenting her arms, and leaning on her elbows on the table.

"Yes."

"And you've decided I'm the one you want to change that?"

"Yes."

"And now you tell me that Coleen is also interested in a...a more physical relationship?"

Regina was close to breaking out in wholly uncontrollable laughter. I think it was the "more physical relationship" that betrayed my uncertainty about what was going on.

"I think that's accurate."

"So Coleen left so we could...make love?"

"Yup, she'll be back in about two hours. If you're up to it and still here... We'd like to share you."

* * * * * * * * * *

I read someplace that almost all men have a few sexual fantasies in common. Younger men often have attractions for older women. I understood that, and I had experienced it. Another is having sex with two women at the same time. Later I would think about that concept and realize that Regina and Coleen spared me the ultimate dilemma in such a situation. They will share me but never were we all involved together. Because, if you were to ask a man what he would do if he had the opportunity to share a bed with two women, most of us would be at a loss for an answer.

Regina may not have had a lover before me, but she sure knew what she wanted. I wasn't sure what her expectations were, but she was willing to do anything on one condition. We needed to be in total darkness. Her caution to me was simple.

"I don't like the way I look naked. I'm sure you wouldn't either."

The way she felt to my touch convinced me I would have liked how she looked if she would ever allow it. Not be able to see her was, in a strange way, more erotic. I told her what I was thinking, but nothing would change her mind.

Regina seemed to be going through the *Kama Sutra* page by page. Some pages we dwelled on. Others we flipped to the next rather quickly. We were playing a game that might not have produced the expected result for all of the experimentation. Then at one point, Regina was straddled on top of me; she bent at the waist and hugged me hard, gripping me with her legs and arms, and I felt a shudder go through her body. After a moment, she relaxed and just laid on top of me.

"Are you okay?" I said.

A long sigh came out of her.

"Oh, yes. I'm more than okay."

"Good." I was wrapping my arms around her and pulling the bed blanket around us, as the sweat we produced suddenly felt cold as it evaporated.

"Women will tell you that the first time is overrated and can be disappointing," she said.

"I'm sorry."

"Fuck them. They just didn't wait for the right guy. I did."

She rolled off of me and laid her head on my chest.

"I showed you where it felt good for me. Now it's your turn."

To say I was motivated would be an understatement.

* * * * * * * * * *

We both fell asleep. I woke up when I felt a hand on my shoulder. I started to get up, but a hand kept me from moving. The bedside lamp was on, but the light wasn't very bright. I could tell it was Coleen waking me up. Looking to my right, I could see Regina was sound asleep, coiled into a fetal position, and erratically tangled into the sheets and blankets.

Coleen held her finger to her lips in the universal sign for silence. She took my left hand and pulled me out of bed. We were both careful not to disturb Regina. We walked down the hall and into Coleen's bedroom. She was wearing a bathrobe, and I was naked. She closed the door and turned to me.

"Are you up for more playtime?" I nodded.

"You are both okay with this?" I said.

"Absolutely. But the question is, can a Catholic boy live with himself if he participates in this much sin?"

"I'll learn to rationalize it somehow."

Her robe fell to the floor. The lights were on.

My soldier came to attention.

"Good, I thought she might have used you all up."

* * * * * * * * * *

In the morning, I was the first one up. I took a visual inventory of what was in the refrigerator. Then I got everything ready for breakfast. When I fixed a pot of coffee, the residents of the house woke up, prompted by the smell drifting upstairs. I had two ladies in their robes huddled around the table while I fixed the eggs and poured the juice. They needled me about not sleeping in and maybe getting second chances. I retaliated by asking them if this meant this occasion was my only chance. They howled with laughter.

"Not unless you don't want any more of us!" Regina said.

The question, what would I do if I had both of them in bed at once, answered itself. It was clear that neither of them wanted to have sex with the other. Once, and it was only once, Regina asked if she could watch Coleen and me. We agreed. After a moment, I had pretty much forgotten Regina was sitting in a chair across the room. When Coleen and I finished, we realized Regina had left the room. I asked Coleen if she was going to ask Regina if she could watch us. Coleen laughed.

"Richard, have you ever seen Regina naked?"

"No."

"What's the chance she's going to change her mind?"

"I guess none, but to be honest, I don't understand her fear of being naked in front of a lover."

"It's called body issues. Regina thinks she is ugly. Look, I've seen glances of her naked, and we have sunbathed semi-naked in the garden patio out in the back. She has the body of a supermodel. She has a mental image that doesn't match reality. In her mind, her body is out of proportion, and she imagines fat everywhere despite evidence to the contrary."

* * * * * * * * * * *

A few weeks later, I went to the house in the afternoon. I was always invited. I never just dropped in. I found a note from Coleen on the dining room table. It said that Regina was sorry, but I came over for nothing. She wasn't feeling well and wouldn't be good company in any case. I walked upstairs to her door and tapped on it. I heard her respond with some surprise.

"Hey. I saw the note. I'm leaving, but I thought I'd check. Do you need anything?"

The voice that answered was like none I'd ever heard from her before.

"No. Thank you for checking, but I just need to rest."

I was concerned because of the way she sounded. I left. But I stopped at the 7-Eleven and used the payphone to call Coleen at work. I explained to her why I was worried.

"Are you busy right now?" Coleen asked.

"No, I had planned on spending the afternoon with Regina."

"Meet me at The Diner on Blake."

When I got to The Diner on Blake, Coleen was already in a booth in the corner. The waitress brought the coke I ordered while I settled into the seat across from Coleen.

“Should I be worried?” I said. “Regina sounded like she was speaking to me from the bottom of a barrel. I almost didn’t believe it was her.”

Coleen just stared at me dead-eyed.

“I didn’t tell you this, okay? She has to tell you, or you don’t know. Am I clear?”

“Yeah, what’s happening?”

“Two things you have to know. Regina and I go back to first grade. We’ve been like sisters for all of these years. Close! I mean, there’s nothing she doesn’t know about me and vice versa. Second, she doesn’t like you, Richard.” Coleen paused long enough to make my heart stop.

She smiled. “She loves you. Regina being a recent virgin, I’m not sure what that means. Nonetheless, she’s into you big time. I volunteered to leave you alone, but she’s afraid if you can’t have both of us, you’ll bolt.”

I started to talk, but she held up her finger, motioning me to shut up.

“I know. You’re playing our game by our rules. I know that Regina, by herself, is worth it. Still, this is a woman who sees fat on her body that isn’t there, right? I also think you’re a horny fucker who would be happy with either of us. But I also think you are a better person. You showed me that most of the time, you think with your head rather than your dick.” She paused to pull herself together.

“Regina suffers from what the doctors call clinical depression. For reasons not apparent to me, she sinks into this mental pit. She can’t do anything. She has no energy. There have been times when I had to feed her like a child and help her to the bathroom. She's taken so much time off from work that they were thinking of letting her go. I convinced her to talk to her boss and level with him about her problem. He's understanding, but she has to show them that she's serious about getting treatment. She's thinking about voluntarily checking into a treatment facility."

"Is that a good thing...I mean, her going into a treatment center?"

"Yeah, but there is one problem. She thinks if she admits all of this and goes into the clinic, you won't be here for her when she gets out. It could be months, by the way."

"Okay." My mind was spinning. "We have to convince her to do what's best for her, that we will support her, and she can count on me. But how are we going to do that unless she admits to me what is going on?" I said.

"You'll have to hang in there for her, no matter what. You've got to know that she might not ever get better."

"I'm using my head here, Coleen."

"She thinks she loves you. Do you love her?"

"I don't know, Coleen. I care enough to try. I can't walk away from her. I care that much."

"Okay, let me talk to her. I know how to get her off the fence."

"What are you going to do?"

"I'm going to tell her that if she doesn't level with you, you probably will move on. My opinion, not your words."

****

Three weeks later, Coleen and I drove Regina to a clinic on the River's Edge north end. Regina didn't know that Coleen borrowed money from her family's trust fund to pay for the treatments. At the time, since Coleen and I had talked at The Diner, Regina had been better. I thought that might signal she didn't need to go into the clinic after all. Coleen straightened me out, explaining to me this is what always happens. Regina would get to a healthy behavior phase and then suddenly go downhill into a depression.

I learned the bus trip out to the clinic was an hour in each direction. I cut that by taking a bike to speed up the last couple of miles, I would have to walk. Coleen and I didn't often go together because she knew Regina wanted to be with me alone for the little time we had.

Regina may have had unreasonable expectations for our relationship. Still, she was with it enough to realize talking about a future together wasn't a good idea either. I didn't rule out a future with Regina, but I didn't want to make promises I might not be able to keep. The Regina I saw on my visits to the clinic was easy to love. Part of the problem was we couldn't express the physical side of our relationship.

With Regina's permission, her therapist told me that she might experience behavioral side effects depending on the drug she was using. It was one of the reasons they kept her so long. Regina was getting talk-therapy, but the drugs they were giving her might worsen her condition. They had to be sure. Her doctor told me that a common reaction was that she might not have any desire for sex or even signs of affection. I didn't think that was the case, as she often prolonged our hugs when we greeted or parted. There was no doubt about what was going on in her mind.

I kept going to the clinic to visit Regina, sometimes every weekend, but no less than every other weekend, until I hit the wall.

Chapter 12
Candice Marlow
Sally Boardman

Regina is like the waif on the cliff edge. That recurring dream is almost like an addiction for me. It's that scene in the movie where the heroine is falling off the cliff, and the hero is holding her hand, preventing her from falling. Well, that's Regina and me. In my worst dreams, my grip on her slips. Regina falls and dies.

* * * * * * * * * *

I'm in my second semester at junior college and working a lot of hours at the restaurant. I see Arliss, but not as much as we had in the past. Arliss is often pissed because I don't spend any time with my parents. She is also concerned about my obsession with Regina and my relationship with Coleen.

Coleen and I get together about once a week, often on Friday evening after I'm through working. We always talk about Regina. Coleen likes to fill me in on their history. To me, the stories are still sweet or funny. She doesn't talk about the bad times, such as when Regina's depression started exhibiting itself.

It was only on a few occasions when we'd had too much to drink that we'd have sex. Regina reassured both of us it's okay if Coleen and I enjoyed each other. Despite Regina's permission, Coleen and I are the ones that think it's wrong. We both felt guilty. It was during one of our discussions that Coleen questioned me about my mental state.

"Richard, you've changed a lot since Regina went into the clinic. You realize that, don't you?"

"I don't know. I don't feel any different."

"That may be, but you're acting differently. You're not as spontaneous, carefree, and fun. You've gotten so fucking serious. You tell me you have problems concentrating and difficulty with making decisions. You need help, man."

* * * * * * * * * *

I took her advice and found myself in the office of Candice Marlowe. Candice is about my Mom's age. She's about five feet two inches tall. Her body is like a ball. She's many pounds overweight. Her hair is in the pixie style. Candice leaves it in its natural color of salt white, pepper gray, and black. She smiles easily and often. Still, I found that as we started my therapy, she could be as serious as she needed to be.

Her campus office is in a convenient site at the Junior College. Her regular office is downtown somewhere. Because I'm a full-time student, I'm entitled to consult with a qualified mental counselor, and the University covers the cost. Candice sees her student patients in this little box with one high window admitting the outside light. Unlike the stereotypical image of a counselor's office, there is no couch.

By the third session, I'm at ease with her. I trust her and find myself unloading my feelings. I share my experiences with Regina and Coleen. I was hesitant to talk about our sexual adventures since I didn't want to sound boastful or proud. While sexual need did have a lot to do with it, I felt the things the three of us did were based on concern and respect for each other. It was not the result of me being such a stud.

"If Ive got this correctly, the facts are that you three at some point agreed that the women were going to share you sexually," Marlowe said.

"Yes. I mean, we didn't sit down and write the rules, but the understanding came together. As far as I know, it was clear to all three of us."

"I'm concerned about your commitment to Regina. You say your friend, Coleen, says that Regina is in love with you and fears losing you because of her depression issues?"

"Yes, Regina also has what I guess you might call 'body image issues.' She imagines her body being out of proportion and fat. In reality, she could be a model if she chose to be."

"Let me tell you why I'm concerned. And please understand, I could be wrong. Regina's helplessness, along with her self-image problems and depressive behavior, could be an unconscious effort on her part to force you and Coleen to accept her right to you exclusively. And let me point out that Regina may not be aware of this herself. Even if I'm correct, Regina could deny it and not be lying. Whatever is happening here, Richard, it's harming you. If you continue with this, it's not going to get better for you. It will only get worse."

"I don't know what to do."

"The first thing you have to do is slow down. This life you are living is wearing you down. You've got issues with Regina and Coleen, your parents, your school, and your work. It's a lot. You've got to get the balance back in your life."

"But how?"

"Richard, start by talking to Regina about reducing your trips to the clinic. Start with every other week instead of every week. Have dinner with your Mom and then your Dad. These events can be short but meaningful get-togethers. You might find it's right for you because I think Arliss has heaped a lot of guilt on you over this. A small gesture like this might be useful for everyone. If you can, cut back on your courses at school and hours of work. Now that is in the order of importance, not necessarily the order of action. Do whatever you feel comfortable doing. Okay?"

"I'll try."

"Why don't we get together in two weeks and see how you've done."

* * * * * * * * * *

I went to my academic counselor, and I found I could drop one course and then pick it up in the summer semester. Tim D'Amato, let me have Tuesdays off until spring. That meant I had three days off in a row. In the spring, I wouldn't have as demanding an academic load. Possibly I could go back to a heavier schedule at the restaurant. Tim was adamant that whatever we agreed upon had to be what I needed to do, and he didn't want to lose me.

Arliss agreed to accompany me to dinners separately with both of my parents. Both dinners went pretty well, but I was glad Arliss was there. Whether she knew it or not, Arliss was preventing both my parents from asking me the tough questions. She may have felt like a sister to me, but she was still a family friend to my parents. Arliss suggested that maybe having dinner with both of them and explaining why I was so upset might help everyone.

So yes, I worked the list backward, but even though I'd had seen Regina in the time between my appointments with Marlowe, I hadn't broached the idea of cutting back on my visits. I left Regina with the sense that nothing was changing.

* * * * * * * * * *

"Listen, I agree with your shrink, Richard. You have to let Regina know what's going on. You are not abandoning her. You're just cutting back for your good. She has to understand," Coleen said.

We were in the living room of their house. Coleen and I had shoveled about three inches of snow off of their sidewalk and driveway. She made some coffee, and we were on our second cup.

"What do you think? Should I talk to her doctor to warn them? I mean, what if she doesn't understand?"

"Why don't you ask Marlowe about that? It sounds smart to me."

****

I reported my progress to Marlowe.

"This is good, Richard. I understand it hasn't been very long, but are you feeling any better?"

"Maybe, but I'm still worried about approaching Regina. Do you think I should warn her doctors about what I'm going to do?"

"That's not a bad idea. The professionals working with Regina may choose to sit in and monitor the conversation. Let me give them a call. Now tell me about how you think these dinners with both of your folks and Arliss are going to go?"

"I'm not sure. Arliss said that she noticed that when we had dinner with them separately, they were both avoiding any conversation that might upset me. But we aren't going to solve anything by not talking about our feelings, right?"

"Yes. What do you want to talk about?"

"I want them to acknowledge that if they were so sure their marriage was over, they victimized me by staying together. I'm angry that they couldn't level with me about their problems. I'm angry because my father cheated on my mother, and I'm angry with my mother that she can't forgive him."

"Wow. No wonder you're tired. That's a load to haul around."

****

Arliss provided the neutral ground. We all met at her house for dinner. I helped Arliss put together a simple meal. We agreed to try to hold the drinking down to the minimum. For the meal, I whipped some potatoes with sour cream and butter. The roasted peppers commanded the top tier of odors in the apartment. The salmon filets were sitting in the refrigerator.

My mother arrived first. Dad might have been sitting down the block, waiting for her to come, because he knocked on the door minutes after she arrived. They both looked so much older than I remembered. It had only been ten months since they separated. Dad took a seat as far away from Mom as possible. Mom didn't even acknowledge him when he arrived.

"I'm sorry, maybe you didn't hear me, but I said hello," Dad said to Mom.

"Huh, I heard from you. Frankly, I don't know why I agreed to do this. I got a divorce, so I wouldn't have to deal with you." The anger in her voice was unmistakable.

"Mom," Arliss said. "We're here to help Richard. You don't have to talk to your ex."

"He talked to me..."

"Mom! Cut it out. You sound like a two-year-old," I said.

She pouted like a two-year-old. "Sorry."

"Arliss tells me that you can't figure out why I'm so angry with you guys splitting up. Well, let me tell you. Now it's obvious you were having trouble long before you got the divorce. All that time, you cut me off from your feelings, intentions, and...quite frankly, your caring about me. I'm sure you were telling yourself that it was for the best. It wasn't. I feel like a fool. You've thrown away a life together for what? Is either of you better off since the divorce? I don't see it. But unlike you, I'm not going to think for you. Tell me, is it better being alone?"

It was so quiet I could hear the salmon sizzling in the oven. Mom moved restlessly in her chair. Dad was bent over from the waist, looking down at the floor. Arliss got up and checked on the salmon. My heart rate was operating at the end of the marathon speed. It surprised me that Dad spoke first.

"Your right, Richard. We kept you out of the discussion. I could give you the reasons, but the reasons are just excuses, and you deserve more than that. I'm sorry."

Mom was looking at him, mouth agape.

"I agree with your Father. I have to say it's hard to recognize your child has become an adult. But as your Father said, that's an excuse, not a reason. As for myself, am I happier? No, but I don't miss him. I miss a family... the one he destroyed when he had an affair."

Dad was in pain. I could see it on his face and in his posture.

"I…she's right; I ruined our family. I can't do anything to change that now. Honestly, I can't get past it. Thinking about finding someone else and starting over is impossible. I'm stuck."

Dad threw his hands up in surrender. I sat there. It was horrible. But, I had asked for this.

"I can't do anything about the two of you. But each of us has to build something that works. I promise to spend more time with each of you so we can mend things. Just remember, I didn't cause this. Anything we have between ourselves has to be new," I said.

Arliss came into the living room.

"Is everyone ready to eat?"

"Yes, I'm starved." My Dad said. He even smiled a little.

Mom got up and began the walk to the dining room. She grabbed my arm to escort her. I wrapped it around her waist and gave her a little squeeze. My action was spontaneous. I had no idea how profound that gesture was until I had a child of my own.

The rest of the evening went pretty well. Mom and Dad never talked directly to each other. The conversation centered around filling them in about my life. Of course, I didn't share my sexual adventures. But I told them about Regina. I could tell they both were concerned about a relationship with someone that was challenging.

"I want to share something else with you," I said.

"I am getting counseling from a specialist. Her services are provided through the University. I have been putting too much on myself. She's helping me get things sorted out. One of the things she urged me to do was to face both of you about my feelings. I think she was right, and I'm glad we did this. Let's be fair here. Arliss has been telling me we needed to do this for a long time, so I owe her an apology."

I paused and looked around at each one of them.

"I hope this wasn't too painful for everyone."

They were either shaking their heads or mouthing 'No' or both.

After dessert, Dad and Mom both excused themselves. They walked out the door at the same time, but I had no illusions that they were going to get together. They harbored their demons. It wasn't my job to deal with that problem.

Arliss turned to me and gave me a big sister hug.

"You are the bravest man I know, Richard. I don't think I could have done that."

"I couldn't have done it without you. There's no way I could have said what I said without you in the room." I hugged her back.

* * * * * * * * * *

When I got to the clinic the following weekend, the desk person asked me to talk to one of Regina's caregivers. I walked down the hall and knocked at the door. I heard something that sounded like 'come in.' I opened the door, and the first person I saw was Regina. She got up and held out her arms for a hug.

As I welcomed her into my arms, I looked over her shoulder. I saw a young woman sitting in a chair within a conversation group setting. She was a small woman with a bright smile. When Regina and I broke away from each other, the woman stood up and extended her hand to me. I took it, and she gestured to another chair.

"Hello, Richard. My name is Sally Boardman. I'm a counselor here at the clinic. I've been working with Regina for about a month now. I thought it would be good for me to meet you. The reason I think it would be helpful is that Regina talks about you a lot." She laughed and looked at Regina when she said that.

Regina smiled. I smiled back at them mainly because I didn't know how else to react. Had Marlowe talked to Boardman? Were we going to talk about how much I was coming to visit? Did Boardman have another reason for bringing me into their concerns? What the hell was going on here?

"So, Richard, I understand you're visiting our patient here almost every week." I nodded. "Regina tells me you don't drive."

I nodded again.

"So, on top of a long bus trip, you either bike or walk the last couple miles."

"Yes," I said. Regina was fidgeting in her chair.

"We..." she nodded toward Regina, "think we should bring you in on her progress and her future out of this place."

My arm was resting on the arm of my chair. Regina put her hand on top of mine.

"Regina has been diagnosed as bi-polar. You may have noticed she sometimes acts frantic and tireless, and at other times she is listless and cannot take care of herself.

"We know this is caused by the inability of her brain to react correctly. Its chemical makeup is not where it should be. The problem is we don't know enough about brain chemistry. We do know some drugs help. What we don't know is how much and how often these drugs should be administered. Also, these drugs may cause more problems than they solve.

"I'm going to give you an example. Say you have a lot of headaches. We provide you with aspirin. It cures your headache, but over time the dosage of aspirin causes stomach problems. I can give you another drug that will help with your stomach problems, but it may have other side effects that we can or can't deal with.

"We adjust her dosage and deal with the side effects the best we can. Some of the side effects are major. Some drugs affect libido. Patients have little or no desire for a sexual relationship. A broad regimen of drugs can cause liver damage over time. There can be debilitating lethargy or loss of ability to focus on anything.

"The other thing that Regina and I are dealing with is her concept of reality, what is normal behavior, and what is this condition dictating. We know that when Regina is manic, overactive, she is not normal. We also know when she's depressed, she's not healthy. On that trip down the scale, there is a period where she is normal. When I say normal, I mean normal for Regina. She has been bouncing up and down in this cycle so long she doesn't have any concept of what normal is. Regina needs that, and so do we. So she and I work together to try and find that through talk therapy. It's a process of trial and error. We'll get there.

After that, Regina's challenge is to stick to her drug dosage and keep working on self-monitoring her actions.

"We know, for instance, that all people have what you and I call good days and bad days. Regina has to learn what is a good day - bad day experience for the 'Normal' Regina."

It was quiet for a moment. Regina was gripping my hand to the point of it being painful.

"Do you have any questions?" Boardman said.

"Yeah, Is there anything I can do to help?"

I heard Regina suck in her breath like a gasp.

"Yes, you can help monitor Regina. You will learn to see the signs. You'll be able to warn her if she's swinging too far out of her normal range and reassure her when she's acting normal. Right now, Coleen and you being supportive is good. Without people who care for her, it's a tough road to travel on her own. But we have another issue here. Does Regina know you're getting counseling?"

"No. I haven't shared that with her. I figure she has enough to deal with."

As I said this, I realized that this is what I raged at my parents for doing to me.

"Do you want to tell her what you've discovered and what you are working on?"

"Okay, ah... Regina, I've been seeing a counselor for a couple of months. We decided that between work, school, family, and you, I'm overextended. In other words, I'm trying to do too much, and I'm not doing any of them very well. I've cut back on school and work. I've tried to mend my relationship with my parents and Arliss. I want to cut back on my visits here, but I'm afraid..."

“Are you giving up on ...giving up on us?” She was close to tears.

“No, I’m not giving up on our relationship. I just need more time to get the stuff done that I need to do. I also want to know what you’re going to do when you leave here. Next year I’m going to transfer to Brighton University. I don’t know how this is all going to work. I do know I want it to work. To start with would it be okay if I come every other week instead of every week to see you?”

I know I wasn’t breathing normally because I could hardly get the words out. Regina squeezed my knee lightly.

“Yes. I’ll miss not seeing you more often, but I get it, and as long as we are okay, I can live with you every other week. I love you, you big dope. I don’t want you to harm yourself. Maybe you could just call me the weekend you don’t visit.”

We hugged. Marlowe was right about the mental weight I was carrying. In those first moments after our conversation, I could feel it slipping off my shoulders.

Chapter 13
Angelica Lopez

Life got better for me when I cut back on the frantic pace I'd previously set for myself. The one important thing I learned in my work with Marlowe was that people could ask you to do anything they want. However, you can say no. Learning to say no is still challenging for me, but at least I recognize the possibility. In this context, let me tell you my boss Tim D'Amato, made me an offer to which I could not say no.

Tim asked, "How's it going?"

"I think it's going well."

"I'm glad to hear that. I've got a challenge for you. I want you to listen to what I've got to say before we start chewing on the cookie."

He shifted around in his chair. Tim referred to dealing with details as nibbling on a cookie.

"I'm rolling out a new restaurant in about six months."

I'm sure he enjoyed my amazement. Tim is a good-looking guy. He was a triple-letter athlete in high school. He went to NCAA Division Three college, where he played basketball and tennis. He graduated with a business degree before he started his marathon tour learning about the restaurant business.

He favors a casual wardrobe. He shows up to work in Dockers, blue button-down collar shirts, a tie, and a sport coat. He prefers boat shoes, but no matter what, his shoes are slip-on. His hair is styled with medium sideburns, and the sides cut to touch the ear lobes. His forehead line is reduced by the hair combed and swept across it.

"The new restaurant will be very different from The Manitou. It's going to feature Mexican food. I'm bringing in a Chef who specializes in a particular regional variation of the traditional menu. The building design will make our customers feel like they are in Mexico. Uniforms for the waitstaff and our hostess will add to the atmosphere. At the bar, I will feature Mexican beers, and more of the cocktails will be made with rum or tequila. This restaurant-style is growing in popularity across the country. We're going to be the first in the State to feature real Mexican food.

"I want to train our staff on this concept. At its simplest, waitstaff will just be trained to treat customers the way we do here at The Manitou. Their knowledge of the menu will be important because we will be serving a customer base that is largely ignorant of this type of food. So, what do you think?"

I will admit, I had no idea why he was sharing this information with me, much less asking me for my opinion.

"I guess the first thing that comes to mind is that I would like to try the menu before I had an opinion about how successful it would be."

Tim clapped his hands together in one loud report.

"Perfect. Great thought. Anything else?"

"Where is this place going to be located?"

"Downtown by the University."

"Why?"

"The marketing people I hired told me that young people would be willing to give this idea a chance. They would be willing to try it and are the demographic segment most likely to enjoy the food."

I thought for a moment, and then I asked, "What if we had a hiring event that included serving the candidates some of this food?"

Tim looked down at his desk.

"Where would we do this? I'm not going to have my restaurant ready for at least four months."

"How about renting the school cafeteria on the campus?"

Tim brightened immediately. Then he considered the idea for a while.

"Done. Can you make arrangements? I'd like to do it in about three months. You know, close enough to opening."

"Could we include a tour of the restaurant even though it won't be finished?"

"Sure"

"You know if we do this, the word is going to get around pretty quick."

Tim gave me a knowing smile with a slight cock to his head.

"Yeah. Won't that be terrible?"

We both enjoyed the idea with a healthy laugh.

* * * * * * * * * *

I didn't think getting this task accomplished would be easy. Tim gave me a stack of his business cards and told me that if anyone was concerned about my authority, I could provide them with his card and ask them to call him. I worked my way up the chain of command at the University. By the end of the second month, I had the necessary agreements to use the cafeteria and staff to put on the event.

Tim told me he had his Chef coming in from California. The Chef was bringing two assistants. I was being charged with escorting them, directing them to vendors and resources. I met them at the airport. Tim rented a small van for me to haul them around and to pick up the supplies we might buy.

I held up a sign printed on a piece of white cardboard. It just said, 'Manitou's.' Two women and a young man responded to my sign. The older of the two women said, "I assume you are Richard."

"Yes. Welcome."

"I'm Angelica Lopez. These are my assistants, Graciela Montenegro and Clark Holstad."

Tim never told me the new Chef was a woman. Angelica had no trace of an accent. I found out later that she was a third-generation Mexican-American. She was striking. Her dark brown hair was shoulder length and framed an oval face with blazing brown eyes and full lips. She was medium height. I didn't notice immediately, but later as I watched her work in the kitchen, I saw that she moved like a graceful dancer. Often she seemed to be gliding rather than walking.

Angelica and her two assistants had worked out a plan before they arrived. Clark's list was in charge of hardware. He looked at the cooking utensils, serving dishes, tableware, and seating capacity. Clark was two years older than me. I would guess he was six-foot-tall. Like a stereo, typical Chef, Clark was on the plump side. He had a shock of unruly blond hair that he stuffed into a knit cap. He laughed a lot. I frequently wondered what he found humorous, but he was fun to be with, and I found him likable.

Graciela was all business. I had the impression she was modeling Angelica's behavior. Clearly, she admired her boss. She was a skinny young lady. She wore her hair like Angelica's, but her face was long. She had brown eyes, a pronounced nose, and a pointed chin. Her responsibilities included food and spices. They brought some spices with them. I guess they were hedging their bet that they wouldn't find what they needed in our supply chain.

* * * * * * * * * *

After two days of list-making and securing or sourcing much of what we needed, we had a meeting with Tim at the School Cafeteria. Angelica produced a detailed drawing of the room, the traffic pattern, and the food stations. After explaining the process and making notes at the margins regarding the challenges we still faced, Angelica addressed all of us.

"Aside from hiring and training a couple more servers, our biggest issues are sourcing some of the meats and a trip to Chicago to get some vegetables and baking ingredients for the tortillas," she said.

"We need a certain type of cornflour for the tortillas, and I'm concerned about the local tomatoes and cilantro quality. Once we open, we will need to work with local vendors to get what we need in quantity, but for now, it's easier to go to Chicago and buy the supplies."

"Take Richard with you, please," Tim said.

"Of course, Tim. Richard has been helpful to us since we've arrived. I'm sure we will need him for the rollout as well as this event."

"You up for this, Richard?" Tim said. "I know you're still going to school, and you have other responsibilities. I don't want to overload you."

"I can handle this," I said.

Angelica took me in hand in the weeks that preceded the event. She showed me how to prepare this fabulous food. Besides the preparation of the dishes, she also had some presentation tricks to show me.

"When I make a Taco, I always place the more colorful ingredients on the outside or top of the dish. The meats and some of the other add-on ingredients like shredded cheese tend to be monochromatic. The tomatoes and peppers attract the eye."

Angelica and I worked together almost every day. I was shadowing her not only in the kitchen, but she included me in her management planning.

"Tim has made it clear that you are supposed to be involved in every step we take in this project. I don't think he expects you to cook once we open, but he wants you to know what's going on in the back."

Tim put me on salary because I couldn't wait on tables and help with the new restaurant project at the same time. The four of us went to Chicago and shopped for the things on our list. All my companions, at different times, quizzed me about how it was to work for Tim. I told them that I had started at the restaurant working for his father.

"Tim is much more aggressive than his father. He's also trained in restaurants beyond our place here. His father would never be trying this concept out. Tim wants what he wants, and he can be strict, but I think he's fair. He's been good for me."

****

Angelica slowly but surely pried my story out of me. I told her about Regina and the challenges we had faced as a couple. She shared her own story in bits and pieces. Over time, I had a good picture of this amazing woman.

When she graduated from high school, she worked in an Italian restaurant in San Francisco. She was working her way up the chain of command. She was eventually recruited by a very prestigious restaurant in San Diego.

"I went to San Diego with such a big head. I was there one week when I thought I had made the biggest mistake of my life. I was so frustrated. After what I considered a near disaster on a Saturday evening shift, five of my dishes were returned to the kitchen because of customer complaints. I went to Chef.

"He took me into his office and asked what the problem was. I told of my feelings about being in over my head. I was near tears. He sat down next to me, and we went through each incident of my returns that evening. In each case, he asked me how I would avoid those mistakes in the future. He told me, as far as he was concerned, three of the five were customer complaints, not errors. He explained that some customers are acclimated to a specific presentation and finish to a dish. They feel if it doesn't fit their experience, they think the meal isn't adequately prepared, and they are comfortable rejecting it. He told me he would either try to talk them into another selection or attempt to redo it in the way they preferred. In either case, he assured me, he would never hold his cooks responsible.

"He said, if I made a mistake but knew how to fix the dish properly, he considered that a correctable performance. If I didn't know how to fix the dish properly, it was his fault for not instructing me. I left his office and rededicated myself to a performance that would never require having that conversation again."

On another occasion, I asked her how she came to master Mexican food.

"Believe it or not, my mother, being second-generation American born, didn't cook a lot of traditional Mexican food. If she had, our grandparents came from a region of Mexico where the food was significantly different from our offering."

Angelica paused and seemed to be considering what she would say next.

"I had an affair with one of my workmates. It was stupid. He was older than I was and married with three kids. He couldn't have left his wife and family even if he wanted to. And honestly, I knew that, but I didn't want to think about it.

"You can't keep a secret like that for very long. When it became common knowledge, it was only a matter of time before his wife found out. Our Chef brought both of us into his office. He told us he was going to fire me. I was about to object when he held up his hand to stop me. Then he dismissed my lover from the meeting.

When we were alone. The Chef told me he was disappointed in my judgment. Still, he understood the heart's feelings, and the body's needs sometimes overrode good sense. He told me he had two opportunities lined up for me. I should interview for both jobs and pick the one I liked. He said that if I found something on my own and considered it better, he would give me a recommendation letter.

"One of the jobs was with a hotel chain. The benefit was that if the kitchen became stacked with too many good candidates, I could transfer to another of their locations and speed up my advancement.

"The other one was a Mexican restaurant. First, I had to inform them I had no background in their food. I remember the manager and the Chef of the restaurant laughing, thinking that I was kidding. When I told them I was serious, I thought I might have lost an opportunity. It was fine with me because I was leaning toward the hotel gig. To my surprise, they convinced me it didn't make any difference. I ended up learning how to cook Sonoran Regional Food. I love it. In a way, it was like coming home."

"Okay, why bring it here?"

"Your boss. Tim and I met in Las Vegas. I was impressed with his knowledge and dedication to the food business. We both went our separate ways, but we stayed in touch. He called me last spring and asked if I wanted to help him with this. I didn't even have to think about it."

* * * * * * * * * * *

In my training period with Angelica, she occasionally turned me over to Graciela. At first, Graciela was quiet and reserved. As we became more involved and had to explain what we were doing, she opened up. She knew a lot about the process.

"So, have you got a girl, Richard?" Graciela said.

"I do, but I don't get to see her often. I haven't seen her for almost a month because of this project."

Regina was responding well to her latest round of drugs. The doctors and therapists talked about sending her home on weekends as a preliminary step to releasing her from hospital care.

I took Friday and Saturday off the weekend that Regina came home for her first visit. I picked her up with the van. I was early, and I ended up waiting in the lobby of the clinic. When she met me, she clung to me ferociously.

"I missed this so much," she whispered.

"So do I. We'll catch up."

I volunteered to pick her up because Coleen was scheduled out of town until Sunday. I guessed that Coleen made this out-of-town trip happen, so Regina and I could have time alone to avoid awkwardness. Coleen and I were not having sex anymore by mutual agreement, but Regina didn't know that. We had all but stopped talking about our previous experience.

"Are you hungry? We stocked the fridge for you."

"I only want one thing now, Richard. You." She smiled and grabbed me by the lapels of my shirt. I put my hands on her waist.

"What are we waiting for?"

* * * * * * * * * *

After we made love, we both dozed off for a while before resuming our passions. I got out of bed about two hours later. I took a long hot shower, dressed, and went to the kitchen. I didn't know about Regina, but I was hungry.

Regina must have heard me working in the kitchen. After she showered and changed clothes, she came out to the kitchen and sat at the breakfast bar, watching me make dinner. I was preparing tempura shrimp with rice and steamed asparagus.

"How's it feel to be home?" I said.

"Great, but then if we had sex like that at the hospital, it might be alright also. I'm thinking Coleen is making this easy for both of us by being out of town?" she said.

"She didn't tell me so, but it's fair to say you're right."

"You aren't sleeping with her anymore, are you?"

"No, we stopped that a long time ago."

"Why?"

"I think that outside of the fun of it, it wasn't important anymore to either of us. Regina, you know that you and I have something special. Now that you've become more stable, I can tell you that I love you. I don't know what that means beyond what we already share, but I want you to know."

She looked at me as if I had punched her in the stomach.

"Richard, I had only hoped that you cared about me. I...I..."

She burst out crying. I walked around the counter and took her into my arms.

"Regina, I didn't want to hurt you..."

She looked up to me, half-crying through a smile.

"I'm not hurt, silly. I'm just so happy."

After we ate, we went to the living room and sat next to each other. We were holding hands.

"I think we have to talk about some stuff."

She leaned over, pulled my arm up around her shoulder, and rested her head on my chest.

"What stuff?"

"Okay, I know they are going to let you out of the clinic pretty soon. What are your plans?"

"Oh, that stuff." She lightly punched me in the stomach.

"I have to ease back into working, but I've talked to my boss at the law office. They do want me to come back to the law firm. It seems several innocent people are in jail because I wasn't there to save them."

"Heartless bitch. And you, not caring and off having a great time. "

"What do you have in mind?" She asked.

"Nothing specific. You do know I'm transferring to Brighton next fall?"

"Yes. But we've done this long separation thing pretty well so far, haven't we?"

"Yes, but I don't want to assume anything."

She sat up and put her face inches from mine.

"Any guy who would put up with the crap I've put you through and still loves me can pretty well assume anything he wants."

"Okay, do you want to get married?"

"Is that a rhetorical question or a proposal?"

"Both, I guess."

"You are such a smooth talker."

At this point, she hesitated. She had thought of this, and her answer surprised me.

"I think we should wait."

I absorbed my shock that resulted from her answer.

"Why?"

"Because we are both young and we have a lot of time. I want you to get your degree. I want to get my certification as a paralegal. I…"

Here was another unexpected turn of events.

"Hey, what happened to you becoming a lawyer?"

She gave me a wry smile.

"Let's imagine we're in the middle of a big case, and the lead attorney becomes unable to continue. No, I think that becoming a paralegal rather than an attorney is a responsible path. Being in the law, being involved in litigation, that's going to be good enough."

"Regina!"

"Richard, I've discussed this with my doctors and my therapists. My condition creates limits on what I can do. Intellectually, can I get a degree? More than likely. Would I be able to withstand the normal pressures of practicing law? Maybe. But the stronger possibility is that it would amplify my condition. I've made my peace with this, Richard."

We were quiet for a long time. Regina slipped into her cuddle position. I felt so bad for her having to place barriers in front of the path to her dreams. She stirred in my embrace.

"Let's go to bed early. I want to get on top of you and see if I can screw you until your eyes cross," she said.

* * * * * * * * * * *

The line into the cafeteria stretched down the hall and outside at the new restaurant's planned event. I know some of these guys had been through the line at least twice. On the other hand, we've offered free food to college students. So what did we expect?

After meal service to the public was over, the students who hoped to work at the restaurant stayed for our pre-announced Q & A. Tim has taken his sport coat off and his sleeves rolled up. He stood on a riser to be easily seen by the group.

"Show of hands. Who likes this food?"

Almost all of the people raised their hands.

"We are going to be opening up in about forty-five days. Before that, we will have a simulated opening for five days. That means we will do thorough waitstaff training in preparation. Our wait staff will have to know how our food is prepared and what ingredients are in it. One day, you will be a customer during this training phase, and on another, you will be the waiter. By the way, during that training, not only will the food be free, but you will also be paid for your time."

He paused and accepted the applause and cheers.

"For the final fifteen days, we will have a soft opening. The customers will pay only for alcohol-based drinks and wine. The food will be free if consumed in the restaurant. Carryout will be 50% discounted. All the customers will be presented with a bill, so they might offer you a voluntary tip based on what they might have paid. If they do not tip you, I will make up the difference.

"I want to caution you about working for me. My standards are high. I don't want to see anyone fumbling with notes when asked about ingredients or food preparation. If they ask a question you can't answer, the response is, 'I'm sorry I don't know, but I will find out.' At that point, you find out.

"Another pet peeve of mine is a waiter coming to the table and not knowing who ordered what. Use whatever mental system you need. Mentally number the chairs. Remember who is wearing what clothing and what the customer requested for a cocktail. I can tell you if you concentrate during the order process, look your customer in the eye when they speak to you, and do these things consistently, you can learn to do this without notes. I have waiters working for me now that can handle parties of twelve without writing anything down. I'm looking forward to this opening, and I hope you will as well. Welcome to Casa de Paco's."

A banner fell open from the ceiling revealing the new logo for our restaurant. Everybody was excited.

I was excited beyond belief. The logo was from a submission I gave Tim just before Angelica and her team came to the city. I had drawn the image of a southwestern mission-style building and then lettered in the name. Regina and I researched the name and made sure it meant in English what we suggested in Spanish. Tim had it put on the banner precisely the way I submitted it. I was in shock when I felt Tim's hand on my shoulder.

"Good job, Richard. I loved it the minute I saw it."

He handed me an envelope. When I opened it later, it was a check for five hundred dollars.

****

Once we opened Casa de Paco's, I got used to working on the restaurant's backside. Honestly, I missed the customers. But I was learning so much that I didn't have time to overthink what I felt. It was all about performance. It was during this time that Angelica and I became closer. She had done her job to teach me how to cook. Angelica taught me the true meaning of a tradition that every cook has to learn, *mise en place*. It's French and means 'putting in place' or 'everything in its place. It is anticipating what you will need for the shift and having all of the ingredients, tools, and plates ready and available in a kitchen.

"Richard, If you are ready for everything, then nothing can stop you from being successful. This is true in the kitchen, but it's also true in life. Something unexpected can always happen, but if everything is a surprise, and you can't handle it, you will fail."

As soon as I realized that this principle applied to anything in my life, things became more natural and meaningful.

Chapter 14
Sydney Polnoski

Two weeks into my transfer to Brighton University, I'm confused, in awe, and excited beyond my dreams. This size of this place gives me the feeling that there is so much to learn and not enough time to sample everything possible.

I'm confused because I have to search for everything from the rooms where my classes are held to the closest grocery store, barbershop, drug store, you name it.

I'm in awe because my classes are enormous compared to my experience in junior college. I already have the sense that the competition for grades is at a new and higher level.

I'm excited because I've reached a place I had experienced only in my dreams. The old cliche about having to pinch yourself to assure what was happening is real finally made sense to me.

From my apartment window, I can hear the chatter of the students coming and going from classes. On a football game day, the band marches right past my building on their way to the stadium. When I circulate in this community, it creates an energy that becomes an element of the air I breathe. The downside is that many of my classmates, because they did all of their underclass work here, know each other. Again, I'm the new student.

While I'm used to being separated from Regina for long periods, the travel distance between us is more significant. I worry about her having a problem, and I could not quickly come to her aid.

* * * * * * * * * *

Im still not sure of my major. I continue on a dual track of business and art. My advisor is a woman, Sydney Polnoski. She seems to have time for me no matter how short the notice or the time of day.

"You've been very understanding and generous with your time. I want you to know I appreciate it," I said.

We were in the cubbyhole office she uses to consult with her students. The sounds of people migrating from class to class seeped through the thin door. The air was stale and heavy in this overheated older building. I'm sure she got a hint of my deodorant because I could detect her perfume.

"Most of my students have been on campus for a year or more. Don't worry. You aren't a pest. You are going to be fine here once you get used to how things work. I see you haven't declared a major yet. I don't know about your ability to conduct business, but your art portfolio is excellent. Would you be open to a paid internship with a design company here in Brighton? It would be for credit."

She passed me a brochure that described the company. Attached to the piece was a business card for Lynn Campo, Artistic Director at *Images Working For You* (IW4Y).

"Give her a call next week. In the meantime, I'll give her word that I've talked to you. You realize she will make the decision?"

"Of course. This is interesting."

"The point is you'll become immersed in what it would be like if you moved toward a career in commercial art and design. You may find out it's not what you want. What's the path in business?"

"My boss back home is expanding his restaurant holdings. He has guaranteed me a spot in his management group."

"Really! That's got to be tempting. What restaurant does he own now?"

"He took over management of *The Manitou* from his father and recently opened *Casa de Paco's."*

"You're kidding. My parents took us for dinner on our birthdays at *The Manitou*. It's a family tradition that we still try to observe. My one sister lives in California, but my brother and I get together as close to our birthdays as we can."

"Have you been there in the last five years or so?"

"Yes."

"I may have cleared your table or waited on you. I've been working there since I was fourteen."

"My God, What a small world. I'm sorry I don't recognize you."

"I might not have either. I cut my hours down when I started classes. If I didn't wait on you or your party was in the house when I was bussing tables, no one remembers their busboy."

Sydney laughed.

"I noticed that you're very comfortable with people. Your restaurant experience explains that to me."

"As I said, I've been working since I was fourteen."

* * * * * * * * * *

Sydney and I met at least once a month. She was candid about the reputation of my instructors. If there were choices, Sydney was quick to push me toward the best fit for me. She'd consider whether a professor was challenging enough to make his class worthwhile.

"Some students want an easy path. They look for professors that grade high and don't ask a lot from their students. We term them 'basket weaving' courses. They typically have a short reading list, a vague syllabus, and multiple-choice exams. I sense that you've come here to learn something. My suggestions may cause you to work more, but I think you will get more benefit from the effort."

Sydney and I were discussing my path through the required math courses. Math was not my strong suit. She was trying to shepherd me into classes where she had success with previous students that suffered from my problem.

"The key is the outlook of the professor. Does he or she acknowledge some students are not naturally adept at the understanding of mathematics? If they aren't empathetic, their ignorance and arrogance predict problems for students like you."

I never got to know her on a very personal level. Still, my association with her was a crucial part of my success in my college. For two years, she had her hand on the tiller of my journey. In my last year at Brighton, one of the courses I needed to finish my degree was full. I don't know what she did, but for me, suddenly there was room.

* * * * * * * * * *

Regina and I continued our relationship. One weekend every month, we would trade off traveling so we could spend time together. Because we had so little time together, we never got to the point that we took each other for granted.

We still were learning about each other. Her meds were working well at controlling her most extreme mood swings. As far as I could tell, the side effects were minimal. Our time was spent with just the two of us. Coleen made sure she didn't get in the way.

When Regina came to Brighton, we'd explore different elements of the campus. I tried to show Regina how I spent my time. We hit all of the college bars and eateries. We did go downtown and took in some theater. After one of the plays, we discussed it back at my apartment.

"Did you notice the set in the theater?" I said.

"Yes, it was excellent. Well, maybe a little over the top. Why?"

"The company I'm interning with designed the set. I was on the team." She bit her lower lip.

"Don't worry. I agree it is a little over the top. It's funny. I saw the play in a dress rehearsal, and it just looked different tonight."

"How did your company get involved?"

"It's a two-way street kind of agreement. The group that put on the play is new. They solicited us for sponsorship. My boss decided that we'd offer to design and build their set rather than give them money. That gave me and some of the other employees a chance to work on a three-dimensional project."

"What did you do?"

"I got in on the drawings of the various concepts we offered them. After they decided which design they wanted, I was on the build team. We got to work with the cast and crew. It was fun, and I learned a lot."

* * * * * * * * * *

Regardless of where we met, Regina was comfortable, lively, and happy. We'd established a way of dealing with the inevitable disagreements. Candice Marlow taught us to take turns working on the issue at the bottom of the dispute. Then we each had the opportunity to state the reason we held our position. We learned not to elevate the issue to personal insults and senseless arguments that had nothing to do with the problem at hand.

Previously we'd been a couple that had to clear the air by shouting it out occasionally. We no longer had that luxury. Any argument that elevated itself to a fight could affect Regina more than someone who wasn't bi-polar. Since I generally dislike argumentative confrontation, it was easy for me to practice Marlowe's method.

Chapter 15
Lynn Kampo

When I went to interview for the intern position at WI4Y, I didn't feel comfortable. I intended to do some research on the company. Because of Regina's surprise visit, the fact that I had just returned from Winter break and was acclimating to a new class schedule, I didn't get time to collect the information I wanted.

Outside of the general category of designers, I didn't know anything about their business. What products were they producing? How long had their company been established? Who were their principal officers? Who was their competition? What was their reputation in the market?

It was cold on the corner waiting for the bus. I didn't have a good overcoat. I put on a good pair of slacks, a dress shirt, a tie with a sweater over the shirt, a jacket, gloves, and a knit cap. When I got to WI4Y, I hung up my coat in the guest closet, went to the men's room, combed my hair, and straightened my tie. When I came out to the reception area, Lynn Kampo was waiting. She smiled at me.

"Good morning, Richard."

"Good morning to you. I'm sorry... is it Miss or Mrs.?"

"I'm one of the new feminists. It's Ms. I'll give you the tour as we go up to my office."

We zigged and zagged our way through two floors of cubby hole offices and studios where a lot of work was going on. She patiently described the stage of accomplishment of the work and which account was being serviced. She introduced me to a couple of people on the way up.

"I might want you to chat with them before we make our decision. You would be working directly for me, but you would be interacting with them."

"In a nutshell, the internship is designed so that you can see our operation in every aspect. Some of us hired on for a job that we no longer perform because we found out we were more interested in some other area. You might also find out you don't like anything about our business, and that's okay. Better now than being ten years into a career you can't stand."

Lynn is in her late thirties. She is style and fashion-conscious. Lynn's vocabulary and speech come from someone who is educated and comfortable with money and power. She appears to be very fit but thin and of medium height. Her hair is styled and colored. I know this because God never created a person with that shade of red. She uses the right amount of makeup. Her face is angular with high cheekbones, deep blue eyes, and full lips. She is what I would call aristocratically attractive. Her ready wit requires you to pay attention lest you miss one of her humorous side-notes.

I realized right away that she wasn't talking down to me. Her tone and manner were congenial. I would find out later that she could be frank in her opinions.

"Your grades are outstanding. When I factor in that you're doing a double major, you are truly impressive. Design and business are not mutually exclusive, but not exactly a natural mix."

"I have been working in hospitality since I was fourteen. A friend of mine exposed me to art. I'm still holding both possibilities open."

"What's the possibility in hospitality?"

"My boss is expanding his restaurant business. He offered me a job once I graduate."

"Okay. I'm fairly aware of a lot of the restaurants in the area. Which restaurant are you working at?"

"I'm not working right now. I worked at a place in Rivers Edge for Tim D'Amato. He owns The Manitou and Casa De Paco's."

"Really! Some friends of mine and I went to Rivers Edge this summer. We ate at Casa De Paco's. We loved it. Any chance he'll open another Mexican restaurant over here?"

"I'll mention it to him."

"Yeah, I liked his logo and signage. Do you happen to know who did it for him?"

I hesitated.

"Look, you don't have to tell me. I'm just curious."

"I did it."

She laughed.

"I know. It was in your portfolio."

I'm sure I looked like a fool. How could I forget something like that?

"Hey. Seriously, I do like it."

* * * * * * * * * *

I waited a week while they interviewed the other people. When I didn't hear anything after a week and a half, I figured I would get a thank you, but we are going with someone else call or letter. Then I got a phone call from Lynn's Administrative Assistant.

"Richard, I'm Shirley Granger. I'm Lynn Kampo's Administrative Assistant. Lynn wants me to schedule an appointment with you to discuss the internship if you're still interested."

I was definitely interested.

* * * * * * * * * * *

After I accepted the job, I did everything an intern does. I got coffee and water for Lynn's visitors. Without visitors, Lynn never asked me to do personal things for her.

I sat in on meetings where it was made clear I was to say nothing. However, after the sessions, Lynn often asked me what I thought and whether I had any ideas. When I told her what I thought, she took my comments seriously, but I realized this process was part of my training.

I got a week off from my internship to take my midterm exams. When I returned, I found Lynn reading a report in her office.

"Guess what? We've got a prospect that is right in your wheelhouse."

She handed me a small stack of paper. The top sheet disclosed a proposed restaurant chain. The prospects owned a local restaurant. They were looking at expanding outside of the university area.

"Our clients are two college buddies who, after they graduated, opened a restaurant that serves college students good food at a low cost. They've been running this business off a plan written on the back of an envelope. They can't change the name of the restaurants they have now, but an upgrade on the same name and theme wouldn't be out of the question. I want you to read it over and let me know what you think of it."

"Thanks."

"You're welcome. Do you own a suit?"

"One, and it's old."

"Do you know where Ambrose Men's Ware is?"

"Yes, it's on the square by the Capitol Building."

"I want you to go there after work tonight. I'll meet you there at about 5:30, okay?"

"Yeah, sure."

"I've got a social/business thing this Saturday evening. I'd like you to go with me. Can you do it?"

"Sure."

"Wonderful."

She walked out of the office with me.

"Shirley, I'll be out of the office for the rest of the day. Richard, I'd like your thoughts on that prospect by tomorrow afternoon. We are having a preliminary meeting with them for breakfast the day after tomorrow. Hold open time for it on your schedule."

She turned and left the office, leaving but a faint scent of her perfume.

"She is something else," Shirley said.

"Yes, that's my impression."

"Yes, and you have no idea how many details she handles. If she left us, half the stuff in this place would collapse."

****

When I got to Ambrose's, I told the young man who greeted me that I was meeting someone.

"Ms. Kampo by chance?" he said.

"Yes."

"They are waiting for you in the fitting area."

I followed him down a hallway and through a curtained-off doorway in the back of the store. Lynn was sitting in a chair while an older gentleman showed her a suit that was still hanging on a hanger. He had tucked a dress shirt with a tie draped around it into the lapels of the coat. She was nodding at it when she realized I was entering the room.

"Richard, what do you think of this?" She gestured toward the suit.

"Ms. Kampo, I don't know anything about buying suits. Hell, clothing in general."

She and the older man laughed. He clapped me on the shoulder.

"Richard, I'm Walter Ambrose. Let me help you decide. Lynn and I were looking at some suits and color options. She based her options on her idea of your skin tone. And now that I've met you, I think she's spot on. Let me get a measuring tape."

He crossed the room and pulled a cloth measuring tape out of a drawer. After each measurement, he wrote it down in a notebook. I could see he had my name written at the head of the page. Off to the right side of the page, he had written Lynn's name. Moving down, he measured my waist and inseam.

"What size shoe do you wear?"

****

Lynn and I were with Mr. Ambrose for an hour and a half. Ambrose had to do several alterations to the three suits. However, I walked out of the shop with two pairs of shoes, three ties, three pocket squares, four dress shirts, six pairs of socks, and two tie clasps with matching cuff links.

When Lynn and I got out of the store, she insisted that she drive me to my apartment. At this point, I'm conflicted. I'm not entirely comfortable. I understand I can't participate in business social occasions with my limited wardrobe. On the other hand, Lynn has just dropped a lot of money on me. What's expected? She took care of that when we got to my apartment building.

"Are you going to get all of that upstairs without help?"

"I'll get into the lobby. It might take two trips, but I'll manage."

"Okay. Let me be clear here. I bought this stuff for you so you can accompany me to business meetings and gatherings. I'm not asking you or requiring you to become my boy toy. What others might think is their business. What goes on between you and me is just business."

"I just want to thank you for the clothing."

She clapped me on the shoulder and shot me a smile.

"You're welcome."

* * * * * * * * * *

The visit by Regina was a surprise, but a welcome one. I wasn't going to be at home for my birthday. Regina showed up without warning to create a one-person surprise party for me. We went to a more expensive restaurant and splurged on a hotel room to have more privacy.

We had spent a lot of time together between semesters. The usual process of catching up wasn't necessary. Still, I admit I sat up and paid close attention the following day when she brought up the new subject on her mind.

"You know, we've never talked about having a family," she said.

We were lounging in bed. I'd ordered a continental breakfast. Regina's hair was in a crazy array of curls and tangles, and her eyes were still blurry from sleep.

"Call me crazy, but don't you think we should get married first."

She smiled, reached over, and fake punched me on the shoulder.

"Maybe. But I don't know if you even want kids and if so, how many?"

"I'll admit, I haven't thought about having a family. In a lot of ways, I don't think I've fully grown up yet. I do know that when we're ready, I do want children. How many? I'm not sure. I want to provide for them, so it may be a matter of how much income we have."

"So, if we're rich, we can have a bunch?"

"Sure, Why have you been thinking about kids?" Suddenly it hit me. "You're not..."

"No. I was talking to your Mom over the holiday, and she asked me about our plans."

"I see."

"I'm in no rush."

"Well, that's good because I don't think that financially we're ready yet."

****

My internship at WI4Y was productive and fruitful. In the months that followed, Lynn included me in every facet of the business. The downside was that I had to stay in Brighton for the summer. To make things a little more worthwhile, I took a couple of summer courses. Regina and I kept our schedule of trading trips back and forth.

I didn't get to see my folks very often. However, I noticed that things were getting better for them. Dad and Mom both had friends of the opposite sex. Dad was far more upbeat about life in general. Mom seemed to embrace her freedom from a live-in partner, and at the same time, enjoy having a social companion.

Arliss was the daughter my mother didn't have. I never saw my mother unless Arliss was with her. They were often as giggly as a couple of teenagers, and they loved to spoil Regina and me. They even picked up Regina, drove to Brighton, and took us to a concert. My mother at a rock concert? At first, I couldn't believe it, but we all had a great time.

Coleen decided that she wasn't getting enough time with me. After all, she had Regina full-time. Instead of arranging to be out of town, Coleen stayed home more often than not when I visited. We even got to the point of talking about the early part of our relationship when I was having sex with both of them.

All of this time, I knew that Coleen had a man in her life, but I never got to meet the guy she was seeing. He was strangely always busy when I was in Rivers Edge. It was only later that I found out he was married. Coleen hired this guy to help with her non-profit. Regina told me that she thought the guy was taking advantage of Coleen, but Coleen was in love.

****

At the end of summer, Lynn called me into her office on a Friday afternoon. I was packed to go to visit Regina. I was worried there would be a last-minute party or some such social obligation Lynn wanted me to attend with her.

After I walked in, she asked me to close the door and gestured to a seat in front of her desk. Usually, we talked in the conversation area. Also, her expression wasn't as friendly as it often was. She was making me wonder what I might have messed up.

"You've worked extensively with Jerry and Ilene, the other two interns, correct?"

"Yes, I worked on a couple of different projects with them."

"Well, here's my situation. All of your internships have run their course. I only have one position to fill. Which one would you pick?"

I realized at once; that this more than likely meant I would not be continuing with WI4Y.

"Um, let me see. Ilene has strong communication skills. She is well organized and has leadership capability. Jerry is more creative. He needs to step up as far as the presentation in team meetings. I guess he thinks the work should stand alone, but I think you and I know it takes some campaigning to get your ideas over the line. So I guess it depends on where you need help as to which one would do the best job."

"I'm thinking about sales."

"Ilene."

"I value your opinion. As I've said in the past, you are more mature than the normal college kid we get in here. I put that down to your experience in the hospitality business. All that being said, I do have an offer for you."

She looked at me for a moment, then smiled.

"Did you think we were going to let you go? Take a breath. You look like you might pass out."

I took more than one breath and willed my heart rate to be at a healthy pace.

"Honestly, I wasn't even thinking about the internship running out."

"Do you remember meeting Clive Bamberger?"

"Yes, CEO at TNA Broadcast."

"He confessed to me the other night, after way more liquor than Clive can tolerate, that he wanted to get to know me better."

"I told Clive I was flattered', which, of course, is code for this ain't goin' nowhere."

"He didn't get the flare I sent up and said, 'but I can't compete with that young guy you're with now.' I said, 'I'm sorry, Clive.' Please note, I didn't turn him down or admit that you and I were a couple."

I laughed.

"Oh yeah, funny. Do you have any idea how many people think that we are having an affair?"

I just shook my head. It's not that I didn't know how people in our company thought I screwed my way into a cushy job.

"I love it!" she laughed and slapped the desktop. I just smiled.

"I know you have a steady, and if you ever have a problem and want me to have a conversation with her, let me know."

"No, that won't be necessary. The first time Regina saw my new wardrobe, I explained what was going on. She trusts me."

"Good. So here's the deal. I want you to form a Limited Liability Corporation, an LLC. This company will allow me to subcontract work to you. I'm doing this as an experiment. I think it's the future. I think more people are going to be working from their homes. The benefits to both parties are numerous, and some of the downsides may be unknown, but we can deal with them as they arise. I'll equip a home office for you, and you can work on design projects in your own time and drop off the drawings or whatever to the office. What do you think?"

I mused for a moment or two.

"Yeah, I think it would be fun. But I'll be able to come into the office for client conferences and team meetings, wouldn't I?"

"Yes. Or just stop by for lunch or whatever else you feel might help you through the day. The idea is you're on your own, and you can work at your own pace. You are a natural for this because you respect deadlines. I've never seen you miss one, and most of the time, you submit days before required."

Chapter 16
Anastasia Domas

I'm in my senior year at Brighton State College. My graduation will be mid-year because of all of the summer courses I took. My home office job experiment with WI4Y is working better than we thought, mainly because I didn't have to schedule my work hours around my classes.

Lynn, however, insists I continue to accompany her to some of the business entertainments and functions. I'm so accustomed to these activities that I didn't notice for quite some time that people we encountered at them began to think I had more power than I did. At the very least, they knew I had Lynn's ear.

I also knew that Lynn allowed suspicions about the intimacy in our relationship to continue. At the time, I couldn't see the advantages to her. More often, on these business/social occasions, I would find myself corralled and gently but persistently grilled.

What did Lynn think of this or that? What's the best way to get her convinced of their project idea or proposal? Often I knew or thought I knew the answers to these inquiries. Still, I never followed up other than to report to Lynn about these questions. Finally, I confronted her.

"Lynn, I want to preface this with the understanding that I'm not unhappy or reluctant to keep things going the way they are, but I'm curious. Why are we operating like this?"

"How do you think we are operating?"

"For starters, as you have consistently admitted, many of the people we interact with think you and I are a couple. I'm trying to figure out where it works to your benefit."

“Okay, You deserve some explanation. As a businesswoman, I’ve learned that most men think they can beat, control, or even just influence you if they can sleep with you. My biggest problem is that if they approach me, I lose no matter what I answer. If I say yes, they win, at least in our contemporaries’ eyes. If I say no, I offend their tender egos. That can be a problem and get in the way of future business. You provide me with the cover, so I avoid propositions. Remember when we talked about Clive Bamberger?”

“Clive and I get along fine, mostly because he was roundly embarrassed about his drunken proposition. Indeed, he’s convinced I’m just fine in my relationship with you and knows to compete is futile.

“My biggest problem is I am a woman, but using my sex to be sexy isn’t good business practice. I can’t use it to flirt or embarrass my male contemporaries. Yet, I can’t be one of the guys either. It’s like dancing on the razor’s edge. Leaning one way or another is inviting trouble.”

“Okay, I guess I understand, but what if you became attracted to one of these guys?” She smiled.

“What makes you think I haven’t?”

“Lynn, you and I have been pretty close for a couple of years now. I’ve never heard, nor have I seen anything that would indicate you were interested in any of the men you contact in business. Are you…?”

“No, and I’m not gay, but I probably have the lowest libido of anyone you know. I get satisfaction from life in being very good at my job. Maybe someday I’ll find someone like you’ve found your Regina. I assure you I do not go home at night and cry myself to sleep because there is no one to share with me. I like things the way they are.”

* * * * * * * * * *

Lynn and I have discussed what’s going to happen when I graduate. I promised one more year in her office-in-home experiment. As far as she is concerned, it's okay for me to move back to Rivers Edge. I assumed she would get another intern to take over my social duties.

In the meantime, Regina and I continue to travel back and forth to keep our relationship on a simmer. I noticed that her occasional bouts with depression are becoming more frequent. Coleen told me what was going on.

"Regina's going through some issues with her meds. God damn her! I told her she should tell you what's going on. Since some of the meds lose their effectiveness after prolonged use, the doctors usually try other drugs or vary the dose. As I'm sure you're well aware, that can affect the onset of side effects. The good news is that unlike many patients who hit a bump in the road, hide it, and make things worse, Regina works with the doctors to find a solution."

"I've been worried. I can only imagine how much you've sacrificed to help Regina through these stages."

"I don't mind. We've been friends for most of our lives. I don't even think about it being a sacrifice. It's just life with Coleen and Regina."

"Which leads me to my next question. I don't know what I'm going to do when I move back to Rivers Edge?"

"You're going to move in here. That's what's going to happen."

"Coleen, that's not fair."

"Only if you don't pick up your fair share of the expenses."

"Are you sure it's not going to cramp your lifestyle?"

"What do you mean?"

"I assume there's a man in your life."

She grimaced and was quiet for a long time.

"I got myself into one of those situations that you know is stupid, but most of it feels so good, so right, that you fucking do it anyway. He's married. To his credit, he never promised me anything but a good time. One of his buddies unloaded on his own wife that if she thought she had it bad, at least he wasn't running around on her like my guy. Then the buddy's wife told my guy's wife, and you can guess what he decided when forced to choose. I'm getting over it, but it's still kind of a fresh wound. But no, you won't be cramping my style."

****

When I moved back to Rivers Edge, I set up my office/studio downstairs because Coleen uses the upstairs third bedroom as a home office. I get a beautiful view of the backyard with the garden, patio, and a faux waterfall and pond with fish from my office. My office is large and comfortable. I laid down some rugs to soften the look and dampen the sound of walking on the tile. Because the back of the house is on a public alley and our nearest neighbor is the coffee shop across the alley, I could walk to its back entrance in minutes if I got the urge to connect briefly with other people.

The garden's solace is outside my window with both flowers in bloom and vegetables for our table. As the spring season progressed, Coleen remarked that the garden is better-tended because I've taken charge.

Waking up with Regina by my side every morning was beautiful and different. My trips to the Brighton office were for a day at most, so visits didn't mean leaving Regina alone overnight. Coleen was building her non-profit, and Regina was doing well at the law firm. I had the house to myself most days.

Our routine established itself rather quickly. I did most of the cooking for our main meal in the evening. The ladies do assist me. I give them a shopping list, and they bring the groceries home.

Everyone kept their own private space clean. I took charge of the kitchen, and the ladies split the chore of cleaning the shared rooms. I did the common laundry because it didn't interrupt my daily work. We all do our personal laundry. Regina and Coleen did the yard work. Our community space was the front porch. During good weather, we would meet in the back garden.

None of us were addicted to much television. We often went to the movie theater located within walking distance from the house. Less regularly, we attended live theater productions or concerts. During the warmer weather, the music concerts at the parks were free.

It was nice living with the two of them. Neither Coleen nor I had to hover over Regina since we communicated regularly on our observations of Regina's behavior. We did find that Regina accepted Coleen's opinion more readily than mine. I didn't take offense to this because I knew Regina's comfort came from their long relationship.

* * * * * * * * * *

Everything was running smoothly. I took the opportunity to check in with Tim at the restaurant.

"Ah, what a sight, for these sore eyes!" Tim said as I walked in the front door. "Here, throw on an apron and see if you remember how to cook."

I laughed. But Tim walked me back to the kitchen and handed me an apron and a disposable head-cover. I realized he wasn't kidding. Moments after walking into The Manitou, I worked the line next to a chef I'd never met. He was as surprised as I was when Tim introduced us and left immediately to cover the dining room.

Quickly the rhythm of working the line came back. Arnie, the Chef, was tentative at first, but once he realized I knew what I was doing, he concentrated on his work and left me to do mine. When the order line was empty, we got a chance to talk.

"Tim promised me to get me some help. I appreciate you stepping in. You're excellent," he said. "Where did you come from?"

"I worked here for years. It's like coming home or maybe riding a bike, whatever cliche works, I guess."

"We got slammed today. I couldn't have done it without you. Are you coming aboard permanently?" I laughed.

"The only reason I came here today was to say hi to Tim and let him know I was back in Rivers Edge. I never thought about working here again."

"I could sure use you."

The idea of getting back in the kitchen felt like a good one.

"I've got a job, but... what do you need? I can't give you much time, but I'd be willing to help if I can." Arnie thought for a moment.

"Would three days a week, Wednesday through Friday, four-hour shifts at lunch work for you?"

"I've got to check with someone first, but I think it could work."

"Get back to me as soon as you can."

From behind us, we both heard Tim's voice. "Sounds like you two are getting along."

"Maybe better than you thought," Arnie said with a broad smile.

* * * * * * * * * *

I checked in with Lynn, Regina, and Coleen. They all had a lot of questions. Lynn was wondering if I was thinking of going full blast into hospitality. I told her I was committed to her experiment of working from home. I argued that this was one of the benefits of the kind of flexibility work from home offered.

“Look at my restaurant work as my recreation... say, like playing golf.”

Lynn said she was okay with it as long as I did the work for her first. I had no trouble promising and reassuring her that WI4Y was my top priority.

“Okay with me. Maybe I should come over there and have lunch sometime?”

“I'd enjoy that.”

“Oh, you wouldn't know until I've experienced your cooking.”

“I'd love the challenge.”

* * * * * * * * * *

I knew Tim was trying to influence my decision on my future. It did feel good to go into the kitchen and set up my station for the anticipated customer rush. Arnie and I got along well. I did think on some occasions that he settled all too quickly for speed instead of quality. I knew that Tim kept an eye on almost everything that went through the kitchen door on its way to the customer. If Tim was happy, I was delighted.

My additional work at the restaurant didn't cramp my home activities, even when I filled in on the occasional weekend shift. I got a kick out of my mother and her friend, insisting on my coming out to their table when they stopped for lunch one day.

I changed into a clean apron before I went out to greet them. No doubt, all restaurant guests turned to see why the cook was coming out to the dining room. Was I going to field a complaint? Was this some table-side prep demo for a particular customer? My mother spoke loud enough for most people in the house to hear.

“Harold, this is my son, the Chef.”

I shook Harold's hand. Leave it to my mother to introduce me to her "friend" in a situation where it could be done in the shortest possible duration. I knew she would eventually ask me what I thought of him. He appeared to be a friendly sort of fellow. He seemed fit and nicely dressed. In the short conversation we had, I noted his vocabulary and diction didn't betray any particular ethnic or regional hints. In my mother's words, he spoke the King's English. They had already eaten their meal. I accepted their compliments as humbly as my mother would allow me. Then I excused myself. I had to help clean up before I left for the day. My Mom smiled and insisted on a hug before she would let me go.

* * * * * * * * * * *

A week or so later, Lynn ambushed me at lunch. Lynn also ate before she asked to see me. Tim told me that a woman asked if she could say hello to me. He didn't mention her name, but I'm sure he guessed who she was.

The rush was over, so I felt comfortable sitting down with Lynn.

"How was lunch?" I said.

"As good or better than anything I've had anywhere else. You guys are good. Don't tell your boss, but you're seriously underpriced." She smiled and patted my hands, which were resting on the table.

"Tim has high standards."

Tim was at the front of the house, waiting for the entry of another customer. I waved him over.

"This is odd. I normally do not get to talk to both of my employers at the same time. Tim, this is Lynn, the life force of WI4Y. Lynn, this is Tim, the owner of The Manitou."

Their handshake was cordial, but I knew them well enough to know they were taking the measure of each other. After all, they both knew quite a bit about each other but only from what I had told them. Looking at them together, it occurred to me how much I owed both of these people.

"I hope you enjoyed your visit with us," Tim said.

"I did. But, it's not the first time I've eaten here, and I've been to Casa De Paco's. I'm impressed with both of your places," Lynn said.

Tim gave her a bright smile. "I'm happy to hear that."

"I think the food was a little better today." Lynn smiled and inclined her head toward me.

Tim chuckled. "That's why I'm trying to convince him this is where he belongs."

"Ah, but he is multi-talented."

I interjected, "Hey, hey, I'm right here. I can hear you. This kind of conversation could affect my ego."

We all laughed.

"I see a customer at the front," Tim said. "I'll leave you on your visit. Nice meeting you, Lynn. Come see us again."

"I will, Tim. It was a pleasure meeting you," Lynn said.

"Nice guy," Lynn said after Tim left.

"He's been like my older brother since he took over the restaurant."

"Oh boy, what does that leave for me?"

I leaned in and spoke quietly to her. She had a slightly pained expression.

"I suppose that depends on who you ask. If you ask some people, we are lovers. Others would say you're my mentor. I'm not sure how I would define us, but I am lucky and grateful to have met you. You've taught me everything from how to dress correctly, how to give a sales presentation, customer relations, and what works or doesn't for design. I owe you so much, Lynn, and don't think I don't appreciate it."

I noticed Lynn seemed upset.

"I'm sorry," I said.

"No, you didn't say much except everything I wanted to hear."

We sat quietly for a while.

"Do you think about your future?" she said.

"Right now, life is going by like a rubber raft down a rapid river. I'm bouncing off the rocks and spinning in the eddies. I'm content to leave things the way they are, and I guess I will be unless you or Tim make it impossible for me to continue."

"For your peace of mind, I can tell you I'm happy with the way things are going. The only thing I'm concerned about is that we've learned a lot about "working from home," but what happens when I don't have a Richard Harrison doing it. I have this nagging feeling that it won't work if we bring someone else on board. You might be uniquely suited for this."

"I guess before you feel comfortable swimming in deep water, you have to jump into the pool's deep end." I said.

She smiled.

"So concise. So wise. Are you fooling me? Are you a lot older and more experienced than I know?"

"If you eventually decide to hire someone over here, I'd be happy to mentor them."

"What if it cramps your hours here?"

"Tim will be flexible."

She slapped the table. "Great. Let me look at my options. I'm thinking of hiring two people. We've got a major customer coming on board. It's a perfect time."

"Who is the major account? It's a done deal, but we are sworn to secrecy until they inform their current agency. It's Jamison & Keefe. Tell no one." Naturally, I felt proud Lynn would trust me.

"Lips sealed."

"I've got to go. I'll let you help me pick out anybody I recruit over here."

"Make it a woman," I said.

She paused and looked at me with a quizzical expression.

"Really,? Why?"

"Just because I think women might be better at this than most young guys. Besides, we don't have enough women in the company. And let's face it, the best employee we have is a woman." I smiled and nodded toward her.

"I'll keep that in mind."

She hugged me, turned on her heels, and walked out the door. Everyone in the dining room watched her walk out. The lady has an undeniable presence.

* * * * * * * * * *

Lynn and I talked a couple of times a week after that, but the subject of a recruit in Rivers Edge didn't come up for six weeks. Lynn called and asked, "What does your schedule look like for next Tuesday?"

"I can make time. What's up?"

"There's someone I want you to meet."

"Good enough. New client?"

"No, it's someone I'm looking at hiring. My candidate has the experience, but she's married, and her husband has a position with a law firm Rivers Edge. Therefore, while she's a good fit for us, but I can't move her to our main office here. The commute is too long for her from there."

"So, she's a candidate for "work from home?"

"I want you to meet her. I need your opinion on if you think she can do the job. I know she can do the work, but can she do it without close supervision?"

"Where do you want to meet?" I said.

"The Manitou, of course. Unless you're tired of the place?"

"What time?" I laughed.

"One o'clock. We will have more privacy."

* * * * * * * * * *

In anticipation of the privacy that Lynn preferred, I reserved a table in the back of the dining room. It was away from the front door and the kitchen traffic.

I rose from my chair when a young Latina came through the front door. She started looking around the room. As Tim was in the kitchen, I walked toward her, noting that she was wearing a business suit with pants instead of a skirt. Her dark hair cascaded over her shoulders in a curly array. She had a round face with large brown eyes, full lips, and her complexion was the color of caramel sauce.

"Hi. Are you looking for Lynn Kampo?'

"Yes. My name is Anastasia Domas." She checked her watch. "I guess I'm a bit early."

"Come on. I'll show you to the table."

She sat down before I could hold her chair for her.

"Oh, goodness, you were going to hold my chair. I'm sorry."

"It's my training as a dining room host."

"Oh, you don't work for Lynn? You work for the restaurant?"

"Actually, I work for both."

I quickly explained what was going on.

"I am the first 'work from home' employee."

"Lynn mentioned you during the interview. I assumed you were working out of the main office in Brighton."

"I did, and then I transferred here. Lynn thought it was time to try the program somewhere other than down the block, so to speak."

"Tell me the best and the worst thing about working from home."

"The worst is not having face-to-face conversations with your peers. You know, like the informal chats in the break room. Like everyone, I suppose I took that kind of interaction for granted. But I've realized there's a lot to be learned in those coffee breaks.

"The best is having the freedom to work when you want. I live with my fiancé, Regina, and our friend, Coleen. I do the laundry and the main meal cooking. I still have lots of time to do my work for WI4Y. If I need to, I can work early in the morning or late at night."

"Sounds great. I talked to my husband about it. He thinks it's kind of weird. He's concerned it will hamper my ability to get promoted."

"I can see that. But here's the thing, and this is just my opinion; eventually, WI4Y will have to open a branch office over here. There is so much business here we could get that we'll need a larger presence."

"Makes sense."

"Again, I don't know what is going to happen. Is there any chance your husband's firm might transfer him anywhere?"

"I doubt it. His firm has an office in Brighton, but the kind of law he practices doesn't require him to work at that location."

When Lynn arrived, the three of us had lunch and discussed various facets of the remote workspace.

"For one thing, you do need a dedicated workspace in your apartment or house. There will be times when you will want to take a break, and you can leave your work out so you can resume working with it without a lot of re-preparation," I said.

"How about client contact?" Anastasia said.

"So far, most of our clients are not in Rivers Edge, so we do have to travel to those meetings," I said.

"That is going to change," Lynn said. "I've decided to put a salesperson over here. It doesn't mean you guys won't be doing some commuting to client meetings, but over time it will mean less."

"How about transportation?" Anastasia said.

"We'll reimburse you for whatever expense you incur," Lynn said. "Richard doesn't own a car. He rents a vehicle when he needs one. You have a good deal with your rental company, Richard. I've checked, and they are more economical than any I've found."

"Do you have any more questions, Anastasia?" Lynn said.

"You can call me Tassy. Everybody else does. No. Not right now."

“Well, I think this looks good. I will send you an offer. I’m sure you and your husband will want to look it over."

"Yes, that will be great. Thank you.”

“I look forward to working with you, Tassy,” I said. “When you and Lynn get the agreement settled, why don’t you and your husband join Regina and me for dinner at our place. I could show you my workspace and how I organize my work.”

I saw some indecision in Tassy’s body language, but she agreed and gave me her contact information. After Tassy left, Lynn and I wrapped up the meeting over coffee.

“I don’t know if you noticed, but when you invited her and her husband for dinner, I sensed some...some, let’s call it, reflection before she agreed.”

“I did. I don’t know what to think, but whatever it is, I think it’s something between Tassy and her husband.”

“Maybe it’s the whole work from home concept. Trust me, I’ve had pushback from the partners. That’s why it’s important; this all works out.”

“What do the people who question this concept object to?”

Lynn smiled and sat up a little straighter.

“They concern themselves with productivity, supervision, and what an employee might be doing during normal work hours. It’s difficult to convince them that our concern should be the quality of the work product and the delivery timeliness. Everything else is not worth talking about. Unfortunately, the lack of direct supervision is a big deal to them.”

“Your experience with me doesn’t change their minds?”

“I’ve never had a complaint about your work, but they think you’re an outlier. That’s why Tassy has to be able to work on her own. I’ve got to prove we can replicate this concept.”

"You can count on me to do whatever I can to see this succeed.”

“That’s fine. It’s helpful for everyone that you mentor her for a time, but ultimately she has to prove she can work on her own.”

* * * * * * * * * *

A week later, I got another call from Lynn.

“I’ve put Tassy on the payroll.”

“Great, What do you need me to do?”

“Remember when we interviewed her, you invited her with her husband to have dinner at your place?”

“Yes.”

“Call her and repeat the invitation.”

“Sure.”

“I hired her, but remember how we both noticed her hesitancy when you invited them to dinner?”

“Yes.”

“I think I know why. When I sent Tassy an offer, it came back with several notes and alterations on it. The cover letter was on her husband’s law firm stationery. It indicated the corrections should be made on a rewritten copy before she would sign it. I sent it to our attorney, and he laughed it off. He told me the corrections neither changed the intent or the content of the agreement. He asked me how bad I wanted this employee. I told him I was sure she would work out. He said he would make the changes. But only because it didn’t change the nature of the document, and it wasn't worth going back and forth. All it would do is cost money for nothing."

"I'm guessing you would like me to give you my opinion?" I said.

"Yes, but keep it close."

"Done."

****

It was a lovely evening. Regina and I decided it would be comfortable to have our cocktails and dinner on the back patio. It meant going through my workspace, so it would be natural to allow Tassy to see how I have it laid out. I planned to fix some chicken on the grill, baked potatoes, and roasted peppers for our dinner.

When they arrived, we all went through the house and into the backyard. I served everyone a drink, and we sat down to enjoy what remained of the daylight. I started the charcoal in the Weber grill.

Curt was a button-down guy. He looked like he got home from work, took off his suit coat, tie, and came to our house. I could tell right away he was uncomfortable as he visually examined our home.

"Tassy, do you want to take a look at how I've laid out my office?" I said.

Tassy didn't say anything. Maybe she nodded, and I didn't notice, but she got up and walked with me.

Tassy and I weren't in my office area for more than a minute or so when Curt wandered in. Without saying a word, he began looking around. Finally, he said, "I need the restroom."

I directed him to the door. Once he was out of the room, Tassy came very close to me and kept her voice down.

"It looks like you're planning to eat outdoors."

"Yes. It's a nice night, and I thought..."

"Would it be an imposition to eat inside? Curt is uncomfortable eating outside."

I could tell she was embarrassed to be asking.

"Of course. Let me tell Regina."

I left her looking over my office while I told Regina about the change in plans. Regina looked at me with some disbelief, but she picked up the table settings and took them upstairs. I got the food out of the downstairs refrigerator and began cooking. Curt was content to talk with Regina and Tassy. I could tell that this is a guy who is used to being in charge. He was opinionated and not going to have his beliefs challenged or changed.

Right off the bat, I did not like Curt. Early in the evening, I felt like I couldn't wait until they left. I noticed Tassy was very quiet and submissive. Curt said nothing about the apparent move inside for our meal. When the food was ready, I asked everyone to move inside. Regina and Tassy helped me carry the food up to the dining room. Curt carried nothing.

From my standpoint, the evening was a failure. I was frustrated because there was nothing I could've done to change it. Curt's behavior let me know he wasn't comfortable in our house, and he didn't care for the food. Through the evening, his comments let me know that he didn't like charcoal-cooked food because it upset his acid reflux. He never wanted peppers. His potato was charred. It was too hot in the house. He was tired and had a big day coming up. They left right after dinner. Thankfully there was no discussion about further social plans.

"What a fucking prick!"

Regina had been visibly upset for most of the evening. She continued to rant.

"You've got to know, I almost slapped that asshole a couple of times. The way he treats his wife is bad enough, but I mean… who can spend any time with that jerk?"

"Okay, I get it. But you have to make up your mind. Is he a prick, an asshole, or a jerk?" I said.

Regina stared at me for a moment, then realized I was kidding.

"There is a question on the floor, sir," she said.

"I will limit or eliminate our having to deal with him," I said.

She mouthed a big sigh. "Thank you. My God, when I see guys like that, I'm so glad I have you."

"I'm sure I have irritating habits."

"That guy doesn't have irritating habits. He is a walking, talking, breathing reason for justifiable homicide."

* * * * * * * * * *

It was a few days later, I noticed Regina beginning to act abnormally. She was quiet much of the time, and when she spoke, her speech was pained and forced. She was avoiding both Coleen and me. Regina was acting very much out of character. Given her history with depression, Coleen and I got together in the kitchen.

"What's going on with her?" Coleen said.

"You know something. I don't think it's the usual depression."

"Why?"

"I think it's because she's quit smoking. And did you notice she turned down a glass of wine?"

Coleen thought for a moment. "Oh, shit!"

"What."

Regina walked in before Coleen could respond.

"Hi, honey," I said to Regina. "Listen, it feels like something is wrong. Why don't we talk about it?"

Regina wouldn't look at me. "You're not going to like it."

Coleen gasped. "You're pregnant."

Regina looked at her in shock. "How did you know?"

"Richard just told me you have quit smoking and drinking. It's not hard to figure out." I said nothing, but I went to Regina and embraced her.

"It's okay, sweetheart, it's okay." I gathered Coleen and held both of them in my arms for a group hug.

Chapter 17
Dawn Rose Harrison

The time passed quickly between the time I knew I would be a father to when I became a father. There was a lot of physical and mental preparation going on.

Regina and I exchanged bedrooms with Coleen because hers was larger, and we needed room for the crib and the changing table. Until Regina was in her eighth month, we waited to make the big moves like buying two cribs at yard sales. Coleen's sister gave us one changing table. We were forced to buy the other one new. Try as we might, we couldn't find a decent one on eBay or Craigs' List.

Then we started shopping for diaper bags and some clothing. Coleen sponsored a baby shower, elements of which surprised me a little. I'd never met about half the women who showed up. They brought wine and gifts, played games, and ate the food I prepared.

Regina, Coleen, and I were ready. Regina and I didn't want to know the sex of the child. However, that didn't work because we were living with nosey, controlling Aunt Coleen. She found out the sex of our child on a visit to the doctor with Regina. Coleen learned we would have a girl. Regina figured it out because all of the clothing that Coleen bought for the yet to arrive, baby, was pink.

I am going to be a father. I'm having a problem wrapping my head around that concept. Nobody is happier than my mother. If not her, it's Coleen. Coleen is more animated than Regina. If she's not giddy, she is hysterically rambling about how good it will be when the baby is here.

Regina is quieter and more pragmatic. She has her to-do lists, and she's checking off the items one by one. She includes me in most of the decisions. One day, I mentioned that we would need two cribs, one for our room and the other for my office.

We had just returned from birthing classes. I talked to one of the other guys assisting his wife with their second child's birth. He had been on overseas military duty up to two weeks before the birth of their first child. He became a stay-at-home dad for two years while his wife went back to work, and he finished his degree at night school. When I told him about our situation, he suggested the two crib solution.

"You're going to end up running up and down the stairs just to make sure the child is okay. The baby will be fine. Ten minutes later, your imagination will have the kid in trouble, and you'll be running upstairs again. You might think I exaggerate, but trust me. When you get one of these little tykes and take charge of her or him, it can drive you nuts. This way, if you're worried, all you have to do is look across the room."

****

After I told this story, Regina thought for a moment. Then she hugged me.

"So, you're going to take care of our baby, huh?"

"Why not?"

"There is no reason at all. I'm just so happy you want to do it. You always amaze me."

"I might need a little training. Seeing I'm an only child, I've never had to take care of a baby. But I don't see any reason I can't learn."

"Down, boy. No one said you couldn't learn." She mussed my hair as she smiled at me.

****

The all-business super executive Lynn Kampo turned into a baby-talking, kissy-faced, wanna-be-momma every time she walked into our house, which was also more frequent than before the baby came. But it wasn't all playtime with Lynn. It always got around to business.

Lynn followed through and hired a sales representative for our area. Jeffrey Ivanovich was a good-looking young man. He was a graduate of a local private college. His family was prominent in the community, so a lot of doors were open to him. He wasn't cocky, but he was confident. At six foot two and reasonably athletic, he had worked hard at school and competed as a swimmer and golfer. His lanky frame carried clothes well, and he was comfortable in the company of older adults. The business started coming our way quickly.

"To be honest with you, Richard, I don't know how long we can hang on to this kid. Either one of his customers or our competition will approach him sooner or later, and he might be gone. I don't know," Lynn said.

"We'll have to make hay, as they say."

"Yes, and I'll have to make sure he's happy with us. There's room for him to move up, but as good as he is, he's not ready for that yet," Lynn said.

"How's Tassy doing?" I said.

"Her work? Excellent. She submits her work on time, and it has great creative content. How is she doing personally? I'm not sure. She's not very forthcoming, but I think she's got trouble at home."

"Well, if she does, she's not going to share that with you or me."

"I'm not so sure about that. Tassy asks about you all the time. I think she wants a better work relationship than you have with each other. I explained that I didn't want anyone upstairs thinking she couldn't work independently or that she needed you to succeed. She understood, but I think she's disappointed."

"Is there any reason we couldn't meet informally as friends rather than co-workers?"

"No. If you want to do that I would encourage it."

"Let me see what I can do."

* * * * * * * * * *

I called Tassy the next day. I asked her how she was doing?

"I'm paralyzed with doubt and confusion."

"I know you're teasing. Do you want to have lunch?"

"I'd love to. Where and when?"

"Any day this next week at my place."

There was a long pause before she answered.

"I don't know, couldn't we meet somewhere, say halfway?"

"I would if I could, Tassy, but you know I have a new girlfriend."

She didn't pick up my joke.

"I thought you and Regina were...what the hell! Of course, you guys just had a baby."

"Right."

There was another pause, but then a confident reply.

"Sure, let's make it Wednesday, okay?"

* * * * * * * * * *

Tassy was less than five minutes in the door when she had Dawn cradled in her arm as she sipped on the ice tea I served her.

"She's a doll."

"Yes, she is."

"Regina is so lucky. I mean, it's got to be tough on her to leave her baby to go to work. But to leave her with their father? Wow, that has to make it easier."

"I have to say it's working pretty well."

"Thank goodness, Lynn is so supportive."

"She'd do the same for you."

Tassy glanced away for a moment. She looked at me while she was trying to make up her mind what to say.

"In my case, it's more like, are we ever going to have a family."

"Oh, well, you know Dawn was a surprise, right?"

She regarded me again for a moment.

"There will be no surprises in my marriage. Having children right now is not considered a good career move."

It was a time for me to think before I spoke. "I'm sorry. I don't get it. What does that mean?"

Her face scrunched up in the pain that she was trying not to express.

"It means he likes the dual-income, and he doesn't particularly want children."

"Did you discuss this before you got married?"

"Yes, but it appears his thinking evolved since we got married."

"So, no kids ever?"

"Appears so."

"I'm sorry."

She bounced Dawn lightly in her arms while holding her close to her face.

"Maybe I could stop over here whenever I needed to exercise my motherly instincts."

"I'm sure you can. I know Dawn is not going to object. She loves the attention she gets."

* * * * * * * * * * *

Tassy did visit at least every other week and spent a couple of hours with us. We didn't discuss business often, and she never brought up her home life. I did notice she occasionally mentioned our sales rep, Jeff. I hardly ever saw him unless Lynn brought him along with her when she visited. I liked him, and he gave me every indication we were getting along.

"How often are you and Jeff working together?" I asked Tassy.

"I guess once a week or so. Jeff and I are collaborating on the Public Securities account. He likes my ideas. I guess the people at the account do also."

"Great."

I changed the subject and hoped she didn't pick up on my concern.

* * * * * * * * * *

I called Lynn.

"Should I be working closely with Ivanovich?"

"I sense a concern."

"Tassy is seeing him at least once a week. Supposedly, they are working on the Public Securities account together."

"Hmm. News to me. Let me check it out. I have told Jeff if he has questions that Tassy can't answer, he can go directly to you. You're telling me he hasn't approached you at all."

“Correct. Look, I’m not worried about my working relationship with Jeff.”

“No, you’re concerned about theirs, and now so am I.”

* * * * * * * * * * *

I didn’t hear back from Lynn for a couple of weeks.

“Can you and Regina get a babysitter for an evening?”

“Sure, what’s up?”

“I’m going to host a dinner for our staff at The Manitou. I’ll be candid with you. I want to check the dynamic of the group. I’m worried about what might be going on with Tassy and Jeff. I want to get your take. Therefore, I will use the spouses as cover.”

“Okay. So what if something is going on between the two of them? What are your options?”

“I have to assess it if it’s going to affect the company and work from there. If there is an inappropriate relationship, maybe it’s as simple as pointing it out and asking where it’s going. I mean, if Tassy is thinking of leaving her husband and taking up with Jeff, I could care less. But what if Jeff is leading her on and there is no chance of commitment?”

“Yes, but is any of this our business?”

“What if you decided to leave Regina for Coleen? Don’t you think that might affect your life? Or worse yet, what if Regina decided to leave you for Coleen?”

I laughed. I didn’t hear it being shared.

“You couldn’t think…"

"I could, and I did." She was serious.

"Isn’t that a little outside…”

"Mister, my whole experience with you has been outside the norm. I don't regret it, but the experience has made me think of things I never thought of. And let me say, they did not teach this in business school."

* * * * * * * * * *

I got us a table at The Manitou. Since Jeff is single and chose not to bring a date, we are an even six. Lynn, Regina, and I are there first. Regina is not aware anything is going on except Lynn is taking everyone out for dinner. Tim comes over to the table and offers his thanks to Lynn for hosting her dinner at The Manitou.

"Only the best for my staff, Tim."

"How's the Dad, Regina?" Tim asked.

Regina brightened up visibly. "The best, but I think I'm losing my daughter to him."

"We miss you around here, Richard, and I don't mean just your cooking. You should drop by when you can with the baby and your wife to say hi, okay?"

"Will do, won't we, honey?" I said.

"Always."

Tim withdrew to greet another couple. As it happened, it was Tassy and her husband, Curt. Tim led them to our table and automatically held Tassy's chair for her. Although it was apparent Curt had no intention of doing it for her, he seemed unable to hide his discomfort with Tim's performance.

It was clear to me that Curt was going to be Curt. I anticipated an early exit after dinner. Tassy, Regina, and Lynn fell into women's talk about fashion and what they were wearing. I didn't plan any conversation with Curt though I did try. He wasn't having it and blatantly ignored me. My impression was that he was pouting. I reasoned that he and Tassy might have had some kind of disagreement on the way over. I settled back and listened to the ladies. Still early, but the last to arrive, Jeff entered and came right to the table.

"Evening, everyone."

"Jeff, have you and Curt met?" I said as Jeff sat down between Curt and me.

"No. Pleased to meet you." Jeff extended his hand. I was a little surprised that Curt not only shook his hand but smiled as he did.

"Nice meeting you." I noticed the smile was not necessarily friendly.

We all ordered dinner. There were several questions about this or that item on the menu. Lynn gave a short but excellent statement about what a good job everyone had been doing for the company. Again the ladies fell into girl talk. Jeff attempted to fall back on the easy conversation piece for men, sports. Curt didn't respond at all. Then out of nowhere, Curt addressed Jeff.

"I see you didn't think it was necessary to bring a date this evening."

While the statement was weird, Jeff didn't even hesitate.

"I'm not dating anyone in particular now. I didn't think it was required."

"Well, and then as long as Tassy's here, you wouldn't need to have a date anyway, right?"

Curt's face was the picture of smugness. The table fell silent.

"I'm sorry, I don't..." Jeff started to say.

"My impression is that you and my wife are close," Curt said.

Jeff recovered quickly.

"I like your wife, Curt, and I respect your wife. I'm sure you don't think she would be doing anything inappropriate, right?"

"Oh, I don't know. You two seem to spend a lot of time together."

I stepped in, but I knew it wouldn't be enough.

"Curt, do you think this is the time and place for this? We are trying to celebrate here." I said.

"Oh, let's excuse Curt. Please," Tassy said. Her tone was uncharacteristically icy cold. "On the way over, I was telling him how happy Regina and Richard were with their baby. He became upset when I told him I found out from my doctor today that I'm pregnant."

No one commented. Curt got up. "We're leaving."

"You might be leaving, but I'm not," Tassy said.

"Tassy, I said we're leaving. Now, get up."

"You go to hell, Curt."

He stood like it would be only a matter of time before she got up to leave with him. As he stood there, our waiter began serving our soup and salads. Accepting the situation, Curt leaned toward Tassy and hissed, "You will regret this."

Tassy turned to him as he left.

"Curt."

He turned back toward her.

"Don't worry about the baby. It's not yours."

Despite that the restaurants light was not all that revealing, I could tell Curt's complexion turned white.

It was challenging, but we all finished our dinners without commenting on the event of the evening. After the main course had been cleared and our dessert order was placed, Lynn spoke up.

"Tassy, do you need some assistance getting home this evening?"

"I can say I don't have a home to go to, Lynn. I will take a cab to my parent's place. They will not be surprised by this news."

"Forget the cab. I will drive you," Lynn said. "Whatever you need, Tassy, let me know."

"I am going to need an attorney." I could tell Tassy was exasperated.

"I can help you with that," Lynn said.

"Seriously?"

"Absolutely. Tassy, I don't know how you put up with that SOB for as long as you did. I think I almost had a climax when you stood up to him."

We all broke up laughing. Tassy looked around the table, laughing with tears in her eyes.

* * * * * * * * * *

In the following weeks, Tassy relocated to her own apartment. She stopped at our place for the first time in what would become our regular bi-weekly visit.

"How is it going?" I said.

She smiled and threw her arms out and up.

"I feel like I've broken out of a cage. Living with Curt was a constant procession of complaints about everything I did. He's one sick son-of-a-bitch. And I know the question that's on your mind. Why did I marry Curt? Believe it or not, he wasn't like that when we dated. I swear as soon as I said, 'I do,' the guy turned into the guy you met."

"How are you doing? I mean, do you have furniture? Were you able to get your belongings out of the house?"

"I wish you could have seen the moving-out episode. My attorney contacted Curt's lawyer, and they arranged a date and time for me to pick up my stuff. I had a list of things I wanted. Curt insisted he was going to 'observe' the process. He was concerned I would try to take something that was not on the list. My attorney convinced me to hire a couple of guys he knew to move my things. When we got to the house, I could tell Curt was going to give me trouble. He got one look at the two guys that were with me, and he knew he couldn't mess with me. It was... It was exciting. The prick went upstairs in his home office, and we never saw him."

"So, you're going to be a mom."

"Yup." She smiled and nodded in a matter-of-fact gesture.

"How do you feel about it?"

"Great. Why wouldn't I?"

"Well, you did say that the baby isn't Curt's. So…?"

"All the better, I don't even have to see or deal with that asshole again. There will be a DNA confirmation that this baby isn't his. Curt already knows it isn't his child."

"How do you know for sure?"

She started laughing.

"To conceive a baby, the male sperm has to be delivered to the female uterus. Curt knows for a fact that his sperm has not been 'delivered' to my uterus in over a year. No, he's trying to save face with his parents. He will be the victim of my indiscretions."

"And the father of your child?"

"I don't think he's a candidate for being part of my or my baby's life. At least I'm not counting on it."

"Okay. Is there anything Regina and I can do for you?"

"No, but thank you for the offer. I see my life kinda like yours, only I won't have a partner."

"Please don't hesitate to ask for help. I would be angry with you if I found out..."

"Don't worry. I know I can count on you and Lynn. She has been a great help. I almost feel like she is my sister."

* * * * * * * * * *

About two weeks before Tassy's due date, she moved in with us. On Tassy's delivery date, she got us up at 4:00 in the morning to go to the hospital. She was in labor for twelve hours. Coleen took care of Dawn while we shepherded Tassy through her child's first hours. She had a boy and named him Paul. I noticed she frequently slipped into her Latina heritage and referred to him as Pablo.

When Tassy was ready to take Pablo to her apartment, her mother was waiting to help her through the first few weeks. She and I talked every day. Much to Lynn and my surprise, Tassy resumed work after being home for only a week.

* * * * * * * * * *

A month after Paul's birth, Dawn and I paid a visit. My daughter seemed to think that little Paul was an exciting toy. Since my little girl could crawl into any possible trouble, our conversation was hampered a bit. I had to keep a close eye on my ever-curious daughter. In our discussions, Tassy mentioned Jeff a couple of times.

"It's none of my business, but... what is Jeff's role in your life? You two seem to be close."

She smiled and shook her head as if to clear her mind before she answered.

"The question you want to be answered, and you're too much of a gentleman to ask is whether Jeff is Paul's father. The answer is no. I could only wish I could find someone like you or Jeff. No, Jeff is too young to take on the kind of burden that you've taken.

"Jeff is just a nice guy. He stops by or calls just to check on me. He's my direct line to sanity. You know as well as anybody how exhausting it is when you're taking care of a baby. He drops by for a half-hour or so. He brings me a milkshake and holds Paul while he's here. He even changed his diaper the other day. Yeah, Jeff will make a great father when he grows up a little more."

"Are you going to wait for him?"

"I don't have any plans for anything past going to bed tonight. It's my Mom's turn to get up with Pablo so that I can sleep through the night.

* * * * * * * * * *

It was a lovely afternoon. The air was fresh, but the sun was warm. A fluffy cloud here and there gave the sky some texture. I opened the stroller and placed my daughter, Dawn into the seat. We paraded down to the park about three blocks away from home. I wasn't a regular, so I didn't know the other moms and nannies who brought their charges to the park on a schedule. We walked the perimeter and then settled onto a bench near the pond. Dawn was crawling and trying to stand up when she had something to hang onto. I was holding her up as she grasped the seat on the bench and got her balance. It was one of those days I will always remember.

I can tell you precisely what happened when Dawn and I got home from our trip to the park. I don't know about other generations, but mine is supposed to remember exactly where they were and what they were doing when President Kennedy was assassinated. And what about Robert Kennedy and Martin Luther King? I could tell you about those things. Equally so, I'm telling you what happened when Dawn and I got home.

The light on the answering machine was blinking, but I took the time to put my daughter down for a nap before checking it. The message was from the County Sheriffs' office. Could I call Officer Jerry Sheffield as soon as possible?

"Sheffield speaking."

"Officer, you left a voice message on my answering machine. I'm Richard Harrison."

"Yes." His tone lowered and became serious. "Mr. Harrison, I'm calling about an accident investigation I'm working on. Is Regina Harrison related to you?"

I felt a flip in my stomach.

"Yes. Regina is my wife." She wasn't. We never did get around to it, but she wore a ring, and we pledged our intentions to each other.

"Mr. Harrison, I'm sorry to inform you that your wife was involved in an automobile accident earlier this afternoon. She was moved to a hospital from the accident scene. Can you meet me at City General Hospital?"

I could not speak.

"Mr. Harrison? Sir? Did you understand what I said?"

"Yes. Yes, I understood. I...I have to make some arrangements. I have to get someone to take care of my daughter and...I don't drive. I'll need to get a cab."

"I'll tell you what. Get someone to watch your daughter. I'll pick you up."

I called my mother. She wasn't home. I called Coleen. She was out of town, but she would be back by six o'clock. I called Tassy.

"Hello."

"Tassy, can you watch Dawn for me?"

"Sure. When and for how long?"

"Now, and I'm not sure. Ah...ahh, Regina has been in an automobile accident. I have to go with the police to the hospital."

"Richard, my God, Regina, was..."

"Yeah, I don't know why or who she would be riding with or anything else about it."

I'm having a lot of trouble finding the right words.

"I'm coming right over," Tassy said.

Tassy with baby Paul was at my front door in fifteen minutes. Officer Sheffield was there a few minutes later.

"Dawn is napping. There's the formula in the refrigerator, diapers in..."

"I know where things are, Richard. Do you want me to call Lynn? She'll want to know."

"Yes, and Coleen. Tell her what's going on and where I am."

"Of course. Richard, I don't know what to say." She hugged me.

****

On the trip to the hospital, I tried to get some details about what happened. Sheffield deflected everything until later. I felt like I was going to throw up, and I told him. He offered to pull over, but I said I'd be alright.

By the time we got to the hospital, I knew she was dead. We didn't go into the ER. We didn't go upstairs where the patients might have surgery or intensive care. We took an elevator down.

Sheffield told me as we walked down the hallway to the morgue. I was okay until they pulled back the sheet covering Regina's body. The attendant pulled the sheet back to just below her chin. Her head was turned to the right. The positioning was deliberate since the damage to her head was pretty much limited to the unexposed side. They asked me if the body was Regina. I just nodded, and then I walked to the sink and threw up. When I got under control, rinsed my mouth, and cleaned a spattering of vomit off my sweater, I turned to Sheffield and the attendant. They had pulled the sheet back to cover her.

"Mr. Harrison, would you like a moment alone with your wife?"

I shook my head, no, and walked to the exit door.

"Can we talk for a moment?" Sheffield said

I nodded, yes. Sheffield opened the door to a small conference room.

He sat me down. "Can I get you something... soda, water, or coffee, maybe?"

"Water would be good." He brought me a cup of water.

"I'm sure you have a lot of questions. I'm going to tell you what we know. Then you might be able to help me. I will try to answer any further questions you have."

I nodded.

"The vehicle your wife was driving was rented from a Hertz location at the airport."

I had been staring at the floor. I moved my head so I could look into his face.

"Excuse me?"

"Yes, sir," he hesitated.

"My wife rented a car at the airport?"

He nodded.

"Then she was driving when the accident occurred?" I said.

Officer Sheffield looked past me.

"Yes, sir. All of that is accurate."

"There wasn't anyone else in the car?"

"That's correct."

"I see."

"Mr. Harrison, when was the last time you saw your wife?"

"This morning, about 8:15. She was leaving for work."

Of course, everything came back to me with clarity. I considered the time Regina took with Dawn that morning, not only dressing her but feeding her. She would typically have left feeding her to me. There was a long hug for me, and did I just imagine seeing a tear in the corner of her eye?

"Was she upset or under a lot of pressure recently?"

II was going to speak, but I paused. I looked at him right in the eye and held his gaze for a moment.

"My wife suffered from occasional bouts of depression. I must say, I didn't see any signs of it this morning."

He opened a file lying on the table between us. In a plastic sleeve was a piece of paper. He turned it toward me so I could read the handwriting. I recognized the handwriting. It was unmistakably written by Regina.

It's better for everyone. I'm sorry

I broke down and couldn't stop sobbing. Sheffield answered the knock on the door. The next thing I knew, Coleen burst into the room. In seconds we were embracing. She was petting my head and murmuring in my ear. "It'll be okay," over and over.

After reviewing information with the hospital later, I realized how long Regina had been planning this. Right after Dawn was born, a lawyer helped us write our end-of-life wishes. Regina wanted to be cremated. There would be a non-religious memorial. Her ashes would be interred in a vault at the cemetery where her parents were buried.

Regina thought of everything. She even insured the rental car. All of her possessions were at home: her purse, jewelry, wallet, and house keys. The only things she had with her were her drivers' license and a credit card so she could rent the car. The police report stated she wasn't wearing her seatbelt.

In the note, Regina said she was sorry. It was going to take me a long time to accept her apology.

Chapter 18
Margret "Midge" Wright

At the age of twenty-eight, I'm a widower and a single father. My daughter is four. Her mother, Regina, has been dead since Dawn was 8 months old. I'm not sure Dawn remembers her mother. Someday, it's going to be necessary to explain to Dawn about Regina's depression and how it took her mother away from us and everyone who loved her.

There is Regina's lifelong friend, Coleen, who was like a sister to her. When Regina killed herself rather than live a life of trying to find herself in a bottle of prescription drugs, Coleen was stunned by what happened. She was still the single woman with a crude outgoing personality. Coleen was never a small woman, either physically or personally. However, after Regina died, I watched and attended Coleen's withdrawal, which was so deep I thought we could never pull her out. Coleen gained some twenty pounds of unattractive weight and carried an tremendous amount of grief and guilt. For over a year, I was afraid that she would be the next to commit suicide.

Now it is almost four years after Regina, my late wife, rented a car and deliberately drove it into an oak tree growing on the edge of a county park. She didn't wear a seatbelt. When she hit the tree at tremendous speed, 'the lack of a restraint' guaranteed she would die of massive head injuries. Fortunately, her last wishes instructed that she be cremated with no public showing of her body.

Coleen and I continued to live together. While our grief and depression fed on each other, I at least was seeking help. My counselor, Candice Marlowe, was concerned that my close relationship with Coleen was holding me back from moving on with my life.

Both Coleen and I had other people trying to help us. My boss, Lynn Kampo, talked to me every other day and visited me at least once a month. My co-worker, Anastasia Domas, who we all call Tassy, and I get together once a week. Tassy is a divorced single mother. Her son, Paul, is four months younger than my Dawn. We alternate going to each other's homes and always bring our kids.

Both of us work for Lynn. We are part of an ongoing experiment to see how working from home can be part of the company growth plan. At this point, the test seems to be proven. Tassy and I have established our value repeatedly, if not to the board of directors, at least to Lynn, our supervisor.

Coleen and I continue our lives as usual, except for the massive hole in our relationship with Regina being gone. It's strange how you take for granted the effect someone has on your life until that relationship is over. Regina was the glue in the group dynamic. Regina's fight with depression was a common element in Coleen's and my life.

****

One evening, after I put Dawn down for the night, Coleen and I relaxed in the back garden. To keep an eye on Dawn, I put her to sleep in the 'big girl' bed, which replaced her crib in my office. Both Coleen and I had experienced a busy day, which drained us of our energy.

I prepared a dinner that was reflective of the attempt to tone down the madness of our workday. I made a chopped salad with a balsamic dressing and served it with Hawaiian dinner rolls and white wine.

We both chuckled when I confessed to giving into Dawn again. As part of our nightly ritual, I had read with Dawn her favorite book, *Good Night Moon*. I was starting to teach her to read, and there were other books I could have read with her, but she often asked me for 'Moon.' I'm not sure, but I think that Regina read the book to her. I explained my theory to Coleen. She pondered it a bit.

"What do you hang onto so you can remember her?" Coleen said

I thought for a moment. There were so many things I did that could have qualified for me.

“I'm not sure. I still miss Regina, but I've gotten past the point where I want to share something with her. For instance, when Dawn took her first steps right after Regina died, things like that, without thinking, I wanted to tell Regina.”

Coleen smiled and touched my hand.

“Did she ever answer?”

“No. I don't do it anymore, either. I suppose I'm moving on and not noticing it. What about you?”

“I was thinking about it the other day. I realize she is not between us anymore.”

“Really. Like separating us?”

“Yes. At least, I don't have to worry about how I feel about you and how Regina might react if I were to tell her what I was thinking."

"Like…”

“Like sometimes, I want to make love with you again, Richard.”

She looked at me with a quiet intensity. It wasn't like her in so many ways. The Coleen I knew would have belted out, “Hey Richard, do ya wanna fuck me or what?” On top of that, she'd enjoy the shock she would create with her audacity.

For a moment, I didn't know what to say. I never got used to Coleen's directness. She knew it and enjoyed my lack of ability to react. But now, she was soft and vulnerable.

“Does this happen often? I mean, wanting to have sex?”

She reached out. I got up and sat on the couch next to her. She wrapped me up in her arms, and I could see the tears in her eyes. I had never seen this side of her.

"I don't want just to have sex, Richard. I want you to make love to me. I want you to forget how we had mad passionate monkey sex before. I need you to make me feel something because I haven't felt anything since Regina died, and I think you're the only one who can do it for me."

Coleen got up and walked with me inside to my office area. Without saying a word to each other, we knew we had to be quiet because if we conducted ourselves the way we had in the past when we had sex, we would wake up Dawn.

So without her telling me loudly and using language both crude and simultaneously arousing because we'd be disobeying so much of what we had been raised to believe was wrong, we began a dance we had performed before. The song's lyrics were the same; the steps we took were similar, but the beat was quieter, and the tempo was slower. The guitar had nylon strings and wasn't amplified. The drummer used brushes instead of sticks. And, no one needed a microphone.

Besides the brushing of our skin against each other and the couch, the only sound I heard was a long breathy sigh when she climaxed. We laid in each other's arms for a long time. I don't know how long we slept like that, but I woke up when the guy from the bar down the alley dumped a load of empty glass bottles into the trash bin. I woke Coleen up. Quietly, she gathered her clothing and went up to her room. I slept in the basement, so I would be there when Dawn woke up.

* * * * * * * * * *

Then there was Tassy. More than once, when we got together, the feeling that we should be living together welled up in me, and I'm sure she shared it. We were parenting our kids. We cooked for each other and recognized our likes and dislikes. I was living in a house that was too big for what I needed, even if you counted Coleen. Tassy was in an apartment too small for her and her son Paul.

Tassy and I were comfortable together, but the idea of beginning a committed relationship with Tassy or Coleen was fraught with problems. They were both close to Regina. I was convinced that Coleen would hold me back from putting my grief for my wife behind me. Tassy might help me move on, but I didn't get any indication of it in our current relationship. Why would I think a commitment would make things different? Then Midge came into my life

****

I was with Tassy at my place on a summer evening. I had grilled outside. We cleaned up as much as I was going to allow, and we were sitting beside each other on separate chairs in the dimming light of the evening. The kids were running out of energy. We knew we would be putting them down soon.

"You remember how you were explaining how odd the woman who cuts your hair acts?" Tassy said.

"Yes. You mean Midge."

"A friend of mine told me the woman is probably autistic. Emotionally, she might have trouble relating to people and acting as we might expect."

"So, it's a mental condition?"

"My friend told me they are just beginning to do serious research on this condition. It has something to do with brain function."

****

The person Tassy was referring to was my new barber. About two weeks ago, I went to a new shop to have my hair cut. The gentlemen that had been cutting my hair for years retired and recommended this shop to me. Three women ran the place. Two of them were sisters, Estelle and Midge Wright. The other woman was their friend Jenna Kent.

At my first appointment, I happened to get Midge as my stylist. Midge appeared to be in her late twenties or early thirties. She was of average height with a medium build. She gathered her hair into a brassy red ponytail. Her skin was a powdery white, and it made her blue eyes stand out like water in a desert.

When she greeted me, I knew something wasn't quite right. Her voice sounded like some kind of electronic simulator produced it. It seemed flat and emotionless. As she swirled a cloth over my shoulders to catch the hair she was going to trim, her motions were jerky. They appeared as if she was trying to be precise about something that didn't require precision.

"Hello, Richard. Welcome. Are you happy with your hairstyle, or should we discuss it?" This all sounded fine, except I couldn't detect any feeling in it. The message was natural, but Midge's voice was monotone.

"Midge, I'm a traditional kind of guy. Just trim it up pretty much the way it is. Thank you."

I couldn't help but notice the other two stylists, though busy with other customers, were paying close attention to Midge and me.

Midge washed my hair and began doing a scissors trim while it was still wet. She started the final trimming around my neck, sideburns, and eyebrows with a shaver. After drying my hair, she applied some kind of product to keep my hair neat after she combed it into place. Midge brought me a mirror so I could look at all angles. It was a great cut. Outside of her greeting, she hadn't engaged me in any kind of conversation.

"Perfect, Midge. Thank you."

"You're welcome, Richard."

"How long have you been cutting men's hair?" She brushed the stray hair off my shoulders and wiped it off my neck with a hot towel.

"Not long, only…" she paused.

"You graduated from beauty school and got your certificate two years ago, honey."

Estelle said without even looking up from the work she was doing on her customer. The comment exposed the fact that Estelle was eavesdropping on our conversation. The tone of Estelle's voice was like a mother reminding a child, but Midge didn't react to the interruption in any way.

"Yes, two years ago, Richard." Midge didn't smile or change facial expressions in any way.

"Well, you did a great job." I handed her ten bucks for a six-dollar and fifty-cent haircut. "Keep the change." I got out of the chair and started for the door.

"Are you going to come back?"

I turned and smiled at her. Her expression had a hint of indecision in it as if to say that she realized she might have spoken spontaneously and out of turn.

"Absolutely. This is a great haircut." Out of the corner of my eye, I saw her sister smile slightly.

"Okay, I guess that's good," Midge said.

I walked toward her. "It's excellent, Midge. You are a good barber."

I felt like I was talking to my daughter. I engaged with Midge's eyes.

"See you in a few weeks," I said.

When I got home, there was a voicemail from the barbershop. The message asked me to call Estelle. I returned her call right away.

"Hello, Estelle, this is Richard Harrison. I got a message to call you."

"Yes, um, I hope you enjoyed your visit, but I have a question for you. Did you intend to leave a three and half dollar tip?"

"Yes, I did."

"My goodness, how generous, thank you. My sister... she sometimes isn't good at making change and things like that."

"I understand. But she didn't make a mistake with me. I told her to keep the change."

"Thank you. Ah, my sister, she is... different."

"I noticed. But she's fine with me. Honestly, that was the best haircut I've ever had."

"Thank you, Mr. Harrison. You're a gentleman, to be sure."

* * * * * * * * * * *

Tassy's friend's evaluation turned out to be correct. I found out from my doctor that the medical profession had traditionally diagnosed people like Midge with incurable mental problems. However, recent research found that these patients could be taught to react in a more generally-accepted way than previously thought.

By the time I went back for my fourth haircut, Midge had become more comfortable with me. Sometimes the subject matter was how I was feeling or what I thought about the weather. However, she floored me when in the middle of my haircut, Midge said loud enough for everyone to hear, "You know if you want to ask me out on a date, it's okay."

It got quiet in the shop. I was facing the mirror. From its reflection, I could look at the rest of the people in the shop. Estelle and Jenna looked as if someone had passed gas, and they were trying to ignore it. I took a moment while I tried to figure out what to say.

"That would be fun, Midge. What would you like to do on a date?"

She kept her comb moving and scissors clacking.

"Do you like movies?" I said.

"I do."

"What kind of movie do you like?"

"I don't like movies where there are a lot of people getting hurt."

"Yes, that can be hard to watch. Can you go Friday night?"

Her scissors flew faster.

"Yes, but I have to be home kind of early, cause the shop is open on Saturday. That's a busy day for us."

"Fine, we'll go to the seven o'clock movie, and I'll bring you right home."

Midge paused her frantic cutting and leaned closer to me and said quietly in my ear, "You know I can't let you kiss me right away, but you could hold my hand."

"I understand. You are a fine woman, Midge. I wouldn't want to do anything that might hurt or embarrass you."

"Okay, I'll go to the movies with you then." She gave me her address.

When I left the shop, I was confused. What the hell had I just done? And more importantly, why? I calmed myself by thinking that I was doing something kind for a nice young woman who probably didn't get to go out a lot. But then I reminded myself that she had asked me out. I was surprised and maybe even embarrassed. What does she want and expect? How far did she think this relationship could go?

* * * * * * * * * * *

When I picked her up that Friday, Estelle answered the door. Midge came up behind her. Midge was nicely dressed in a dark pair of slacks, a white blouse, under a lightweight green sweater. I told her that maybe we should just walk to the theater since it was so close. Midge just nodded. Estelle put a hand on my shoulder. The look on her face was a look of confusion. On the one hand, I think she was happy her sister had a date; on the other, she was worried about how it would turn out.

Almost as instinctively as I would with my daughter, I reached for Midge's hand as we crossed a busy street on our way to the movie theater. After that, she didn't want me to let go of her hand for almost the entire evening.

The theater was showing a romantic comedy. Midge didn't always laugh at the movie's funny parts, but she did get upset when the guy and the gal broke up, as they always do in that kind of film before they get back together before the end of the film. When they did reconnect, Midge was happy. We walked out of the theater into the cool darkness of the night.

"So, did you like the movie?" I said.

"I didn't like it when he hurt her feelings," Midge said.

"Yes, but you could tell he was sorry. He loved her so much," I said.

We were out of the theater in a little over an hour and a half. I offered to buy her a drink from a bar on the way home. She declined. We proceeded to her house. Just before she reached to open the door, she said, "I'm not like other people. I don't always know what to say or do."

"That's okay with me. You're a nice person. I like you, and I thank you for going out with me."

"You are the first person whoever took me out on a date. I like you a lot. Is that okay?"

"Yes, I'm flattered. Did you notice how many people looked at us tonight? I'm sure they were wondering what such a good-looking woman was doing with a plain old guy like me."

Midge didn't comprehend my attempt at humorous self-deprecation.

"I like you, Richard. You can kiss me if you want to."

I leaned over and kissed her on the cheek.

"Thank you, Midge. Good night."

* * * * * * * * * *

It wasn't going to be our last date. I admit I was unprepared for any kind of close relationship with a person like this. The questions cascaded through my mind. What kind of future is there with a person who's dealing with this problem? Or is there a future? I liked her. Her innocence was both charming and dangerous. What could I bring to her life that she needs, and how much harm could I do without even realizing it? I also recognized that I was developing a heightened sense of protectiveness and concern for Midge. The white knight was in full armor and mounted on his faithful steed.

The shop was closed on Monday, and I invited Midge to have lunch with me. Soon every Monday became lunchtime with Midge. I did not ask her at my house. There were many reasons not to do that. My biggest concern was giving anyone the impression I might take advantage of Midge.

Midge knew I was a single dad. Occasionally, she would ask about Dawn. It was hard for me to judge if Midge had a genuine concern or something that she thought she should bring up.

Midge would often say something that indicated she was interested in having a more physical relationship. It was pretty apparent to me that she didn't know about sex other than what she had read, seen on TV or movies, or heard in conversation.

It started with that one peck on the cheek. That led to a hug and peck on the cheek. Then the hugs lasted longer. She wanted to hold hands when we were sitting and talking. Sometimes she would pick up my hand and put it on the side of her face or her leg if we were seated. I could sense this activity mildly aroused her. I called Estelle.

* * * * * * * * * * *

"Listen, Estelle, I can't explain fully to myself why I care so much for Midge, but..." Estelle interrupted me.

"I can tell you why. It's because she is a person who exhibits both adult and childlike activity. Like me, you are torn between trying to make her show her feelings, and at the same time, you want to make sure you don't hurt her. Richard, the rules for how to treat Midge are not fully understood. Trust me, I've lost sleep over the answers to those questions. I talked to her counselor about her relationship with you. I did it as much for you as I needed to know for myself. Make no mistake about it. Midge has a full set of normal reactions to sex. She probably wants to have sex with you, but she doesn't know how to tell you or show you what she wants."

"Estelle, I can't take my relationship with Midge to that level. I just can't. It's not fair to Midge or me. Generally, I'm not in favor of sex with people who don't know why they are doing it. I've had sex with women who I knew just wanted to have sex, scratch the itch, or just have fun, whatever you want to call it. But I think we both know that Midge will never understand that. No, I think the bigger question is if Midge wants to have sex with me, then what's next?"

"I guess the question is, what is possible, Richard? I don't think you want to commit to anything with Midge, right?"

"I know this is going to sound crazy to you, Estelle, but I don't think I'm good enough for her. I don't know what she needs or what she wants, but I'm also convinced that she doesn't know what I would expect and need. I could learn. I could love her enough to care enough to try and make her happy. Unfortunately, I also believe she isn't capable of changing. I don't know if I could live with that."

"What if she wasn't the way she is? What if she was more normal, whatever that is?" Estelle said.

"If she were another woman who I met and knew what she was doing by having a relationship with me that included sex, it would be a risk I might take. But Midge doesn't know this, does she? How would she feel if we began the kind of relationship that included having sex, and I decided to stop it? Or what would Midge do if she wanted to stop it?

"Hell, Estelle! There are times when I think of her as a sister and other times like my child. How can I imagine having sex with someone I feel that way about?"

Estelle and I talked some more, but the only thing that came out of our conversation was that we both were happy that Midge and I shared a friendship. Midge needed to have an adult friend, and Estelle trusted me. We also were both concerned about where it might go in Midge's mind.

We didn't talk about the one thing I would learn about later. Midge's special ability that made her unique.

* * * * * * * * * *

Midge and I had another date. Yes, we are now calling it dating at Midge's insistence. There was a performance by a popular singing group at the casino. This group had a resume of several hit songs from twenty years ago. Midge would have been about five, yet she knows and loves their music.

During the show, Midge was as animated and happy as I had ever seen her. Smiling and bouncing in her chair to the music, she became a person with feelings and automatic excitement.

As we walked out of the auditorium, I became aware of another facet of Midge that I'd never observed. Our casino is designed so that you must walk through the gambling area before exiting. It's like putting the candy at the checkout counter at the grocery store. You know the kids will ask mom for some, and mom will often say yes.

As we walked, I noticed Midge kept looking at the activity in the casino. Then she stopped by one of the blackjack tables. We were watching the players.

"Does that look like fun to you?" I said.

She just nodded.

"I don't know how to play the game well enough, or we could try it," I said.

"I know how to play," she said.

"Really," I wasn't sure what to do. "Would you…?"

Before I finished speaking, Midge walked to the table, sat down at an empty chair, and put down a twenty-dollar bill. The dealer took her money and gave her chips. The next twenty minutes flew by. As I watched her play, I couldn't believe what I saw.

When I thought back on the evening, I knew immediately I needed to learn a lot more about Blackjack. In my research about the game, I came to understand two crucial things about playing the game. Once I learned about these things, I knew how Midge accomplished what she did.

First, she sat down as the dealer was shuffling the six decks of cards and loading them in the "shoe." The shoe is the name for the box the dealers use to hold the cards when dealing. The cards come off of the top of the stack consistently. The dealer can't pull a card from another part of the deck.

What this meant to experienced players is that every possible combination of cards was available. The odds of winning were slightly to the advantage of the casino at this point. As each of the cards is used and taken out of play, many combinations are not available, and the odds begin to change in favor of the players. But this is only valid if the player can keep track of all of the cards played. It isn't even necessary to know the exact cards, but more which groups of cards have been played.

In the gaming industry, it's called "card counting." Some players have trained themselves to do it. But after I learned more about the game, I found out that Midge appeared to be naturally adept at card counting. On top of that acquired skill at card counting, she had another advantage.

Card counters can be spotted. If they are identified, they can be banned from casinos. That evening, Midge had turned that twenty dollars into six hundred and fifty in thirty minutes. At that point, I thought she was just lucky.

To the developing mind of a child, many behaviors are modeled by example. How do you greet people you don't know? Thank people that serve you, such as check-out cashiers, wait staff, and valet car parkers.

Estelle pointed out to me that as Midge spent more time with me doing things adults do together, she learned more about how to make small talk with strangers. I taught her to avoid something she shouldn't talk about and helped put some boundaries on her public conduct.

I also knew that once people had spent time with her, the childlike innocence she projected defined her. No matter how much she won at the blackjack table, no one would dream of thinking that Midge was smart enough to count cards. But I learned all of that after the fact. That night I was lost in awe of it all. I called Estelle the next day.

"Did Midge tell you about last night?"

"Yes, she enjoyed the music. She's such a fan. Did she overreact?"

"No, she was having a good time. What I was surprised at was the money she won at the blackjack table."

It was quiet on Estelle's end of the line.

"I wondered if she would play. I should have warned you about that. I'm sorry."

"So, she has done this before?"

"Oh, yes, many times."

"How did she learn to play the game that well?"

"She learned to play the game in one of the group activities she attended when she was a kid. Early on, when we knew why she is the way she is, it seemed to help her when we put her with others with similar conditions. I don't know if someone taught her how to keep track of the played cards or if she figured it out by herself. Regardless, she does it. There's that, and the paradox is she understands the mathematics behind the game, even though she sometimes has problems with making change.

"All of this took us some time to grasp. Once we did, you can imagine my dilemma. Midge could legitimately make a living playing blackjack where it's legal. She is not cheating. But it's gambling. Could she make the wrong kind of person upset to the point they would hurt or even kill her? Or, could someone exploit her talent for their gain? She has won thousands of dollars from all of the times she has played in a casino, and she's never lost.

"At one casino, they asked her to leave. But I could tell they were unsure of what they were seeing. They didn't ban her from playing there again, but I didn't let her go back there for a long time. When she did go back to that casino, I made her quit after she won a few hundred dollars so she wouldn't draw attention to herself. And that's pretty much the way we do it when we do go to play.

"So that you know, I put all of the money she wins in an account for her. So far, she hasn't spent any of it. It's become clear to me that she doesn't do it for the money. I think she just gets a kick out of being better at something than other people."

* * * * * * * * * *

In many ways, my relationship with Midge was similar to the one with my daughter. Dawn was no longer a baby. Dawn liked being with me, but she didn't like constant supervision. When we went to the playground for a picnic, Dawn always wanted to see me, but she ran off to play with other children and didn't want me hovering over her. Sometimes, she needed to be cuddled. At other times, she wanted to be left alone.

Dawn was aware she didn't have a mommy. She knew that she was different because her dad brought her to the park when all of the other kids came with their mothers. To further the confusion, she had Coleen and Tassy, who acted as mothers. Both of them were more than willing to fill the role.

I was committed to Dawn. She is my daughter and has a right to my unconditional love and protection. Midge did not have a right to those expectations. However, I had the same problem with Dawn and Midge because I had no way of knowing what they were thinking. Dawn was getting better at expressing her needs, but she was a kid and just beginning to understand some things about the world around her.

Midge was somewhat in the same state. However, when you looked at Midge, you quite naturally had expectations of behavior and trouble understanding that she didn't possess despite her adult appearance. In both cases, I did enjoy seeing that my relationship with them helped.

I asked Estelle and Midge over to our place for a backyard cookout on a Sunday afternoon. Coleen would be there, as would Tassy and young Paul. Midge and Estelle were the last to arrive. I had told Estelle there would be other people. Either Estelle didn't tell Midge, or Midge didn't consider what that meant because I could see that Midge was uncomfortable. She was like a child in a group of people she didn't know. Dawn was familiar with everyone except Midge and Estelle. Dawn played with Paul. Later Coleen was playing in the sandbox with both of them.

Midge was at my elbow all afternoon. I put her to work, helping me prepare and serve the meal. She sat next to me while we ate. I don't remember her saying anything to anyone unless she was asked something. Coleen complimented Midge on the scarf she was wearing and the pin holding back her hair. Midge kind of smiled and thanked her. Tassy talked to her about hairstyles and promised she would call for an appointment.

I don't know how it started, but at one point, I looked up and saw that Midge, Paul, and Dawn were in the sandbox playing in the sand. And like children will do, they were playing at being adults. I heard Dawn say to Midge very matter of factly, "You are the oldest. You get to be the mommy. Paul and I will be the kids." Midge nodded without enthusiasm. "Okay. You have to be good, though."

And while I relaxed with the other adults, the 'kids' continued to function as a make-believe family. We, adults, tried not to think that anything unusual was happening.

After that afternoon, Midge would ask about Dawn and Paul. Dawn kept asking me when Midge would come over again. Tassy told me Paul was fascinated with Midge. I checked in with Estelle.

"She didn't have much to say to me when we went home. However, the next day she chewed off Jenna's ear. She loved the kids. And she thought it was funny that they chose her to be the mommy. Did you know that Dawn asked Midge to come over the next time she and Paul sleepover? Oh yeah, Midge had a great time. I wouldn't be surprised if she has thoughts of moving in with you, Richard."

I was quiet.

"You know I was kidding, right?" Estelle said.

Chapter 19
Lee Anne Dobson

My life is a version of Dorothy in The Wizard of Oz. My companions in my journey are the excitable Coleen, the autistic Midge, and the earth mother, Tassy. I don't have Toto, the dog. I have Dawn, my eight-year-old daughter. My counselor, Candice, might be cast as the Good Witch.

During my bi-weekly appointment, an idea is planted. A picture begins to grow in my consciousness. I shared with Candice, "I have so much going on in my daily life. I love every facet of it except something is missing."

"What's missing?" Candice said.

"I'm not sure."

"Can I make an observation? We've talked about your responsibility to all of the people in your life and how you appreciate them. We've explored having you establish boundaries. What I don't see in your life is balance. Is there any time just for you?"

I wasn't ready for that. I just hadn't thought of it. Candice was right. I couldn't think of any time that I did something just for me. I go to the gym at least three times a week, but I go with either Coleen, Midge, or Tassy. Sometimes I take Dawn, who usually is taking swimming lessons, while I sit in the bleachers watching lest she drowns while no one notices.

I rarely eat alone, if you don't count my working lunches where I chew on a sandwich while I work at my desk. I can't remember the last book I read just for the pleasure of reading.

I know why I quit putting time for myself into my schedule when I became a single parent with an 8-month-old child. Dawn forced me to be a twenty-four-hour guardian and provider. As I pondered this situation, I remembered a conversation I had with Tassy about the playground moms I encountered.

When I began taking Dawn down to the park, I would run into the same moms with their children. They were polite but kept me at arm's length. I figured that was because I was a man in a woman's world. Eventually, they welcomed me into their circle. I knew I was trusted when they began telling jokes about men and didn't excuse themselves.

"You know why, don't you?" Tassy said.

"No, I don't. I just figured when I kept coming to the park, they became more trusting."

"That could be part of it. I think it's because the mothers knew you could relate to them and their experience of being the child's primary caretaker. You and I have discussions I wouldn't want to have with other men. You know both the effort and reward of being a single parent."

As Dawn has grown, she is more challenging mentally as opposed to just physically. Dawn bathes, feeds, and dresses herself. However, now she asks all of those curious kid questions and expects me to know the answers.

The complex inquiries for me to handle are about her mother. So often, I've rehearsed the speech about how and why your mother died, but I need to wait until Dawn is ready to understand it. So far, Dawn has asked questions such as, "was my mother pretty, smart, or kind?". These are simple kinds of questions, and it was easy for me to assure her that her mother was all of those things.

* * * * * * * * * *

At my next counseling appointment, Candice said, "So you've thought about all of your commitments and the value they have to you, but you haven't come up with a plan to put 'me-time' into your life. So, what are you going to do about that? What aren't you doing today that you were doing before Dawn came into your life?"

Bingo! I called Tim the next day.

"Hey, do you guys have any need for a part-time cook?"

It's not like I hadn't seen Tim for four years. I took him up on his invitation to visit. He was at "Uncle Tim" status with Dawn. He always found time for us and never mentioned me coming back to work for him. I'm sure my request surprised him.

"What are you thinking?" he said.

"A couple of shifts a week. I don't care about which shift, lunch, or dinner. I just need it to be consistent so that I can schedule."

"I've got a new chef at The Manitou. Why don't you drop in for lunch, and I'll introduce you," he said.

I dropped Dawn off at school and went for lunch with Tim. During lunch, I told Tim why I wanted to cook again.

"I need something in my life that is just for me. I know that sounds whiny and selfish, but I'm buttering the bread with a brush, and I need a knife."

"I think I understand," he said.

"Look, I don't need a charity thing here. If you don't need..."

"Don't worry about that. You have no idea how difficult it is to find good people in our industry right now. I just don't want to force you into a team that's working pretty well at this point. I'm sure you'll fit, but I want them to have the last word."

Later, looking over Tim's shoulder, I saw a tall woman in kitchen whites walking toward our table. She was a slender woman with her graying hair pulled up inside of the traditional chef's hat. On her long angular face were two glowing blue-grey eyes, and between them was one of those tremendous french-hawk noses and a tight smile with thin lips. Her stride was smooth and so effortless you might have thought she was on roller skates. As she drew closer, I noticed the lines that framed her face. I guessed she was in her late forties. Her smile simply gushed as she arrived.

"Hello, Richard. How was your lunch?"

"I had the walleye. It was fabulous."

"Not overcooked?"

"No. It was perfect."

"Did you season it?" Her smile became quieter.

"I squeezed a little lemon juice on it."

She nodded as she sat down between Tim and me. Her query was a test. I think I passed.

"Tim has a lot of praise for your past work."

"I was at it for a long time and worked with some good people."

"I'm fussy. Even anal-retentive."

I smiled at her, even though I knew she was serious.

"I know I'm going to have to work myself into shape to handle the job. But I'm more than willing to learn from you and comply with your standards."

"Good," she said.

We agreed to a lunch shift on Monday and Wednesday. I had to be in by nine o'clock, and I had to stay until two o'clock. I would be able to take Dawn to school and pick her up in the afternoon.

I informed Lynn about resuming work at The Manitou and why I was doing it. She was sitting across from me in my downstairs office. When I finished, she let out a big sigh.

"I'm sorry. If it's a problem, I won't do it," I said.

"No, you go ahead and do this. I can tell it's important to you. I was worried that you were quitting WI4Y."

"Christ, no. I never thought in terms of quitting the company. Lynn. I can't imagine leaving the company."

* * * * * * * * * *

My significant challenge was getting back into shape to work the line so I gained my new Chef's confidence. Lee Anne insisted everyone called her Chef in the kitchen and Lee when we weren't working. She wasn't a person who yelled or threw things at her workers. No one I've worked with has ever done that, despite what you might see on TV cooking shows.

Lee was very discrete with her commentary. Often it started with a question: Why was I doing what I was doing? If she was satisfied with the answer, she would smile, nod, and move on. If not, she might suggest an alternative. If she noticed you weren't complying with her suggestion, you got a stern look, and "I thought we agreed that...?" Ultimately, she was far more comfortable to work with than I originally thought.

Lee and I were having a beer after my shift about a month and a half into my hire.

"How am I doing, Chef?" I said.

She smiled, put down her beer, and put her hands on my shoulders.

"I couldn't be happier if my children worked for me, and they performed like you. You know if I wasn't here, you could take over, and no one would notice."

"Lee, I seriously doubt that no one would notice, but thank you for the compliment. So, do you have children?"

Her expression darkened a bit.

"No. I haven't been lucky enough to find a man I wanted to have children with, and now it's a bit late for me to have them. You're lucky. Although losing your wife is a difficult thing to face, you do have your daughter."

I was a little surprised that Lee knew that much about me, but I appreciated her comments.

"Part of the reason I'm the best dad I can be is that I come here twice a week and work."

She smiled and put her hand back on my shoulder.

"Think about how good you'd be if you worked here more." She grinned, turned, and walked to her office.

* * * * * * * * * * *

It's interesting how you can look at someone you are accustomed to seeing in one environment and what happens when you suddenly encounter them in another.

Dawn and I were building up our appetite by strolling around the local park. It was a school holiday. Lee was sitting on a bench feeding the birds and a couple of aggressive squirrels. I almost didn't recognize her.

What initially drew my attention was her hair. A gentle breeze blew her unfettered hair off her shoulders. It was like a flag marking some kind of prominent spot. Then I noticed her clothing. She was a little overdressed for a stroll in the park. Her high-heeled boots were knee-high, her skirt was flaming red, and her coat was a conservative dark blue.

Dawn expressed an interest in the birds that were, "Flying around that lady." Lee turned to look for that voice and saw Dawn. She looked up, saw me, and smiled. I experienced a mental gasp at how radiantly attractive Lee looked.

Lee said, "Oh my goodness, it's you, Richard. And this must be your daughter."

"Dawn, this is Chef Dobson, the lady I work for at Uncle Tim's restaurant. Lee, this is Dawn, my daughter."

Lee got off the bench. It caused a flurry of suddenly ignored birds and the mad dash of squirrels looking for a haven in the trees. She crouched to get more eye-level with Dawn and extended her hand for a welcoming shake. Dawn reacted immediately and extended her hand in greeting.

"Nice to meet you, Dawn. Your Daddy talks about you a lot. He tells me you're a smart girl. How are you today?"

"I don't have school today," Dawn said.

"How nice you can spend it with your Daddy."

"Yeah, but I'm going to Aunt Tassy's later to play with Paul."

"Well, that's nice too."

"You have pretty hair."

Lee chuckled. "Thank you, Dawn. Most people don't flaunt their gray hair. It's nice someone thinks my hair is pretty."'

She looked at me and smiled.

"We were just about ready to turn for home and have some lunch. Would you care to join us?" I said. Lee thought for just a second. "I'd love to."

Lee moved to the other side of Dawn. We began walking, three abreast with Dawn in between us, holding our hands.

Most of our conversation was directed at Dawn. We noticed the geese and ducks in the pond and egrets wading along the shore. Dawn fell in love with a small dog on a leash tethered to a large man who seemed embarrassed to be holding on to such a little dog. The man good-naturedly allowed Dawn to pet the dog. Her attention got the dog very excited, and the little lady peed on the sidewalk. The owner and the dog resumed their walk. We continued the opposite way.

When we got back to the house, Dawn entertained Lee while I prepared lunch. I added some tomato bisque to the menu because it was chilly outside, and I thought it would be nice to warm us up. The sandwiches consisted of sourdough bread with mayo, mustard, ham, lettuce, and tomato. I put out a bowl of kettle chips, and Lee accepted my offer of a bottle of beer.

"Nice house," Lee said.

"I'll show you around after lunch."

"I'd love that."

Tassy showed up to pick up Dawn for her playdate with Paul. I introduced Lee to Tassy. Tassy knew I had work to do that afternoon, so I sensed she was confused about why Lee was there. Dawn explained without being asked how we met.

"Daddy and I found her at the park today."

"How nice." Tassy smiled at Dawn. There was never a doubt in my mind that Tassy and Dawn had a strong bond. Dawn was always glad to be with Tassy. She looked forward to her playdates with Paul, but I suspected it was more about being with Tassy.

When they left, I showed Lee around the first floor of the house. Naturally, we spent more time in the kitchen. She noticed how I set up my kitchen as best I could to reflect my experience in a professional setting.

We went downstairs to my office. Some of my artwork was mounted on a cork board.

"Wow, I can see why you're in demand in this profession. This stuff is stunning."

I thanked her. She continued to take in the rest of the space.

"Would you like to sit down?"

"I'd love to. You're sure I'm not keeping you from something?"

"No. I'm ahead of schedule on this one."

She was curious about my background. I felt like a reporter was interviewing me. I, in turn, inquired about her history. Then the conversation took a turn I could never have anticipated.

"What's it like working with me, Richard?"

I was taken back.

"I'm not sure what you mean?"

"Okay, How have you come to put me in your life? Am I boss, co-worker, friend...?"

I am ashamed to admit that my first inclination was wondering: What is this about? Was it calculated? Is there an expectation?

"Okay. You seem to be stuck. I'll go first," Lee said.

We were sitting on the couch. Lee picked up my left hand and put it between both of hers.

“I’m of two minds about you. You are either the guy I’ve been hoping to meet or the guy I wish was my son. Now our age difference tells me it should be the latter, but my libido tells me it could be the former.” She looked at me with an expression of honest inquiry.

I was stunned. I stammered my thoughts out.

“Lee, I’ve never thought of ’us.’ I mean, you’re my boss in one sense. In another way, while you are an attractive woman, if I ever found my thoughts going in that direction, I would have stopped deliberately. I guess because if I acted on that kind of relationship, I’d imagine you’d reject me.”

Lee leaned closer to me. “Right now, what I want to do is kiss you,” she said.

Slowly we both reached for each other. I am sure it was because I hadn’t had sex for quite a long time that my reaction to kissing her and the feel of our bodies as we embraced went through me like lightning bolts. Still, I was confused. Where was this going? She answered that without a word.

Lee began unbuttoning my shirt. She engaged me with a stare and kissed me softly on the lips after each button. I reached for the buttons on her blouse, but she took my hand away.

“I’ll do all of the work this time.”

Of course, this time implied there would be more of this sometime later. Everything was moving fast, and I was not opposed to what was happening. I was just having a tough time keeping up.

She unbuckled my belt, pulled my shirt off, and I kicked my shoes aside. Lee was down to her bra and panties so quickly I didn’t notice how she did it, but her clothes were deposited neatly across my office chair. She pulled off my undershorts.

She cocked her head to one side and smiled, “Nice.” Then she did that behind-the-back reach that only women can do and make it look easy. She handed me her bra, and I draped it neatly over her clothing.

She was standing like a dancer at rest, with her feet slightly spread apart, her hands on her hips, and her head back. In an exaggerated upright stance, her gaze dared me not to become aroused. There was little danger of that happening. She peeled off her panties and walked out of them in one graceful move.

For such a moment of unexpected passion, we took our time. When we began, she whispered in my ear, “I'm not a glass vase. I won't break.”

As it was when I was working for her, Lee's instructions and expectations were expressed clearly, and compliance was rewarded. We played. We explored. We had fun. At least, we laughed a lot. When it appeared we were finished, I was afraid that I hadn't been generous enough. She dispelled that notion innocently enough.

We were lying side by side, staring at the ceiling. After what seemed to be a long time, Lee rolled onto me, draping her leg over my legs and putting her head on my chest. At the height of our passion, our age differences fell aside. Yes, her face was beginning to wrinkle, and gravity was working its evil on her body. It made no difference to me.

“I'm going to tell you something I probably shouldn't,” she said

I kissed her.

“You are an unbelievable lover. Rarely do things work out where it's better than you thought it would be.

"I have another confession. I wasn't in the park by accident this morning. I didn't know how I was going to turn that into an opportunity for us to make love, but when I woke up this morning, that was my plan."

"And you knew I was going to be there because…?"

"Because you told me that was what you were going to do on your daughter's day off from school. Next week we can…"

"Next week, Paul, Tassy's son, will be coming here for a playdate. Tassy, and I alternate."

She thought for a moment.

"Then we're going to have to figure something out for those weeks. Less than once a week with you is not enough for me."

Yes, I know. Once again, I am involved with a woman calling the shots, running the show, claiming me like a midway circus game prize.

"My time is more flexible than you might think," I said.

"I hope so. My God! You're ready again."

She propped up on one arm, looking down at me with an amused look on her face.

"Can you…"

"Yes."

"Will you…"

"Just tell me how you want me to make you feel good."

"Do you have body oil?"

"I do."

I went to the bathroom and returned with the bottle.

"Do you want me to apply it?" I said.

She laughed and gushed out dramatically, "Absolutely."

Chapter 20
Jennifer Dale

My daughter, Dawn, is ten. Many things have changed, but in some ways, nothing has changed.

Coleen sold her share of our house to me before she moved to California. Why this departure? Her business took her there for a seminar. Coleen fell in love with the idea of living there. Forget the problem of moving her company; it had grown to be almost coast to coast anyway. Compared to succeeding with her do-gooder project and despite her wealthy family's opposition, moving the company headquarters was nothing.

As far as our family is concerned, adjusting to her decision was no small task considering the bond she had with my daughter and me. While the practical effect of her sudden departure was tremendous, the mental adjustment was mountainous.

As the years passed by, Coleen and my relationship had become even more brother and sisterly. This was despite our 'sham incestuous' habit of having sex. Or, as we might say more politely, we had a history of being occasional lovers.

When Coleen moved, Dawn and I had more space. That space was empty for quite a while because neither Dawn nor I needed it. The emptiness made the place feel cavernous. Any noise created almost an echo chamber effect.

Dawn has visited her Auntie Coleen twice since she moved away. I live in particular fear that Dawn will go for a visit one day and not want to come back. When she returns from those visits, Dawn always tells me she's glad to be home. I think she's trying to redirect my fear of losing her, but she's just not selling me. It takes some time for her to reconnect with our life. I'm sure the difference between our northern midwest climate and California's weather is part of the attraction. I also know Dawn misses Coleen as much, if not more than I do.

Despite that change in the household, Dawn and I have a good life together. She's a good student, even though I don't think I've done an excellent job motivating her to excel.

Dawn hasn't gravitated toward any particular interest outside of travel. Because I recognize her passion for traveling, Dawn and I have gone all over our State. I was hoping she would develop more interest from the variety of the geography and the quaint villages in our State's remote rural parts.

Here in Rivers Edge, I've been exposing her to theater, film, and art. We are fortunate to have enough of all of these things. Dawn is taking piano lessons, and she is an enthusiastic participant, if not a natural talent. On her own initiative, she has developed a romantic affection for New York City. I've promised to take her there for her twelfth birthday.

* * * * * * * * * * *

I'm still working out of my home, but I'm freelancing instead of being tied to WI4Y. Another firm, Brighthouse, bought the company. The stockholders in WI4Y received a generous offer for the company that the Board of Directors could not turn down.

To Brighthouse's credit, they realized that a large part of its value was in some key employees. They exhibited that by insisting on employment contracts that included non-compete clauses. That stipulation in an employment contract could prevent people from leaving the company and working for the competition or starting their own competitive company. I was initially okay with that and intended to sign the agreement until I learned from Lynn that they wouldn't continue to let employees work from home. Lynn told me that there were other reasons to be concerned.

Looking over the terms of the sale, it was understandable that our stockholders were more intent on getting a reasonable price for the company than negotiating a good transition for the employees. If I refused the new contract, the severance package from the company was minimal. However, the incentive to stay was considerable. The healthcare and retirement benefits were far more generous. I'm sure many people took it without question, a bird-in-the-hand kind of outlook.

I had some initial meetings with the Human Resource staff and my prospective supervisors. I felt that they had purchased our company because they saw our way of working was more in line with the future.

Unfortunately, they had a tough time letting go of their more authoritarian management approach. The explanation for that was simple. The management staff was all-male. They tended to be older, white, and, frankly, stuck in the past. It was clear they liked our staff's creative talent but could not relinquish top-down control.

Lynn and I talked late into the night on a couple of occasions before I had to make a decision. We tried looping Tassy in, but she had a different set of objectives. I couldn't blame her. Her son, Paul, was in school. She was dating a nice guy, and it looked like they were planning a future. The money and security were too much for her to pass up. Besides all of that, Tassy didn't see herself as a career person. She was happy just to have a secure job. Paul was old enough that he didn't necessarily need to have a mom home with fresh baked cookies on the kitchen counter when he got home from school.

It was clear to Brighthouse management that Lynn was the face of the company. They wanted her for her reputation and relationships in the market; however, they were not comfortable leaving a woman in that position. This attitude made no sense to either of us. Lynn had forged her relationship in the market through hard work and innovative management practices. Brighthouse recognized the value of her career, but not her as the person that did the job. Instead, they selected an assistant for her without allowing her to interview him. He was a middle-aged man, Brett Cummings, who management clearly wanted to be her eventual replacement. They specifically asked her to introduce him to her contacts and customers. Since they didn't have a position to promote her, her career track with the company was predictably sideways into the proverbial office with no window. This approach was just a subtle way of getting her to walk into the career trap. Lynn recognized this and knew she was not going to sign on. There was a price for her knowledge. They have to pay for it, and it wasn't just money. They might have known what they were doing. Fortunately and predictably, Lynn had an alternative plan.

* * * * * * * * * *

"We made a lot of money, creating an image for customers. Our accounts want to be recognized in the marketplace as something outstanding. WI4Y drilled down on that desire and provided the graphic interface that propelled them forward into the market.

"What I wanted to do is start with doing the whole package. I want to build our clients from the beginning. I want to develop them as a brand name. And if they diversify their products and services, we create the brands within the brand."

"I don't understand the difference," I said.

"Okay, let's say you've developed a company like Sears. They tell you they want to have their brand of appliances, so you create Hot Point. Then they want their brand of tools you bring them, Craftsman. There are so many food processors and retail companies in our market that need this approach."

"Okay, why don't we do that now?"

“We were going to do it, but the board got a hard-on for the buy-out, and anything to do with change or future development went to the bottom of the priority list. That is with everyone except me. I've got a file on this larger than the NYC white pages. This is my vision, my idea. They didn't want to work on it. The hell with them!

“I know you've got a decision to make, Richard. You've had to decide what is best for you and Dawn. However, if you can hang on for a year or so, I will have a spot for you. I want you to work for me..”

Lynn knew what I had in my retirement fund. She also knew I could get along by working for Tim. I couldn't turn her down, and she knew it. Yup, there I am in another relationship with a woman that controls the game and makes the rules.

****

Then there's Midge. In a lot of ways, Midge took Coleen's place as the sister-in-close-proximity. She didn't live with us, but she often visited. Despite her autism, Midge was competent and trustworthy.

Midge was my first choice to watch Dawn if I was out of the house. I've left Dawn with Midge for as long as couple of days. Dawn has been exposed to Midge for so long that she isn't disturbed by her sometimes odd behavior. I suppose the only thing I had to get used to was that often, I found that Dawn had talked Midge into styling her hair into yet another look.

Midge and I are still close. The tension of possible sex between us died a natural death. It was probably because I avoided anything that would encourage her, along with her sister's council. I learned I couldn't prolong the inevitable hug that Midge and I habitually shared coming and going from our meetings. Her sister told Midge that I was interested in being a friend but not a lover. Then there was 'the conversation.'

Midge was sitting with me in the back garden. It was early spring and a little bit cool. Still, the winter season's length and the desire to sit in the sun overruled the necessity of wearing more clothing layers.

"Richard, why can't we be like you are with Lee?" Midge said.

I was surprised by this question, and I wasn't prepared to answer it. I could have responded with some trite remark, pointing out that Midge was too young for me. But seeing as she was pointing out my relationship with Lee, who was twelve years older than I was, that wasn't going to work. Mentally I was still stumbling when I blurted out something close to the truth.

"Midge, I'm afraid… and let me say, I've always been afraid that if you and I crossed that line, it could ruin one of the best friendships I've ever had."

"Really, Richard. I am one of your best friends?"

"Midge, we know that some people think there is something wrong with you."

"There is something wrong with me, Richard. I'm not like most people. My mind doesn't work the way most people's minds do."

"See, that's just it. I've learned by being your friend that there is nothing wrong with your kind of difference. It's just different, not wrong."

"Why can't you love me?"

I knew that this was the edge of the cliff.

"Midge, I do love you. I love you like I love Coleen... like a sister.

"But you made love to Coleen, Richard. Why can't you do that with me.?"

'Shit,' I thought. She has me there.

"Yes, Coleen and I had sex together, but it wasn't right, and we had to learn that. That's why I don't want to make that same mistake again."

"What mistake?"

I looked at her. I'm sure my expression betrayed my frustration. It wasn't the questions that made it hard. It was my lack of ability to put my feelings into words.

"Midge, just because you feel like having sex with someone doesn't mean you should. Many people can't have sex with someone just for the fun of it. There has to be some feeling of certainty about a complete relationship. When you go to someone completely naked, you are very vulnerable. Not only is your body bare, but so are your emotions. Lust, the desire to have sex, is one of those emotions. But the need for unconditional acceptance and understanding is underneath that powerful feeling of lust. After you have sex, those needs become more important. They become the most important."

"Okay, but I still don't know why it stops us from having sex."

"Midge, when I was younger and didn't know all of this, I didn't think much about anything but the feeling of wanting to do it. Now I feel that having sex with a new partner is like jumping out of an airplane with a parachute. The thrill of falling through the air is from desire. The only reason it is enjoyable is if the parachute opens when you pull the cord.

"Then there's the other part. I have to be secure in the thought that I know there is more to it than sex. I am not sure you understand that, Midge. That is why I won't have sex with you. You have to know it is not because you are not desirable. It's not because I don't love you. I just don't love you that way."

I'm not entirely sure she understood everything I said, but she appeared satisfied, if not happy. I leaned over and kissed her cheek. I was utterly unprepared for what would happen because of this conversation, but that won't happen for quite some time.

* * * * * * * * * *

Besides losing my close contact with Coleen, I have felt another relationship's pain gone off the rails. Lee informed me, even before she told Tim that she was leaving. Not only was she quitting her position at the Manitou, but she was also moving to Arizona.

As I cautioned Midge, my affair with Lee became far more than sex, although we certainly kept each other happy. Lee's enthusiasm for sex was terrific. Her need for experimentation and variety was challenging yet thrilling to me.

Our affair became common knowledge at the Manitou. I knew that Tim knew about us. We spoke when Lee had a day off.

He said, "So I hear ah… I hear that you and Lee are…"

I didn't wait to acknowledge the truth of what he already knew.

"Yes. It's been a little over a month."

"Good for you. Good for both of you," Tim said.

He never said another thing about it until she quit.

"I'm sure you're aware that Lee is leaving," he said. "How do you feel about that?"

"I guess I have to accept that she has to follow her dreams. We never made any plans together. As far as timing, I'm as surprised as I'm sure you are."

I talked tough, but I was hiding a lot of pain. As we continued our relationship, Lee and I got past the 'it's all about the sex part.' We opened up about ourselves to each other.

"Christ, Richard, I didn't know your wife committed suicide. I knew she died, but suicide. Damn, how were you able to handle it?"

"To begin with, I was distracted because Dawn was just a baby and needed so much attention. Then I went to a therapist. And I had a lot of friends that stuck with me through the tough parts. When all of the turmoil and disruption after her death calmed down and sunk in, I was angry with Regina. I wondered, why did she do it, and why couldn't she talk to me about carrying that much pain? I felt helpless. But then, working with my therapist, I've made my peace with it."

"But you've admitted you have had affairs but no committed relationships. I mean, don't you think that's part of it?" Lee said.

"I'd never thought of it that way. Maybe you're on to something. I don't know. I don't think about it that often. I used to have to deal with Dawn's questions about Regina. Dawn hasn't asked me about her mother in a couple of years. I suspect she will someday. But for now, we've both put that part of our lives in the memory book."

After that conversation, Lee and I went through a period where she cuddled me like a child and loved me like a man. When I pointed that out to her, she pondered her answer for quite a while. The one thing I had learned about Lee was it was better to give her time to think things over rather than getting confrontational. I'm sure my point hit home, but her treatment of me was something she hadn't realized or she was trying to ignore. It took some time. Finally, Lee opened the mental box and spilled out what was going on. Lee shared with me both the recognized feelings and the causes she had been hiding. The reasons she had for justifying us.

"You want to know my story. Well, it's not a new one for sure. I was in my early twenties, right after I'd graduated from college, living with a guy I thought would be the person I was going to be living with for the rest of my life. Can you believe that? Can you believe I was ever that naive?

"Anyway, in short order, I got pregnant, and he moved out. My father passed away while I was in college, and my mom was living on Social Security and my Dad's pension. I thought about getting an abortion, but I couldn't do it. I carried the baby full term and put him up for adoption. I saw him for a couple of minutes after I delivered him, and I've been looking for him for all of my life."

"I'm sorry," I said.

"Yeah. I know. You've got a heart, Richard."

She started to choke up. I had seen her angry, frustrated, and bored, but I had never seen her cry. I embraced her. She began to weep onto my chest. I stroked her back while holding her in my arms. It was the only time I ever saw her exhibit real vulnerability. She pulled back so she could engage me with her eyes.

"I know it's why I haven't been able to settle anywhere. It's why I get into impossible affairs like you and me. I mean, Richard, you know there is no future for us, don't you? I will leave you."

I nodded, but I pulled her close to me again.

"Not right away, though," she said.

She pulled back and looked at me with a teary smile.

"I'll tell you something though it might ruin you if you know it. You are, by far, the best lover I've ever had. And, my sweet Richard, you're the best man I've ever met. So I'm not going to be running away from you anytime soon. But be aware, it's going to happen, no matter how hard you or I try. Okay?"

It was time for me to hide my uncertainty and vulnerability.

"I'll pretend I didn't hear all of the complimentary stuff and keep on trying to impress you with my devotion. That way, when you do leave me, I can have an excuse to feel hurt and abandoned."

She thought I was kidding. I should have won a prize for acting because the words came naturally to me. Lee might have thought I was using humor like trying to put frosting on a burnt cake, but I meant every one of those words. Long after Lee left, I finally told Tim how surprised and hurt I was by her abandonment.

****

I got some help from someone I would never have thought to turn to. Jennifer 'Jen' Dale appeared to be a tough but simultaneously a grandmotherly woman. She looked like the older woman she was, but she was as tough as any woman I've ever met. I hired her after I started working for Tim and into my affair with Lee.

In the beginning, Jen cleaned. Previously I was splitting chores with Coleen, and that worked fine. However, when Coleen moved away from us, maintaining the house became too much for me. I had too many balls in the air.

Jen was the third cleaning person I hired, mostly because the first two didn't pass the Dawn test. I hadn't realized that Dawn had to put up with the person I hired. While my cleaning person would be working, I would be either in my office downstairs or at The Manitou. When she came home from school, Dawn became part of Jen's job. I didn't think in terms of my housekeeper being a nanny for Dawn.

Jen could not stand dirt, and she knew where to look for it. She found some dust bunnies in my wardrobe closet that looked big enough to ride. Jen moved the stove away from the wall every time she cleaned the kitchen. In a nutshell, she was meticulous.

Jen established borders in her relationship with Dawn. If Jen saw something that concerned her, she would ask Dawn, "Does your Dad know you're doing that?" Enough said. Dawn knew I would hear about it. After I offered her the job permanently, Jen accepted, but only if we would replace the vacuum, cleaning solutions, and supplies.

I'm not sure exactly when she became our cook, but we just accepted that after a while. On the three days a week she worked, she would cook dinner. Jen knew I cooked professionally, but that didn't seem to bother her. She used whatever I had in the kitchen to make wholesome tasty meals. She never asked for advice or any unique ingredients.

"Smells good," I said.

"Gonna be good too."

"If you're going to keep this up, I will expect you to join us for dinner."

So it happened. Jen became part of the family. She got used to Dawn, calling her Grandma. At first, Jen had trouble with Midge, who was often included in our dinner plans, usually at the last minute. Still, she understood after I explained Midge's condition to her.

Jen was in awe of Lynn. She always made special meals when she knew Lynn would be dining with us. Somehow she learned about Lynn's sweet tooth and fixed desserts that catered to her taste.

Whenever Lynn got Jen aside and talked with her alone, Jen would become so animated it was like seeing another personality. If I heard one sentence from Jen that started with some form of "Lynn was saying the other day…" I heard it a thousand times.

Jen trusted and confided with Lynn. Because of that confidence, Lynn was able to fill me in on Jen's backstory. That story facilitated another considerable change in our lives.

Jen had three grown children. She raised them as a single mom after her husband died in an accident on a construction job. A piece of lifting equipment failed, and he was crushed to death when it fell on him. An insurance settlement and his union pension helped her get by, but providing education opportunities for the kids sent her back to work.

It appeared that her kids were on good terms with their mom. As young adults, they had all moved out of the Rivers Edge and were more than likely unaware of her plight. Undoubtedly they were uninformed because Jen wouldn't admit to them she needed anything.

****

Lynn found out that Jen was living hand-to-mouth in one room of a repurposed motel on the edge of town. Jen didn't own a car, so she was at the mercy of the bus system. The system was pretty good in Rivers Edge, but out where she was forced to live, it wasn't.

"Jen, I heard from Lynn that you are living out in the county. Isn't it tough to get transportation back and forth?"

"I get by," she said without looking at me.

"Well, I've got a problem, so I think we can make things easier for both of us."

She had turned off the vacuum cleaner. As she looked at me, the expression on her face was not welcoming.

"Look, I've got other customers. I can't be taking on more work without..."

"I want you to move into the spare room full time."

It was almost pleasurable to shake her up. Jen was always so calm.

"Excuse me, I'll be right back," she said. Then she turned quickly and went into the bathroom. I'm sure she wasn't aware that I could hear her through the door that she failed to close completely. She was crying. I sat down and busied myself with a magazine. After a time, she came out with her attitude intact. The evidence of her upset was apparent around her eyes.

"So you were saying you want me to move in with ya, huh," she said.

"Yes, I think it would good for both of us," I said

"Why would I wanna do that?"

"A couple of reasons. First, you'll cut down on your travel time. I'm assuming your other clients are here in the Rivers Edge?" She nodded. "It's not like you'll be working all of the time you're here. I think you know what we expect. You can set your schedule when you want to take care of us. The rest of the time, you are on your own. Lastly, you won't have to pay rent. The only thing extra you have to do is shop for groceries."

"What's in it for you? You don't seem to be asking too much."

"We'd be getting the company of someone we've come to enjoy and appreciate. Before you ask, I've talked to Dawn about this. She'll be damned hurt if you say no."

Her answer was yes, but not before she left for the bathroom one more time.

* * * * * * * * * *

Over time, many of the rough edges to the independent, strong-willed Jen began to be smoothed. Like any other extended family, we brought different things to the table. Jen extended our family even further over the coming months as we got to know her kids when they visited her. One thing became clear. They hadn't visited her in quite a while. I reasoned that it was because she didn't want them to see how she was living.

During a visit from her son, Kyle and I went out for a bike ride. When we took a break at a local park, Kyle told me what it was like growing up, and I told him what I knew about her recent history.

"She never expressed any interest in finding someone to fill in at the dad spot. I'm not sure what she thought about, but I'm sure you know a lot is going on in that head of hers that she isn't going to share with anyone. I can't complain. She encouraged us to aim high and did the best she could for us. When I was a kid, I wished we had a dad, but I realized later she was pretty good at filling both roles. My older sister stepped in as the par time mother because Mom often worked two or three jobs to make things go. When I was old enough, I told Mom I'd find a job and help out. She told me in no uncertain terms that I was to concentrate on school and enjoy my teen years. You know, it was a version of 'you'll have the rest of your life to work.'

"When I graduated from high school, she sat me down and told me that I could live at home if I stayed in school. If I didn't stay in school, I'd have to pay for room and board. I started at Community College and got a job as a part-time night clerk at a motel. When I transferred to the university, the motel chain I worked with had a franchise there. I graduated three years later with a degree in Mechanical Engineering. I got a job offer from a company in Minnesota.

"My older sister got her nursing degree, and my little sister is a CPA. The girls moved away because they got married. She doesn't know it yet, but my older sister is pregnant. She's going to be a grandma pretty soon. I kinda knew she was in a tough situation, but every time I'd bring it up, she'd shut me down."

"We love your Mom. She has a home here as long as she wants. All of you are welcome to visit."

"You are kind."

“We are lucky to have her. She’s the Grandma Dawn doesn’t have anymore and someone I can count on when I’m not around.”

* * * * * * * * * * *

This happened a year and a half before Lee left us. And I mean she left us. No phone call telling us her automobile trek to Arizona was successful. No mail to pass on her address. She was gone. As bad as I felt about her leaving us, I resented that she knew where we were, but she wouldn’t let us know anything about her life.

Dawn was off at a piano lesson. Jen caught me taking a break in the garden patio. I was guzzling sparkling water with a real orange flavoring. I was replacing it for an increasing beer habit, which was expanding as fast as my waistline. Jen sat down next to me.

“How’s it going?” I said.

“It ain’t none ah my business, but you remember the other night at dinner? You and Lynn was talking about Lee. I got some thoughts I want to share, but I figured it’d be better if we was alone.”

“Shoot.”

“You was complaining that Lee knew how to get ahold ah you, but you can’t find her. I think Lee has to have it that way. If you was to call her, it would just reopen the hurt we all had when she left. Not only that, she knows you would do that if you could.

“On her end, she always has hope. If she needs you, she can call. She ain’t going to do it. She’s like a guy I knew who quit drinking. He was drinking too much, and he knew it. He said he was going to quit drinking before he became an alcoholic. This guy always kept a bottle of his favorite scotch in the cupboard. He told me the reason he had it there was that it gave him hope. He hoped one day he’d trust himself to drink again. He ain’t going to do that, but the opportunity was comforting.

"I'm sorry if what I'm going to say hurts you, but I know too much about lost love and the hurt it causes not to say it. Richard, Lee's not coming back. And she's not going to ask you to go to her. There will be nights and times when she will be tempted, but she won't. She won't push that button cause she loves you too much, and she don't think much of herself."

* * * * * * * * * * *

I didn't think I was showing my grief, but I was. Tim knew it, and partially out of need and mercy for my pain, he asked me to fill in as full-time Chef at The Manitou until he could find someone else.

"Look, Richard, I don't know if this merger thing affects your game plan, but I need a Chef at the Manitou right now. It's yours if you want it. Take it and tell me to look for someone else in the meantime or just take it. It's up to you."

As it happened, Lynn came to me and told me that she'd be ready for me in six months, and I could work out of my home if I wanted. At that moment, I had only begun to realize how demanding the full-time responsibility of running a restaurant kitchen was. I was missing a lot of Dawn's extracurricular activities and my time together with my extended family. The essential things in my life became The Manitou kitchen and the people that worked there. I told Tim to look for a Chef and why I couldn't take the job permanently. He took it well and kept his word to find a replacement.

"Welcome to my world. I'm sure the only reason I don't feel the same is that I've never known anything different. I've been doing this since I've been old enough to remember. I'll do what I can."

He wanted my opinion before we hired another woman. Darcy Brin was younger than Lee, but she had some great experience in her resume. Her only drawback was the question of why she was taking the job? Tim and I both thought Brin was moving backward on her career path. We were afraid she would realize it after she took the position and would quickly move on.

When we questioned her, we got an answer neither of us expected.

"What do you mean moving backward?" she said. "I don't know if you're aware of your reputation here, but I and others I know have kept an eye on this spot since Lee Dobson took it. The longer she stayed, the more I became convinced you guys would be a great fit for me. Lee was like my hero and my fantasy mentor. I've looked up to her through my whole career."

Tim and I mulled over the unexpected response we got. Not that we said anything at the moment, but before we could react, Darcy spoke out.

"By the way, do you guys know where she is? I've lost touch with her."

Chapter 21
Vivian Brantwood

I first saw 'Viv' Brantwood in person at a lunch event for volunteers for the *Bootstraps for Single Mothers,* a cause I had been supporting for two years. The organization helped single mothers get a toehold onto a successful path for themselves and their children. Our counselors help the applicant devise an individualized plan to get these women where they wanted to go. This plan would look at housing, childcare, medical, and educational needs. Then the organization reached out to our members looking for the resources to help the client.

Being a single parent, I thought I knew some of the problems. However, since most of our clients didn't have the advantage of being male, educated, and financially stable before becoming single parents, I found I had a lot to learn.

We were being wined and dined at Brookside Golf and Country Club. There were opportunities to contribute to the organization, including a silent auction and lottery tickets. Female volunteers attired like 1930's nightclub cigarette girls roved through the crowd. With their high heels, push-up bodices, thirties style makeup, hair, and short skirts, they circulated amongst the Bloody Mary and Mimosa lubricated group soliciting ticket sales.

I felt a tap on my shoulder. When I turned to respond, I was eye to eye with a striking woman. The first thing I noticed was her smiling dark eyes. They sat on either side of a patrician nose set upon an oval face with generous but not overly plump lips.

Vivian had her hair in an appropriate style for the costume and period. Still, unlike many of the women of that particular age, hers was not colored. Vivian left her hair with its natural salt and pepper grey. Even with the premature greying hair, she would have no trouble passing herself off as ten years younger. She was a fit and attractive woman in her late thirties. Some of her height was attained with the high heels, but she graced those heels with long legs and a lithe body.

"Richard, can I interest you in some lottery tickets?"

I wasn't sure how Vivian knew my name. I was a soldier in this group. She was one of the commanding officers.

"I am."

I came prepared for this eventuality. I handed over a one hundred dollar bill. The cigarette ladies had a cardboard tray wrapped with foil and a strap around their necks to simulate the real thing. I placed the bill in the tray. She peeled off the tickets and handed them to me.

"Extremely generous, Richard."

"My daughter and I talked about how much we should contribute. After exhaustive discussion, we agreed on this."

Her face lit up with a smile.

"How much did your daughter chip in?"

"Twenty dollars. Dawn waits tables part-time."

"Wow, she sounds like a great kid. How old is she?"

"Dawn is eighteen. She will be going to Brighton next year."

"It seems you've done a good job raising her."

"Thank you. I've tried."

"And Mother?"

I never got used to answering that question without feeling like I was bragging instead of grieving.

"Her mother died when Dawn was eight months old. Fortunately, a lot of people have helped me along the way."

She flinched but otherwise kept the conversation going despite my bump in the road answer.

"Well, thank you for your contribution, Richard. It's been nice talking with you."

We hadn't been introduced, but then, I knew who she was, and it slipped out.

"And you, Vivian."

She shot a quick contemplative look, nodded, and moved on.

* * * * * * * * * *

When I arrived at the event, I had checked to see where I would be sitting and who would be at my table. By looking at the seating cards, I found that I didn't know half of the people at the table for eight. I didn't know the people who sat on either side of me.

When we took our seats for lunch, the place to my right was empty and remained that way as they started serving the soup course. The seating card was missing. It occurred to me that the person canceled for some reason. While chatting with my neighbor on the left, Harry Vetters, an older gentleman from the banking community, I felt someone slip into the chair on my right. Sitting next to me, arranging a napkin on her lap, was Vivian "Viv" Brantwood.

"We meet again," I said

Vetters could damn well talk to someone else. This lady was going to get my complete attention. Vivian gave me an accomplished return handshake. I'm sure she learned how to do this in kindergarten. Along with the handshake came a sincere smile.

"Yes, how nice."

I could describe Vivian Brantwood in several ways. This much I knew from reading about her in the newspapers, magazines, and from her appearances on local television. She came from a well-known wealthy family. More than one building in Rivers Edge had her family name on it. All these buildings were gifts from multiple generations and various branches of the Brantwood family tree.

Vivian graduated with honors from Princeton. After a stop at the Sorbonne - Paris, she received her MFA from NYC. She acted on Broadway for a time, appeared in a couple of successful films, and then got behind the scenes as a producer and director.

Vivian and I talked during lunch, but she knew how to work the crowd. Vivian got everyone at our table conversing together, and that's a tough job. Generally, with a table of eight, you would have three, maybe four exclusive conversations rather than one round table discussion, but Vivian managed it effortlessly.

Soon after the closing speeches, people began excusing themselves and taking leave. Not long after, Vivian and I were alone. She showed me no signs that she was in any hurry to move on. To get out of the way of the staff cleaning the dining room, we adjourned to a cocktail table on the patio overlooking the eighteenth green. The day was warm, but the umbrella kept us both out of the sun, and a light westerly breeze kept us cool. Vivian had changed from her Cigarette Girl costume. She wore a navy polo shirt, caramel-colored skirt, and deep brown pumps.

"So, Richard, tell me what should I know about you that I don't?"

"Since I'm still trying to figure out how you knew who I was when you hit me up for the donation, I'm not at all sure what you know about me in the first place."

I was grinning and hoping she knew I was kidding her a bit. She put her forefinger next to her mouth, looked aside, and then looked back at me.

"Coleen Bero is one of my oldest and best friends. I was visiting with her on a trip to LA. Your name came up. Then she couldn't stop talking about you. After that conversation, I was bound and determined to meet you."

I was stunned.

"If Coleen told you all she knows about me, you know everything important."

"I'm a little surprised. She didn't mention you lost your wife at such a young age. I met Regina a couple of times, but I didn't know her well."

"I know why Coleen didn't share that with you. Regina and Coleen were girlhood friends. The three of us lived together in the same house for years, even after Regina and I were together; actually, we never married. Then, Dawn was born. Regina… ah… she… Regina committed suicide."

Vivian leaned forward and took my hand in hers. I was tearing up. I couldn't help it.

"Oh, damn, Richard. I'm sorry. I can see it upsets you. We don't have to …"

I was surprised at my reaction, but when I started talking about the grief that Coleen and I shared, it all came back to me. I tried to grin away my anguish.

"You wanted to know something about me you didn't know."

I looked up at her. There was a tear flowing down her right cheek.

"I'm so sorry."

Vivian spent the next hour pulling my life story out of me. At the same time, my inability to get the conversation to be about her got me nowhere. Reluctantly, I told her I had to get going. Dawn had a volleyball match that afternoon. I promised Dawn I would watch her team play and take her out for Pizza.

"I enjoyed this conversation, Richard."

"Well, since it was all about me, I don't know if it was all that stimulating, but I enjoyed being with you. You are a charming person, but I'm sure you hear that all of the time."

"A woman can never hear that enough. I'm going to New York on business for a week. How about I give you a call when I return, and we can get together ?"

I'm sure she noticed my surprise.

"I think that was supposed to be my line."

She let out a full-throated laugh.

"Okay, I get pushy. Can I call you?" she said.

"Can't wait."

* * * * * * * * * * *

In the back of my mind, a caution flag unfurled. Vivian Brantwood is one busy lady. She doesn't need the company of a guy like me. I doubted if she would follow up. So I wasn't going to be surprised if she didn't call or if I would ever see her again.

Though surprise will be a regular feature in my relationship with Vivian, the next unexpected occurrence came from another quarter. The phone in my office rang mid-morning the following day.

"What the hell, man!" It was Coleen.

"What the hell are you "what in the hell" about, lady?" I said.

"I was on the phone for an hour with Vivian Brantwood yesterday. Good God, man, you've got her panties wet. What is going on?" This was so Coleen.

"Coleen, girl. Let's slow down. Vivian and I met at a charity thing. She just happened to be seated next to me, and we had a nice conversation."

"Okay, Stud. Let's get your facts right. Maybe I should be sorry about this. During a recent visit from Vivian and me having a little too much wine, I engaged Miss Brantwood in a lengthy conversation about my good friend Richard Harrison. Okay! And she just didn't happen to sit next to you. She engineered it with the deft exchange of seating cards. And 'nice conversation!' She thinks you walk on water, Dude."

"I like her, Coleen, but you know she's out of my league."

"Don't. God damn it, Richard! Don't give me that shit. She's a wonderful person, and so are you. Everything else is crap. Just because she is who she is doesn't mean she has to fit the stereotype."

"Okay, but when I think of the possibilities she has, I don't see where I might fit in."

"Richard, do you know what smart women look for in the men in their lives? They want a guy who feels something besides loyalty to some God damn sports team or his army buddies. You fucking cried when you talked about Regina committing suicide. Richard, I told her that was the genuine you, even though it's been over sixteen years. She's not shallow, Richard. She's a great gal, and that meant something to her. Open your heart, asshole. This relationship could be good for you and her."

* * * * * * * * * *

It was Saturday evening. Dawn was out with friends. I was downstairs trying to figure out what's wrong with one of my paintings. The phone rang. The moment it rang, I checked my watch. It was 9:30 and a little too early for Dawn to be calling me for a ride home. Besides that, I thought one of the girls she was out with had driven and promised me she'd bring her home.

"Richard?" At first, I didn't recognize the voice.

"Yes."

"Am I calling at a bad time?"

I realized it was Vivian.

"No, it's not at all. How are you?"

"I'm coming back tomorrow morning. I wondered if you would like to have dinner with me."

In my mind, there was no doubt I wanted to be with her doing anything.

"I'd love to Vivian but can't. I'm committed. I always spend Sundays with my daughter."

"Do you two have plans for the day?"

"No, not really. I was looking at the weather and thinking we might go for a hike or something."

"Why don't you pack a bathing suit, and the two of you could come and relax by the pool."

At this, I'm of two minds. One thought is, 'Yes, I'd love to see you in a bathing suit.' And the other is 'What if Dawn ends up bored out of her mind?" The image of Vivian in a bathing suit prevailed.

"That would be fabulous. What time?"

"Be here around three. We'll eat about six-thirty."

* * * * * * * * * *

I didn't see Dawn until 8:30 the following day. She, with a bowl of cereal in one hand and a glass of OJ in the other, slumped into a seat next to me on the couch in front of the TV. She kissed me on the cheek and settled in. I was watching a new show I liked, CBS Sunday Morning with Charles Kuralt. When the commercial came on, she put her empty cereal bowl on the table next to the couch and asked, "Have you got plans for us today?"

"Yes, I do. We've been invited to a pool party."

"Who's having it?"

"A woman I know, Vivian Brantwood."

Dawn straightened up from her slouch, her eyes and her mouth opened wide. She blurted, "You know Vivian Brantwood?"

I chuckled at her excitement.

"Yes, we are invited to her house for a pool party. Don't you want to go?"

"Not if we don't go to the department store, so I can buy myself a new bathing suit. Mine looks like crap."

"Okay."

"So Dad, tell me this isn't the kind of a thing where I am looking at her, and she's looking at me, and you need approval from both of us to have an affair with her, is it?"

I laughed partly because the line of questioning was coming from the influence of Coleen. I had no answer to her 'what is this about?'

"Let's just go and enjoy ourselves, honey."

* * * * * * * * * *

While the buses ran near Vivian's address, it required a fifteen-minute walk to finish the trip. We rang the doorbell and waited. I was anticipating a maid, a butler, or some member of the hired help to answer the door. Instead, Vivian did.

"Hi. Come on in. I'm sorry I took so long. I was in the kitchen. I have something going into the oven that needs to be taken care of."

She led us into the cavernous home. After Vivian tended to her kitchen chore, we all met on the patio next to the pool.

"Vivian, this is my daughter, Dawn."

"Hello, Dawn. I must tell you I've heard a lot about you from your Aunt Coleen."

That startled me, but I don't know why. Vivian and Coleen must have gone deep into the weeds about both of us. But the following exchange got my attention.

Dawn said. "I know. She's shared a lot about you with me also. But you know Aunt Coleen... It's hard to keep her quiet about anything."

And there it was, their acknowledgment of their commonality in the sisterhood of women. Of course, Dawn noticed we were the only guests. We changed into our suits. Dawn talked me into buying a new one also.

"Make sure you get all of the tags off it before you put it on," Dawn said.

"Do you think I'm that kind of a dork?"

"No comment as far as the dork thing goes. However, if this woman is attracted to you, I don't want something stupid like that to be a deal killer."

"Do you think she's that shallow?"

"Right now, I'm not considering what she is. I'm questioning her taste."

She playfully punched my upper arm and went into the ladies changing room.

We swam for about half an hour. As we swam laps, I became aware that I was falling further behind Dawn at every turn. Dawn was now a stronger swimmer than I was.

I didn't notice Vivian until I heard her enter the pool with a splash as I turned my head to take my breath on a stroke. Vivian was a blur of color traveling the pool's length underwater. I got out of the pool and settled by a table with lemonade and snacks.

While Dawn and Vivian continued swimming, Dawn paced her laps back and forth in the pool. I didn't know what her intention was, but her stamina was impressive. As it turned out, she was merely counting laps to see how many she could do before she got tired and quit.

Vivian had a slower, more relaxed pace, but it was plain that she was a well-trained swimmer. Like many things about Vivian, her stroke was smooth and perfectly executed.

Vivian seemed to be intent on strengthening her initial bond with Dawn. They talked about Dawn's plans. Dawn didn't share anything with Vivian that I didn't know. Until…

"Are you going with anyone?" Vivian said.

"No. But I've got my eye on someone," Dawn said.

"What's so attractive about this guy?" Vivian asked.

"He's a little older. He's at least as interested in me as a person as he is in getting into my pants. That makes him special in my crowd. What about you? Anyone special in your life?"

Dawn grinned. I didn't think she was expecting the answer.

"Yes. Because of my initial encounter and a glowing recommendation by your Aunt Coleen, I'm trying to better understand your father. What do you think?"

I was squirming in the chair with a ridiculous smile, trying to pass this off as good fun. Dawn went on, "I know I'm supposed to be distancing myself from him to become my own person, but I'm not looking forward to it. Richard is a 'what you see is what you get' kind of guy. Nothing up his sleeve, and he's not going to pull quarters out of your ear. On the other hand, when I compare my upbringing with some of my friends, I recognize this guy has knocked himself out, making sure I was raised ready to go out in the world. He's fun. He's brilliant and talented. I'm going to miss not having daily contact with him."

I'm not squirming anymore. I am not smiling anymore. I've got a lump in my throat, and I'm trying not to tear up. Dawn hasn't looked at me since she began this conversation.

"He's getting choked up, isn't he," Dawn said.

I was sitting behind Dawn. She was looking at Vivian. Vivian is looking at me over Dawn's shoulder. Vivian is a bit in awe of this situation. She nods yes to Dawn.

"Well, there you go. A guy that shows his emotions and cares about people." Dawn turned to me, touched her lips with her two fingers, and blew me a kiss.

"Okay, that was nice, but enough about me, okay?" I said.

As I walked to the men's room to pull myself together, I heard Dawn say in a lower voice, "He gets embarrassed when he becomes the center of attention." They both laughed.

* * * * * * * * * * *

Vivian's roasted pork loin dinner was marvelous. She served whipped potatoes, roasted peppers, coleslaw with oil, and vinegar-based dressing rather than the mayo. Dessert was a baked peach cobbler and topped with vanilla ice cream and caramel drizzle.

After dinner, the conversation centered on Dawn's expectations for her education at Brighton. Vivian shared some stories from her college years. Most of her stories involved professors she valued and what she had learned from them.

I chipped in with my story about my internship with Lynn and how it changed my life.

Dawn said. "But have no doubt, Vivian, his life in the kitchen is as strong as his design experience. Every so often, Uncle Tim will call him, and Richard's back in the kitchen at The Manitou, slicing, and dicing."

I said, "I'm interested in how somebody who is on track to have an exciting career in theater and film ditches it for producing."

Vivian responded. "My acting career wasn't as promising on the inside as it might appear on the outside. I had some traction, but the scripts and auditions I got told me I had become a 'type.' I didn't like what the industry thought I was, so I decided to produce something to demonstrate my range.

"After we finished the project, I realized that I enjoyed production more than acting. Film and theater are highly collaborative processes. However, the producer/director has a lot more control than the lead actress will ever have."

We all helped to clear the table and do dishes. We had just sat down with a fresh cup of coffee on the patio when the doorbell rang. Dawn popped up out of her chair.

"That will be my cab," Dawn said.

"You're leaving?" I said.

She smiled at both of us.

"Yeah. I think you guys need some time alone together. Besides, I've got stuff to do at home."

Vivian got up and hugged Dawn. She stepped back from their embrace, with both arms at full extension with her hands on Dawn's shoulders, and beamed a smile.

"You are a jewel. Let's talk. Call me anytime."

"Thank you. I will. I enjoyed your meal, the pool, and this beautiful house."

Dawn came over and hugged me.

"I approve," she whispered in my ear.

Dawn grabbed her beach bag and gave us a wave and a smile as she left.

Vivian and I went back to our chairs and our coffee.

"Wow, that is some young lady you've raised," Vivian said.

"I can't forget Coleen and the many others that helped me along the way."

"I'm sure that's true. However, I also think that you are very much the captain of that ship."

We talked for about an hour. I took my cup to the kitchen and put it and the saucer in the dishwasher. Vivian was standing behind me with her dishes. I took them from her and put them beside mine.

"I should get going," I said.

"Already. What are you doing tomorrow?"

"I've got a client meeting at ten o'clock downtown."

"If I promise to get you there on time, would you spend the night here?"

I didn't anticipate this. I hesitated.

"I need something from you," she said.

"Oh, yeah, What would that be?"

She approached me, put her arms across my shoulders, and kissed me.

"I need you to make love with me."

There was no way I wasn't going to help with that request.

* * * * * * * * * *

At first, I didn't know what motivated Vivian to have a love affair with me. It was just wonderful being with her, and I didn't want to question it. She was passionate about almost everything she did. We didn't talk very much about our work other than to share the occasional people and experience stories. Over the next few months, it was as if we were sharing our lives by experience rather than an explanation. We spent time at each other's homes.

I visited her office when she conducted her philanthropy and worked on her film.

Vivian sat and watched me work in my studio. I even got her to work at The Manitou when I cooked one evening to help Tim.

When Dawn moved to college, Vivian would stay overnight at my place. She often offered for me to stay at her home for more extended periods.

"I'd love to have you come here for a hot meal. We could rent a movie… you know, just like an old married couple." Vivian said

We'd laugh and did just that. When Vivian wanted sex, she preferred it to be done slowly with feeling at every juncture. I don't know how many times in my life. I mentally thanked Lisa Duffy for teaching me how to kiss. I wouldn't know how to react to a woman's need for passion if it weren't for Audrey Becker. Regina made me use my senses to discover my lover's unsaid needs, and Coleen taught me how to have fun in bed. Lee showed me that taking care of my lover's needs guaranteed that my needs would be satisfied. It all came together with Vivian.

* * * * * * * * * *

There is no question that Vivian had lived her own experiences. I did my best to let her know that she could tell me what she needed, and her request would be met. She tiptoed into those waters. Once she found that I kept my word, she no longer tiptoed.

Did we have arguments? Oh, yes. Vivian was raised in an entitled atmosphere where she got what she asked for without question. When we did have disagreements, my habits with Regina created an automatic reaction. I wouldn't allow myself to get pulled into irrational rants or name-calling. I tried to let her know that what she was saying was hurtful and unnecessary. At the same time, I wanted her to realize we could deal with things that made her angry.

I don't know what conditioned her to be argumentative on some occasions. I think she learned that she didn't need to be that way with me to get what she needed. Her needs were not simple. Sometimes her passion became almost violent. I didn't understand some of it, but then came the night of confession.

We had played hard that day. We took a long hike along the lakeshore, followed by laps in the pool. After that, I cooked, and she relaxed by the pool with a bottle of sparkling Rose wine.

I put together some of the tacos Angelica taught me to make. People who'd never eaten at Casa de Paco's would be amazed by the combinations. My refried beans and Spanish rice were also far better than most Mexican restaurants that sprang up after Tim's Casa de Paco's produced a market. I added refried beans, rice, and a covered dish of soft corn tortillas.

Vivian wasn't slurring drunk, but I could tell from her first words that she felt the effects of the Rose wine she was drinking. She put together a taco with the ingredients she liked. Taking a small bite, she savored it.

"These are fucking fabulous, Chef."

Vivian was using words she wouldn't use if she were sober.

"Good, try some avocado. It's better than butter if you can believe it."

She had a slightly drunk happy look.

"You've got me in the mood. You're getting to me, mister."

"Really. Should I be worried?"

"No, I should be."

"Why."

"I've never lost someone I loved like you did with Regina, but I've had men I loved leave me."

"Fools."

"Oh, no, my lover man. Don't be so sure. You might leave me someday."

"I'm sorry, my lady. I can't imagine why."

She paused and then said, "I'm not sure why but eventually they all do. I was going with a guy in college. Like me, he was a trust baby, so I knew he wasn't attracted to me because of money or the Brantwood name. I had a spate of that kind of attention, and I was wary. We were the Ken and Barbie of fraternity/sorority row during our junior and senior years. When we graduated, he went back to L.A.and I came back here. I never heard from him again. It became obvious that to him, I was just a classy piece of ass and acceptable arm candy."

She stared out into the fading daylight. I sensed that part of the reason she was drinking was to get the courage to broach the subject of us and our future. There was an ocean of possibilities.

"Vivian, let's be candid here. I don't know why you're attracted to me in the first place. From my perspective, you are an exceptional person. You're smart, educated, well-traveled, and successful. Oh, and by the way, drop-dead gorgeous. I can't speak for the others, but I understand that many men couldn't stand the competition you bring to a relationship. I guess living up to your standards can be difficult. Being your date or maybe even a friend with benefits might work. But a committed relationship? That's another thing altogether."

She quit staring at the sunset and said, "So what would you want... friend, a friend with benefits... occasional date…?"

"I want to be with you, committed to our relationship, but what do you want, Vivian? We've both have a history and complicated lives. We can put it all together, but if you think I'm attracted to you because of your social status or money, we've got a problem. I know this is all new to both of us, but I would be lying to you and myself if I didn't admit that I love you, and I've known this for some time. In a way, I've been looking for you for a long time. But I was looking for you, Vivian, not your money, social standing, or fame. If all of that is a barrier to our future, then somehow we have to get past it."

She smiled a dreamy drunk smile and said, "You know what was one of the best times we have spent together?"

"No. From my perspective there have been so many."

"It was working at The Manitou that night. I've eaten in hundreds of restaurants. I never really thought about what was going on on the other side of the kitchen door.

"I watched you and your companions produce food on the level of great art. You did it so easily. I realized that many people I don't know, have never seen, and haven't thanked for what they do, make life easy for me. I can see that one of the things you bring to our relationship is to ground me in reality. For the creature comforts, I can offer you, you give me a solid dose of how other people live. I need that. Let's make a deal here. Anytime you think I need a lesson in humility, you call me out."

She raised her glass for a toast.

"For love and happiness," she said.

We were quiet for a time.

"I also need one more thing," she said.

"What's that?"

"Please get used to calling me, Viv. Every time I hear someone call me Vivian. I remember my mother. If she used my full first name, I knew I was in trouble."

* * * * * * * * * * *

And so it went, the twists and turns, the ups and downs of our life together into a new relationship that grew stronger and tighter every day. We didn't fight. It didn't mean we agreed on everything. We had long conversations, most of which came to a mutually acceptable conclusion. Sometimes we just decided to disagree.

I began thinking of the experiences that got me to this point. I think my patience and ability to discuss came from my relationship with Regina. Mentally, Regina was so vulnerable.

I saw the downside of unresolved conflict in my mother and father's relationship. The stone-cold silences that prevailed in our home after the behind-the-doors shouting matches failed to reconcile the differences.

I learned from dealing with Midge a few years ago when she was diagnosed with breast cancer. Midge began to understand that any kind of relationship with her was delicate. She couldn't feel what other people felt and wasn't sure why.

Before Midge passed away, she and I had more of a relationship than before she was diagnosed. It was easier for me because I knew if I didn't say things while she was still with me, I would never have the opportunity.

I confessed to her that I had fallen in a kind of love with her. I couldn't commit to a relationship that she imagined because I knew it would be based on believing that we could somehow have a healthy life together. There was nothing I could do that would change her. I told her I gave her everything I could because I did love her, but I knew it was not enough to make her happy. She asked to do one thing.

"Kiss me like you love me," she said.

I did. It was easy. I put everything in that kiss that I wouldn't have done before. Before Midge passed, she asked me to do it again a couple of times. I did it because it meant something to her and me. Each time I kissed her, she kissed me back, returned my passion, and became aroused the way anyone would in receiving a wanted kiss. I even began to question my previous decision to distance myself from her.

Being Dawn's father taught me so much about the differences in the way women look and experience life. And I don't mean adjusting to the mood swings. Women find they have to learn how to live in a mans' world. For much of my life, I didn't even realize that this is a man's world. After all, my mother didn't accept the expectations that society had for her. Raising Dawn helped me to understand that she needed Coleen and other women in her life. I had to learn that they weren't plotting against me. They were collaborating on how to deal with me and all of the other men in their lives.

Dealing with Dawn after she lost a friend due to his silly teenage behavior, I realized that the last thing any woman wants to hear is platitudes about how many more opportunities there are. After all, it took me a long time to get over losing so many relationships in my life. Telling her that the terrible hurt will go away and things will be better wasn't that helpful when what she needed was just to feel the grief and let it heal in her own time.

When I was learning that lesson, my thoughts went back to Dedra, so long ago, when I was a teenager. I wonder if it took her a long time to get over all of the hurt in her life and how long it took to get over me. I know it took me months to not think of her. Part of it was the lost opportunity to have sex with her. After all, I was a young inexperienced horny kid. But as time went on, I thought more about the time we spent together and the conversations we had instead of the fading memory of her bare breast under my fingers. I hoped that Dawn would have the same experience of recovery from a loss.

****

Viv and I were happy and were out in public as a couple. When I proposed, I did it to let her know I was ready to commit. I wanted her to know that what we had was real, and I wasn't going anyplace. I wasn't surprised when she said yes, but the rest of our world was.

It came to light in many ways that many people thought I was her boy toy. They tolerated me because who was going to tell Viv I was not in her class? As long as she wanted me around, they would continue to accept me. When she sent me packing, they would swear that they had told her so. It would be, 'he was a nice guy, but' story.

For our wedding, we flew to Las Vegas with Dawn and her current friend Ethan. Tim came to be my best man. Viv asked Coleen to be her Maid of Honor. When Viv initially told me that she knew that Coleen and I had been lovers. Viv smiled and told me that Coleen let it slip about how she and Regina had shared me.

“I guess the only thing I'm curious about is after Regina was gone, why did you two never make it together?” Viv said.

“Coleen and I could never be alone. Regina's memory was always with us. Our relationship with Regina was competing with a bond between us. I think Coleen knew it all along, But until Coleen moved to California, I didn't realize that.”

“Coleen told me that she wanted you, but when Regina told her how she felt about you, Coleen stepped back.”

“I know that, but she shared that with me after Regina passed.”

“Then, it's over between you two?”

“It was over long before I met you, Viv.”

The ceremony was simple. We exchanged vows that each of us had written ourselves. Afterward, our whole group went out for dinner. Later, when the group was having fun playing roulette, Viv and I excused ourselves. Making love that night included the relief and pleasure we felt from making our commitment.

Chapter 22
Ellen Roth

The first time I saw attorney Ellen Roth, she was sitting behind her desk in her office on the fifteenth floor of a twenty-story tower referred to as the "Spike" because of its unique appearance in our city skyline.

"First of all, Mr. Harrison, I want you to know that I'm genuinely sorry for your loss."

* * * * * * * * * *

Viv and I celebrated our tenth anniversary in Cannes, France. Viv's film company produced a film presented at the festival and got some support for an award. Viv and I invited Dawn, Tim, and Coleen because they witnessed our Vegas wedding.

As it happened, Viv's film did not receive any awards. She did make secure distribution contracts, which guaranteed a good return on the film. It would be seen around the world.

We were trying to treat this like a vacation with friends. We didn't intend to get involved in the action of the festival. However, Viv needed to circulate because of her film company's interest. Viv was well-known in the film industry because of the kinds of films she's made. Many of the more renowned actors and production people in the movie business wanted to work with her. It certainly wasn't because they were going to make a lot of money, but they would be making exciting films. Plans aside, we allowed ourselves to partake in the celebration enhanced by the star-studded atmosphere. Honestly, it was hard not to get sucked into it.

However, I did get to spend time with Tim. He told me he thought it was time for him to retire. Since Tim married his wife Roseanna, a widow with two adult children, he felt the need to be rid of the restaurant responsibilities.

"Richard, I never dreamed that I would acquire such a desire to be a grandfather to little children at my age. But my step-grandchildren love me. Children don't guard their feelings if they love you; they love you and show it. And... well, I suddenly need that. What can I say?"

I know Tim is feeling me out. Do I want to take over the business? My problem is that I'm up to my back pockets in other things. After Lynn told me she wanted to retire, we decided to sell our design business. The sale of our company made Lynn and me very wealthy overnight. I thought I was ready to retire because I had discussed the eventual situation with Viv.

In that discussion, I told Viv, "I have to admit the longer I'm in the design business, the less creative work I do, and the more paper I'm pushing so others can do the creative side. I'm burned out."

We were on the patio. I had grilled some salmon. We were relaxing with an after-dinner drink, watching the sun go down.

"Okay, but you're still young and have a lot to offer someone. What are you going to do after you cash out?" Viv said.

"I'm thinking. I could do more volunteer work with any number of organizations. I'm going to research the opportunities."

"I'll give you one idea and a way to make an immediate impact."

"Honey, as much as it would be fun to live the fantasy, I don't want to be your pool boy."

She faked a punch to my upper arm.

"Get serious. I'm thinking about *Bootstrap*. Let's face it, your house would be a great emergency short-term refuge for them. You certainly won't need it when you're retired. God knows, you hardly use that studio space now."

I pondered her idea. As for my art projects, I was slowly but most assuredly moving my studio into her home, which has become our home. However, I hadn't decided where in the house to put the studio. My belongings were becoming a noticeable traffic problem in the garage and the mudroom entry.

Initially, I kept my house because I needed to know Jennifer Dale had a place to live. We were just fortunate her granddaughter moved in with her the last year before Jen died. At this point, I was using my house for storage more than anything.

"We have space in the bonus room above the garage for your studio. I assume you want to keep working on your art," Viv said.

* * * * * * * * * * *

As it happened, maintaining the old house and converting it to help *Bootstrap* so they could provide their clients with short-term residence brought significant and unforeseen issues. First of all, we had to consider zoning regulations. It turned out as long as I wasn't charging anything to allow families to use my house for semi-permanent lodging. We only had to comply with the city ordinance with occupancy limitations of no more than two persons per bedroom.

It made sense to split the residence into separate apartments to enable more than one family to live there. We renovated the first floor quickly since it has two full baths. The centrally located kitchen would serve all the units. By moving some of the walls downstairs, we added a third living area.

Initially, I thought this third apartment would be available to clients like the upstairs apartments. I found out that unless I wanted to be commuting every time, there was a turnover of clients, issues between families in residence, or physical problems, I'd need to hire a building manager. I was looking through the *Bootstrap* organization when I discovered the ideal candidate for the job was closer than I thought.

* * * * * * * * * * *

Arliss White was moving back to Rivers Edge after leaving her job in Chicago. She needed an apartment and was willing to take responsibility for managing the operation. It was good to see her. Although we kept in touch while she was away, she didn't often return for a visit. The last time I saw her was at my mother's memorial service.

I knew Arliss could apply compassion and authority in the appropriate amounts. The clients we got were all single mothers who were homeless or on their way to being without shelter. Our house was a stop on the way to more stability. While the families lived in our house, *Bootstrap* would be working with them on jobs, healthcare, and childcare.

Our biggest security problem was with the uninvited visiting fathers or stepfathers of the children involved. While some of these men had genuine concern and love for their children, many had unresolved anger about their loss of control of their children and their wives. Some of them were violent, and many of them had drug or alcohol addictions that could make dealing with them difficult and dangerous.

These fathers were intent on getting control over what most of them believed belonged to them. They blamed the do-gooder social workers, the judges, their wives, anybody but themselves.

Immigrants, who came from a male domination tradition, could not understand how a man's family could be taken away from them for conduct they had been raised to believe acceptable. To them, it was emasculating and an assault on their rights as the head of their household. Domestic violence issues suffered from systemic myopia from the legal system and insufficient social support for families.

The primary issue had to do with their finding out our location. Often this information was something they were not supposed to know. Nonetheless, some predatory men found out one way or another where their family was sheltering. Sometimes a naive family member would disclose the location. This well-meaning family member, be it child, mother, or grandparent, often was conned into divulging to an angry dad where his family was hiding. This brought about some ugly confrontations. Some dads tried to seduce their wives with sympathy and empty promises. They would appeal to the children who were often not told the whole story of why their parents were having problems. Some of the men menaced their wives and children with threats and intimidation.

Although we installed alarm systems and counseled clients that anything they did to reveal their location could endanger them, leaks occurred. Teenage girls didn't think their teenage boyfriends would share the location of the place they were hiding. Young children, missing their fathers and frightened by the situation, imagined that they would be the ones to bring the family back together if only mommy and daddy would kiss and makeup.

The police were summoned on a couple of occasions. Not only did these police calls create problems in our organization, but I was also concerned about my neighbors. We'd told our nearest neighbors what we were doing. We had brought up the possibility of some trouble. No one objected until it happened.

* * * * * * * * * *

"Do you want any protection?" I asked Arliss.

We were having an on-site meeting with John Clay, a senior case manager from *Bootstrap*, Haley Marsh, from the city police department, Arliss, Viv, and me.

"What do you mean... like bodyguards?"

“I’m thinking more like weapons, mace, a club, guns,” I said.

“Whoa there, Richard,” said Marsh. She and Clay were almost coming out of their seats. “If we’re going to think in terms of weapons of self-defense, Arliss is going to need a professional trainer. Anyone of the things you mentioned can be used against her if the invader gets ahold of them. Plus that, you’re surrounding her with children who could find the weapons and use them accidentally or on purpose.”

“I understand, but in the middle of the night…”

“I can stop this right now,” Arliss said. “No guns. No clubs. Maybe mace.”

As Marsh carried on about Mace, I listened to her explain how you safely store it, make it quickly available, and a complete description of what works and what doesn’t. I mulled this over. Did I ever even dream of having a conversation like this?

The reason for this all-hands-on-deck meeting was a need to review the latest failure of our system to keep out a violent father, George Pritchard, from finding his family. The incident ended in a confrontation where Pritchard’s wife was injured, and there was damage to our property.

Marsh filled in the story by saying, “He accosted the daughter’s boyfriend, Jimmy Patton. Give the kid credit. George beat the shit out of him before he finally disclosed the location. Jimmy is still in the hospital. If a neighbor hadn’t interrupted the beating and got the kid some help, it might be worse than it is.

As soon as the EMTs got to him, Jimmy told them what happened. The police rolled in here and woke me up. When we went upstairs, we interrupted George as he was trying to get the family to leave with him. His wife, Diana, was resisting. When we came through the door, he had just started beating her.”

“How did he get past the alarm system?” I said.

Marsh answered, “George has done a couple of stretches for burglary. He knows how to disarm alarm systems. George is in custody, and I doubt if he'll get a bail offer. I'm hoping we can get him for attempted murder for the beating he gave Jimmy Patton.”

“I'll get a couple of volunteers out here to fix what is damaged, Richard.” Clay said.

"That would be great. Haley, can you make a couple of house calls with me to help calm down any neighbors that may be frightened?” I said.

* * * * * * * * * * *

We got better at providing security. One method was having one of the former resident families explain to the new clients how dangerous it is to believe that a violent, out-of-control dad will act any differently without a lot of intervention.

Individual counseling with the kids helped. It clarified that because their father forced them into seclusion, ripping apart their family lives, they needed to understand the bigger picture.

I got the neighbors involved in helping with security. I gave them phone numbers to call if they saw some suspicious activity.

The most effective deterrent we had to prevent location disclosure was clear information and rules for newcomers and showing them the path to a better future.

Often the disruptive fathers ended up in jail for long terms. This allowed some families to move back to their own homes and safely resume their lives.

We were doing pretty well and getting better by the day. Arliss confessed to me that for a while, she had been ready to quit. Seeing the help that *Bootstrap* did for families convinced her to stay.

* * * * * * * * * * *

Jason Anderson was a serial wife-beater and petty crook. Books and medical papers are written about guys like Jason. Abused as a child by his parents and later by step-parents, violence, and insecurity were normal. He hated authority and authority figures. Jason didn't have any idea how to be a good husband and father. How any woman puts up with Jason's behavior is beyond understanding.

We knew about Jason when his family, a thirty-two-year-old wife who looked like she was forty, a ten-year-old daughter, an eight-year-old son, and a five-year-old daughter, moved into our *Bootstrap* program.

One look at this family told you two things. First, Jason may not have fathered any of these children. Their appearance varied significantly from the older girl with Hispanic features, the boy as mixed-race, and the five-year-old's Caucasian features. These weren't similar to either his Mother or Dad. The second thing was that the children's life was bound to duplicate Jason's if someone didn't intervene.

Arliss struck up an incredibly close relationship with Jason's wife, Margie Anderson. Margie came from a stable family and knew her life with Jason was neither normal nor acceptable. She admitted that her children were not Jason's. Margie confessed to Arliss that she was forced to have unprotected sex with Jason's thug buddies. What finally got her to risk Jason's rage and the danger of leaving him was her awareness that her oldest girl would be the thugs' next sex toy.

At this time, I was checking in with Arliss by phone every day and stopping by once or twice a week. We never told any of the clients I owned the house. To them, I was just a volunteer helper. We maintained that story because we didn't want to encourage anyone to go behind Arliss' back if they thought it would get them something.

I learned the hard way that it was often difficult to effect change in these families. At best, it was a complicated process. Primarily because of the psychological and physical damage done, it was hard to provide what would be something like a typically safe environment. How could a child who lived with one of these monsters ever feel safe?

Arliss kept up with some of these families after they moved on. She told me if the whole family got to something that worked and allowed them to prosper independently, it was because the mother stepped up and turned things around. Sometimes it was the oldest child who took the role of parent and raised their siblings. Another improvement scenario was a kid who got out of the troubled family and made his or her own way to a happier life.

"It's never pretty, Richard," Arliss said. "I often come out here to work in the garden just to help get myself back together. It is bad enough when I'd hear a woman talk about how her husband isn't so bad and how she is sure this time her husband understands and will come around. It's tough hearing the younger kids crying because they want their daddy. Often we can't convince them that daddy is sick and needs to get better. I can't tell you how many young girls have come through here that I am positive have been sexually abused by their fathers or adults he brought into the picture... uncles, buddies, you name it."

"Do you need a break from this?" I said. She leveled her gaze at me., "Yeah, I do. Am I going to take it? No. I honestly feel that if I leave here for any amount of time, something will happen to a mom or one of the kids because I wasn't here. And Richard, if that happened, I don't know if I could handle it. No, I'm not taking any breaks."

"You know, Arliss, we could refuse clients for a while and empty the house so you would be able to take some time. I'm concerned here.

You're being stressed. I don't like the probable consequence of pushing you too far."

Arliss would disagree right away, but I could tell she was considering it. I took the initiative and had Clay block new clients from the house. He understood not only the problem but the motivation.

Clay told me, "I have to monitor my staff constantly. It's a well-known problem among the people who work in this field. The condition is similar to a soldier who is on the front lines too long... battle fatigue, PTSD. Call it what you want, but the road ends at the same place, with serious mental problems."

Arliss finally agreed to a two-week vacation as the house emptied. She planned on visiting her sister in New Mexico. Clay warned me that while Arliss needed to take a break, we might find that she didn't want to come back. I thanked him for the heads up.

Arliss did return. I think she was more motivated than ever. During the first couple of weeks after her return, the Anderson family moved in. They were on track to get a more permanent home. The schools would be better for the kids, and Margie would work toward a nursing certification. Her husband, Jason, was in therapy. Margie disclosed to Arliss that Jason's supervised visits with their kids disturbed her. Jason seemed more interested in seeing his wife but became upset when he was told Margie didn't want to see him.

* * * * * * * * * * *

I was having lunch with Tim. These occasions were getting to be pretty predictable. First, I'd have to listen to a good half hour of his wonderful grandkid stories. That would be followed by veiled offers for me to take over managing his restaurants. I was thinking about it. My idea was to sell Casa de Paco's and get the job down to operating The Manitou. Tim had already quit serving lunch on weekdays. He served brunch on Sundays. If I took over, I wouldn't have to be on the floor every night, and his staff, as usual, was top-notch. My new mobile phone rang. I excused myself and found some privacy to answer it.

"Mr. Harrison?"

"Yes."

"Mr. Richard Harrison?"

"Yes. Who is this?"

"Mr. Harrison, I'm Officer Tom Handly of the City Police. We are on a service call at a property you own. I need you here as soon as possible."

"I'll be there in about twenty minutes, Officer. Can you tell me what's happened?"

"There has been a shooting, sir. And there is a loss of life."

Walking out the door as he told me this, I quit the call and got into my pickup truck. I made it across town in fifteen minutes. When I turned onto the block, all I could see was blinking hazard lights at the house. There were police, fire, and EMT vehicles blanketing the street outside the home. There were uniformed police, firefighters, and emergency medical people moving in chaotic choreography. I identified myself to the officer assigned to perimeter security. He escorted me through the cordoned-off area around the house.

The first detail I noticed in the scene was Viv's car parked in the driveway. I had to steady myself, considering the possibility that she was hurt or worse. Officer Handly took me to a quieter area of the scene.

"Mr. Harrison, I'm sorry to tell you that we're dealing with multiple deaths in your house. I understand it's a temporary family shelter. Is that right?"

"Yes, Officer. Can you tell me who is..."

"Mr. Harrison, as difficult as it might be, I was hoping you could help by identifying the victims. I'll warn you, it is not a pretty picture. If you don't think you can handle it, I understand."

I immediately responded, "Sure, I'll help. But I have to know if my wife is among the victims."

"I don't know that, sir. Again if you don't feel you can help us, I understand. Maybe it's best..."

"I'll do it." I had to know what happened to Viv.

"Okay, first, we have to put booties on your feet. Then you and I will go in there. Do not touch anything. Do you understand?"

I nodded. He gave me the booties to cover my shoes and had me put on some disposable gloves. When we walked through the front door, I was surprised. It looked fine. Nothing was out of place. When we walked into the Anderson's apartment's living room area, there was some broken glass, and a chair was overturned.

When we got to the master bedroom, it was heart-stopping. The oldest daughter was on the floor with multiple gunshot wounds. The youngest girl was halfway under one of the beds lying in a pool of blood. The boy was face-up by a dresser. His body also had multiple gunshot wounds. I identified each one of them by name to a uniformed officer who was taking notes for Handly.

We went into the kitchen. The entire area was a mess with broken dishes and upside-down furniture. Everywhere I looked was stained to varying degrees with blood. Damage caused by bullets marked many places on the cupboard, walls, and ceilings. I wasn't aware at the time, but the number of rounds and the pattern of bullet damage indicated that the killer was using an automatic weapon referred to by police officers as an Uzi. The gunman was using 22 Caliber ammunition. They found six empty twenty-round clips in the house.

In the passageway leading to the lower level of the house was the blood-stained body of Marge Anderson. As I identified her to the Officer, it became clear that anyone in this house when the killer invaded it was dead. I felt sick knowing that we might find Arliss and Viv among the victims.

We walked down the stairs past Margie's dead body to my old studio. As we exited the stairway, I was surprised to see minor damage. Behind the back of the couch was the body of Arliss White. She had fallen to the floor and appeared to be trying to crawl away from her attacker.

My heart was pounding. Sweat was coming off my forehead even as I continuously wiped it with my shirt sleeve. I was beginning to feel dizzy and unsure of my balance. Where was Viv? Unable to continue staring at Arliss' body, I walked to the window that looked out over the garden and saw Viv. She was sitting in a chair. While she was presumably in shock, she didn't appear to be wounded. Most importantly, she was very much alive.

As soon as I opened the door, Viv saw me. I got to her before she could get up. I kneeled next to her and hugged her. She was shaking uncontrollably and was breathing as if she couldn't get enough air.

The police officer who had been sitting with her was an older guy in his late fifties. He looked like the kind of guy who would have hugged a victim to offer comfort. He didn't say anything right away, but he put his hand on my shoulder to let me know it was okay. Viv was incapable of speaking.

****

Later, the officer told me, "When we cleared the house, we found her locked in the bathroom. It's a good thing she was lying in the bathtub. The guy must have emptied a whole clip into that door, but he couldn't get in. None of the bullets hit her. The small wounds you see are from wood chips and tile fragments the bullets created. Given time, she will be okay."

I knew Viv would be okay physically. Psychologically it would take a lot of time. Fortunately, while she knew the others were dead, the only body she saw was Arliss'. Even then, the police covered Arliss with a tarp before Viv was allowed to leave the bathroom's shelter and go out to the garden.

They found Jason five blocks away from the house in the parking lot of a small manufacturing company. He was slumped over the steering wheel of his pickup truck. He had put the gun under his chin and fired it up into his head.

* * * * * * * * * *

Two days later, in the middle of consoling my wife, sorting out my feelings, and arranging for Arliss' memorial service, I answered the phone.

"Yes. I'm Richard Harrison."

"Mr. Harrison, my name is Ellen Roth. I'm an attorney. I represent the estate of Arliss White. You are the named executor of her estate, Mr. Harrison. We need to get together."

"I'm sorry. I'm the executor of her estate?"

"Yes, sir. This document I'm looking at showing you as executor is signed, notarized, and witnessed."

"I see. When was this document...?" Suddenly, it came to me. "I do remember. It was signed four years ago, right?"

"Yes."

"We were writing up a contract for Arliss, and she insisted that I agree to be the executor of her estate. How urgent is this, Miss Roth?"

"It's Mrs. Roth, and I hope you haven't completed her funeral arrangements."

"No, I've made inquiries and gotten some pricing, but no, I haven't committed to anything yet."

"Well, that's good because she left some very detailed instructions for you."

* * * * * * * * * * *

We didn't need a coffin. Viv and I found the vase in which Arliss specified her ashes be placed. Unfortunately, her request to donate any organs was nullified by how she was murdered. Arliss had purchased a crypt in the local cemetery building used for cremation remains. She even set aside money for her memorial service that specified that it be held at The Manitou. We sent out notices to known friends and published a statement about the memorial dinner for others who knew Arliss. We got one hundred RSVPs. Tim and I created the dinner menu. We picked food that would be reasonable in cost and easy to serve. We decorated the tables with flowers, which I knew from our garden conversations that Arliss favored.

We attended the funerals of the Anderson children and their mother. Viv and I had to leave early when it became evident that Viv was suffering from survivor's guilt. Watching those caskets wheeled in and out of the church was more than she was capable of handling. It would take a long time and a lot of counseling to put that experience behind her.

Ellen Roth attended Arliss' funeral. It was clear that Arliss was living well below her means and was planning on early retirement since her estate was quite large. Ellen told me that when she and Arliss devised her Will and the estate structure, Arliss was working in Chicago.

"She told me the Chicago work was highly unsatisfying to her, and she felt like she was cheating her employer. When she started working for you, all of a sudden, things changed for her. Arliss told me she felt needed and valued in a way she had never felt before."

"I'm sure it was the clients that motivated her."

"I agree, but she valued the trust you put in her and the support you gave her."

"Thank you. I'm trying to think of a way to forgive myself for exposing her to the kind of danger that ended up killing her. It shouldn't have been a surprise. We've had several incidents that could have gone to this level before."

"I think she was aware of that."

"Yes, but can anybody ever believe it's going to happen?"

"What did they find out about the killer?"

"He left one of those drug-addled, self-deluding proclamations about how he would show everybody they couldn't just push him around. I can't get the picture of those kids out of my head."

"The police should have never allowed you in there."

"They didn't force me. I needed to know what happened and find out how my wife was."

"Still..."

"I know. Hindsight? But at that moment, I had to know."

****

In my meeting with Ellen one afternoon, I thought we were finishing with the estate's mechanics. Ellen changed the tone and tenor of our discussion. She came out from behind her desk and sat next to me in one of the client chairs. Almost immediately, her administrative assistant, Sheila Grant, brought in a tray with glasses, an ice bucket and laid it on the desk in front of us. Then Sheila went to a cabinet at the back of the office where various liquor bottles were visible. She looked at Ellen.

Ellen said, “Richard, would you like some Scotch?”

“I would love some. Does this mean we’re done?”

“Hardly, Richard. We’re barely started. Now that we know what we’re dealing with and where she wants the proceeds of her estate to go, we have to distribute it.”

Sheila handed both of us a drink and then left the office. Ellen then began my introduction to the responsibility of being an executor.

“I think you’ll agree that is one heck of a pile of money for a woman not born to wealth, nor did she necessarily make a lot of money during her life.”

“Yes, it still surprises me.”

“Arliss lived way below her means, saved, and invested in accumulating this small fortune.”

Ellen paused to let what she had said sink in.

“Then, she selected you to take care of this money after her death."

Her pause is long this time. I begin to feel uncertain about where this was going.

“I’m going to tell you something that I think you should know. Arliss loved you and admired you deeply.”

“I do know that. Arliss was like the sister I never had. She and my mother were very close. She was family.”

“Her feelings for you were deeper and more than just sisterly. I know she wanted to be closer to you, but for some reason, I don’t know why she couldn't confront you with it. I also know she never resented the fact that you couldn't see her feelings about you. Arliss was content to love you from afar. Her moving to Chicago was deliberate. She needed to create space between the two of you."

I was shocked. I didn't know what to say. Ellen was just sitting there, sipping her scotch, waiting.

"Ellen, this is right out of the blue. I never had any indication that she… she felt that way about me."

"And why would you? No, I am not chastising you for not being observant. I know nothing other than what was shared in my conversations with her. The talks Arliss and I had were prolonged, detailed, and sometimes emotional. I'm sure she presented herself as your surrogate sister convincingly to you.

"I just want you to know that she trusted you. She trusted you with everything she had. She doesn't have any children. No family. You are this combination of brother, should-have-been-lover, and friend. It's up to you, Richard. How are we to use this money to honor her? Let me say this much. Arliss never told me what she wanted to be done with it, so the page is blank."

* * * * * * * * * * *

I had the job of cleaning up the mess at the house before we could sell it. I had Arliss' estate to manage. We set up a foundation and began funding *Bootstrap*. We made plans to build a short-term residence building to replace my original house. It would be more significant, safer, and named after Arliss. Her estate would provide some funding for the construction, furnishing, and maintenance. *Bootstrap* would lease the building to provide income to reduce the loan on the project. *Bootstrap* would also manage the building and the clients they housed.

I went into a state of deep introspection. I tried to see myself as I imagined others did. Being decisive and a leader? I felt that Lynn had always trusted me as her second in command. Tassy felt comfortable with me in charge.

I noticed how I was regarded on those occasions when I got on the kitchen line. When I donned the white coat and chef's hat, I still was to my staff, 'one of the guys' who got needled, encouraged and welcomed. I could fill any position where I was needed, including acting head chef. As the manager, I was more respected and liked than resented and feared.

Included in this mixed-salad of feelings was my relationship with Viv. After she was involved in the massacre, Viv was in counseling for the next couple of years. We were also doing joint-counseling, and our home life was challenging. We didn't seem to be able to face our problems without a counselor serving as a referee.

Viv couldn't shake the classic survivor's guilt. While she would admit this in therapy, she kept retreating into a shell of silence at home. It seemed nothing I could do would penetrate that shell.

I also had guilt. I felt I had failed to protect all of them; Margie Anderson, the kids, Arliss, and Viv. I must have gone over the situation a hundred times, looking for ways I might have made a difference. I fantasized with my therapist about how, if I had been at the house when Jason showed up, I might have stopped him.

"Richard, that kind of thinking gets you nowhere. It's over. Yes, people are dead, but I can't see anything you could have done to stop him. You're deep into hindsight information, Richard. What you know now you couldn't have known then, so that you couldn't have acted on it. You know what would have happened if you had been at the house. Jason might have killed you too, Richard."

****

Viv was able to find distraction by working with her film company and her philanthropy. People she worked with would often comment to me about how well she was doing, considering what happened. This situation seemed to be circular for us. It might seem to be getting better, and then we would slide backward. I worried if we could make it through this. Nothing seemed to show us a way out, but it was coming, and it would come from a place I would never have imagined.

Chapter 23
Dana Camille LaFleur

I have been managing The Manitou for about three years. Tim had been meeting with me for lunch every Wednesday unless he and his wife were traveling. Both of us agreed that the ownership of The Manitou should transition into an employee-owned company. It was a little strange to be working for the people I was supervising, but we were making the transition. I was grooming a woman, Janice Stanfield, to take my place. She had a degree in Hospitality Management, which is common in our industry nowadays. Janice and I have already agreed on a transfer of responsibilities date.

When Tim passed away in his sleep, I missed him so much. He had been the voice of my better angel. His death forced me to look down the road. I had just so much time left in my life. I wanted to spend that time on meaningful things. One thing I knew for sure was that I was entrusted with an iconic business. I owed it to Tim and his father to keep the business going.

In the restaurant business, an establishment like The Manitou is unusual. It had been in business for over sixty years. Most restaurants last from less than a year to a few years at the longest. Family-owned and nationally franchised brands have the best chance of making it longer.

So many things can ruin an otherwise successful operation. The neighborhood can change in character and become undesirable. The restaurant needs to be maintained, which is expensive and often ignored. People's tastes change. It's challenging to keep up with dietary demands and fads. Keeping good help can be challenging.

Tim had always had a close, almost parental relationship with our employees. Because of that, our retention rate was spectacular. Tim always said he didn't mind retirement parties for employees but hated it when an employee left us to work someplace else or when he had to fire someone.

Our business competition came and went. Some of the theme restaurants closed when the fad that bred them died. Then someone would open them up with a new look. Others faded away into the food critic's memoirs. One of the competitors I had to deal with was a place called Frenchy's. Frenchy's is run by a young man from Montreal, Andre Dominic LaFleur.

* * * * * * * * * * *

The Manitou continued to be what most people would call a supper club. Our bartenders knew how to make traditional cocktails like Old Fashions, Martinis, Manhattans, and Grasshoppers. The Manitou is still known for its extensive wine cellar.

We still put the crackers basket on the table for customers to enjoy cheese spread, liver pate, or flavored butter. We had a salad bar, which was included in the cost of most of the entree selections.

The entrees are the Midwestern American menu standards: sirloin and tenderloin steaks, pork and lamb chops, roasted chicken, and duck. Our fish options included shellfish, lobster, and oyster; ocean fish: cod and haddock; freshwater fish: salmon perch and walleye. The Manitou has always been renowned for its desserts, so popular that the so-called after-theater crowd would often stop by just for dessert.

At first, we noticed our customers were trending older. No doubt, we were still getting the business trade from the expense-account crowd. The Manitou still had the reputation of being a place where people celebrate big occasions, be it an anniversary, a birthday, prom dinner, or graduation. Having dinner at The Manitou put the stamp of importance on it. On the other hand, Frenchy's was a competitor we had to keep in mind. We started by offering lower prices on 'Daily Special' items. We turned that into our lighter plates regular menu, which didn't include the salad bar.

I wouldn't say we were at war with this young guy, but Janice and I agreed he was a good competitor and taking some of our business.

Dawn, my daughter, gave me an idea. "Why don't you have a meal at Frenchy's? You might learn something."

* * * * * * * * * *

Viv and I needed a night out. Her therapy was beginning to get her back on an even keel. I had to accept the diagnosis of her therapist and doctors. She can reach a place where she can function, be happy, and rejoin the rest of us in a familiar environment. The mental wounds would heal, but the scar would always be there. Our life together was reforming around her progress and mine. As I said, I had to accept that Viv would never be quite the same. But neither would I. My guilt and the sadness I felt from losing Arliss were hard to face.

Ellen was right to tell me that I had missed Arliss' signs regarding her feelings about me. I went over every occasion where Arliss might have tried to get my attention. While it's true, her bold and ballsy personality had mellowed, I still kept trying to forgive myself for missing her cues for a more intimate relationship.

I allowed myself to consider what might have happened had Arliss and I paired up. The picture was light, with an aura of a humorous and easy-going relationship. I could see the compatibility of a sex life, but what I couldn't see was any purpose to our pairing off. Our likes and interests in life were just very different. She was a shot and a beer gal. I am the guy who drank wine with dinner and Scotch after. I was a live-theater fan. She preferred popcorn on the couch at home with a B movie. Indeed those differences weren't insurmountable, but I had nothing else to compare.

Uncontrollable thoughts like these were helpful to no one. I was sure that both Viv and I were still committed to overcoming our psychological dilemmas and not let them ruin the more profound love and need we had for each other. It was exhausting to rein in thoughts of all those that died that day.

* * * * * * * * * * *

Dawn finished her rotations and got her license to practice medicine. She told us, "I'm going to go into primary care. It's not as lucrative as some of the specialties, but it will mean I get to know my patients. I just want to have meaningful contact with them. It's where I get my satisfaction from being a doctor."

She had dated while going through medical school. Still, no boyfriends kept her from accepting rotations in other cities and other parts of the country. We thought she might stay in San Diego or Seattle. However, when she settled down and got her license, she chose to stay in Rivers Edge and didn't live that far away from us. We got used to seeing her often. There's no doubt it was helpful for Viv and me to have contact with her.

Dawn asked Viv if it was okay for her to call Viv "Mom" and introduce her to people that way.

"I don't like stepmother," Dawn said. "I don't even remember my mom. You're the closest thing I have had to a mother since Aunt Coleen moved to California."

It meant a lot to Viv to hear Dawn say those words. She answered Dawn by embracing Dawn as she whispered, "Please, yes, Do call me Mom; I love you so much."

Now back in Rivers Edge, Dawn joined a practice with an older Doctor and two younger ones. The elder doctor was looking to retire and was not seeing new patients. The clinic's reputation was well known and widely appreciated in our area. Dawn had no problem fitting in and becoming a contributing partner in the practice.

* * * * * * * * * *

Taking Dawn's advice, Viv and I planned to go to Frenchy's. I didn't want to make the guy think I was sneaking in to spy on him. I called him, told him who I was and that my wife and I would like to meet him and have dinner in his restaurant. It was apparent he already knew who I was.

"It would be an honor, Sir." I could hear a little of the French Canadian accent. "Might I be so bold as to ask you to be my guests and let me join you for dinner?"

"I think that would be great."

When we arrived, the hostess immediately seated us at a reserved table that was set for three. On the way to the table, she mentioned that she had sent a busboy to tell 'Dom' that we had arrived. We had no more than reached the table when he presented himself.

"Mr. and Mrs. Harrison, I'm so pleased to see you." He held the chair and seated Viv. A waitress took our drink order.

"I heard our hostess refer to you as Dom," I said.

"My full name is Andre Dominic LeFleur. When I got to cooking school, I picked up the nickname Dom. If you hear anyone call me Andre, it's my family or friends from Montreal."

The restaurant decor leaned toward a fashion Viv called "Parisian," meaning frequented by the neighborhood locals. Dom laughed and agreed with her.

“The restaurants in Paris that cater to tourists tend to give them a more stereotypical decor. In the locals’ neighborhoods, it’s much more about comfort. People linger over meals and spend time casually communing with their neighbors.”

“I see you’re preparing to serve on the patio when the weather gets warmer,” I said.

“Yes, it’s funny, you know, in Paris and even Montreal, people eat out or enjoy a coffee in colder weather than Americans. But you’re right. We think it will draw. I just hope my kitchen is big enough to handle the volume we could generate.”

We talked shop for a while longer and then ordered our meals.

Dom said, “Mrs. Harrison, I must tell you that I admit to having a crush on you as a young man. I can’t believe I’m sitting here dining with you.”

Viv smiled.

“Dom, please call me Viv. Tell me, what film of mine have you seen?”

Dom laughed, looked at me, and then back to Viv. He said somewhat sheepishly, “All of them. And to be honest, this isn’t the first time we’ve met.”

He pulled a pamphlet from the breast pocket of his sport coat. “You autographed this for me about eight years ago at the film festival in Montreal.”

She looked at the film festival program. Looking over her shoulder, I could see her signature on the cover and a ‘Best wishes for my fan, Andre.’

“Am I supposed to be jealous?” I said.

Viv smiled at both of us and directed her remark to me. “Of course, you are supposed to be jealous.”

"You know," Dom said, "I know that what I think of you is based on the roles you've played. I hope we all can become friends, so I get to know the person you really are."

I didn't know it then, but Dom's admiration was a catalyst for Viv's recovery. After that evening, Dom and I didn't see each other often, but we did stay in touch. Meanwhile, Janice Stanfield asked me for permission to interview with a hotel chain in New York. I couldn't stand in her way if it was an advancement of her career. In the end, she took the position in New York.

* * * * * * * * * *

Dom consistently impressed me in the way he made his presence felt in our community of restaurants. One spring Rivers Edge had a terrible storm in the river valley. The river flooded over its banks, something that hadn't happened in anyone's memory. Thirty families were displaced for about a week or longer. They had to find temporary shelter while their homes were repaired. Dom came and asked me if they could use our dining hall to serve meals for the victims with food prepared by his crew. All those displaced victims had to do was call us to plan for the number of people eating. Some victims were staying with their extended families or friends, so they didn't come often. Many of them needed to come every night.

Dom and I agreed to a temporary sign in the dining hall that 'Frenchy's at The Manitou.' Dom and I split the cost of the food, and our staff volunteered some of their time. Dom got the local theater to donate movie tickets. Both of our team's worked together on planned activities for the children. After that intense time of working together, we would have lunch at least once a month. At this point, I was tempted to see if there was a way that I could make a deal with Dom for him to run both Frenchy's and The Manitou.

* * * * * * * * * *

Dawn called me one day "Dad, I've met someone, and I'd like you and Viv to meet him."

I have to say I had mixed feelings about Dawn's call. I knew from meeting some of the guys she dated that she had a pretty good eye for men, but she previously never announced that she wanted me to meet any of them. We'd meet them, but it was because she'd bring them out with us for a double date to the theater or include them in a family get-together.

"Tell me about him?"

"He's buying us dinner at Frenchy's. You can meet him then."

I called Dom.

"Listen, Dom; my daughter wants to introduce us to some guy. She is serious about him. He's reserving a table for dinner at your place. Could you just make sure I get the check?"

"Absolutely. She's serious about this guy, "It's the first time anything like this has happened. I guess so."

* * * * * * * * * *

Viv and I were both excited and apprehensive when we got to the restaurant.

Dawn was already seated when we got there. I didn't notice, but my sharp-eyed wife commented as we approached the table, "It's a good thing we're getting a large table. Look at all of the flowers on that thing."

Dawn stood up as we approached. She hugged us both, and when I released her, Dom was standing by the table. Both Dom and Dawn were grinning at us.

"Dad, Mom, I know you are friends of Dom's. What you don't know is that he and I are engaged."

We all looked at each other for a moment.

"Dad, I thought you'd be happy."

I felt my voice shaking. "I am sweetheart."

"Then why are you tearing up?"

She hugged me again.

I wondered how they met? When I thought of all of the time I had spent with Dom, none of it included my daughter. Their story was romantic in a movie script kind of way. Dawn told us their story.

"Dom rushed to the clinic one day with one of his young kitchen workers. The young lady had cut herself badly when she reached into a sink full of soapy water and sliced open her hand on a knife someone dropped into the sink.

"He was frantic when he barged into our office. Our receptionist didn't even bother to tell him he should have taken her to the ER at the hospital. My schedule was open, so she asked me if I'd treat the girl. I got her patched up, but I was concerned about how much blood she had lost. I arranged for her to be admitted to the hospital for overnight observation. When I went to visit her the next day, Dom was in her room.

"After I checked her over, I told her she would have to take a couple of days off from work. I explained how to take care of the wound and asked her to make an appointment to see me in a week. Dom immediately jumped in and told her not to worry. She wouldn't lose any pay. When she returned to work, he'd make sure that she was completely healed before she was required to do anything that would endanger her. Then he waited until we checked her out of the hospital, and he volunteered to drive her home.

"A week later, she was back for her checkup. When I came to the waiting room to bring her into my office, Dom just followed us. Then I gave her instructions on her further care and checked her out. While we were walking out, she got ahead of us. I said to Dom, 'Your girlfriend is lovely.'

Dom said, "She's not my girlfriend. Frankly, she's a bit too young for me. But you know, I was going to ask you if you were attached. I told him I wasn't."

Viv was chuckling.

"So Dawn, were you trying to find out if he was single?" Viv said.

Dawn looked at Dom and then back to us.

"Right up to this very moment, I've let him think that I was that crafty. Was I interested? Yes. But I really thought she was his girlfriend. Do you know why I was convinced? He just cared about her so much and was so concerned for her. When he told me she wasn't his girlfriend, I was even more interested in this guy who was so empathetic."

* * * * * * * * * *

Two years later, Dom and Dawn provided the glue that put our family back together. Our first grandchild, Dana Camille LaFleur, arrived. Her arrival made me understand why Tim wanted to spend more time with his grandkids than work.

Dana was born to two people that love her and a family that adores her. Dom is an only child. His parents visit from Montreal frequently. Because Dom has the restaurants to run and Dawn can be on call quite often, Viv and I get to take care of our granddaughter regularly. We found that something about sitting on a couch with your mate and a grandchild between you can be healing.

When you carry the kind of guilt Viv and I did, there is forgiving, and then there is forgetting. Forgiveness is the easier of the two. Slowly you begin to realize that your self-loathing is a burden you have given yourself for surviving. It is a burden we came to know we shouldn't carry.

Forgetting is more difficult when you consistently allow yourself to wallow in the terror and the horror of the memories we carried. We did it because we thought we'd be dishonoring the dead if we began to forget, and we didn't have that right. We slowly accepted that the dead didn't care, and if they could, they would have forgiven us a long time ago.

Viv and I were finally able to bury that terrible time in our lives. We had a responsibility to be grandparents to this lovely gift our daughter and her husband gave us. It was more important than what turns out to be the selfishness of prolonged debilitating grief. Simply put, Dana Camille gently restored the love Viv and I had for each other.

Dana has a lot of experiences most children wouldn't have. While she's too young to know this, evidence of this will be around for her to see when she is older. For instance, she has been an inspiration for many of my sketches and paintings. Viv has used her in two of her films. And Dom has named a cocktail and a dessert for her.

At the Manitou entrance, there is a photo display of Tim, his father, and me. Next to that is a family photo with Dom's parents, Viv and me, Dawn, Dom, and Dana. I paint a new portrait of Dana that goes up every year on her birthday.

The End

Acknowledgements

I've been writing stories, essays, and novels for as long as I can remember.

When I went to the Writers Institute In Madison, Wisconsin, I became acquainted with Marshall Cook and the number of writers he brought into the gathering to instruct and inspire us wannabes. Cook taught me many things about the craft and pointed me to other sources that have polished my skills. One of the first, and maybe the most important thing he taught us, is that if we write, we are writers. We may not be good, published, or recognized, but we are writers.

Writers write because they have to. We feel a little uneasy if we don't have something in process. We have to produce, however, not for money, fame, or recognition. Frankly, if any of those things are the primary motivation for you, it takes away from what you're supposed to be doing, writing.

I have a lot of people who have encouraged me in this addiction. Gail Cohen and Susan Dennison, who I initially met at the Institute, have become collaborators and friends.

I herald Pam Frautschi, who went word for word twice through this book with me. She made it better in so many ways. If there is a mistake in punctuation, spelling, or word usage in this book, it's because I didn't listen to her.

My daughter, Mary Jo Moegenburg, designed the cover of this book. Her loving support and keen design talents are priceless.

Anna-Marie Opgenorth allowed me to edit the Historic Milwaukee quarterly newsletter, *Echo.* I learned about deadlines and processes from that experience.

I have to recognize John Croce for giving me a chance to write for *Appleton Monthly Magazine* about Regional Theater and Restaurants in the Fox Valley. When I wrote for them, my editor was Rebecca Zornow.

I can't fail to mention the opportunity I have in writing for *UrbanMilwaukee.Com*. Co-Founders Dave Reid and Jeramey Jannene, and editor Bruce Murphy gave me the chance to spread my wings.

Nothing in this book is autobiographical. I'm the kind of person who chats with strangers. Over the years, I've had some rather interesting conversations. Some of the stories in this book are loosely based on those conversations. And some of them came in my head, usually when just about to fall asleep.

www.ingramcontent.com/pod-product-compliance
Lightning Source LLC
LaVergne TN
LVHW050408010725
815048LV00004B/111
* 9 7 8 0 5 7 8 8 2 6 8 5 1 *